EMELE'S
NIGHT GODDESS

Steve Pierce

PublishAmerica
Baltimore

Softcover 9781462637423
PUBLISHED BY PUBLISHAMERICA, LLLP
www.publishamerica.com
Baltimore

Printed in the United States of America

EMELE'S
NIGHT GODDESS

YOUTH'S CURSE

Ivan Dracula was born in Transylvania from a loving couple that was very well off. His father had the foresight to travel to Africa and buy land that he thought would be rich in diamonds or gold. He was right. This brought the small family much money, but took much traveling. Ivan was loved much by his mother and father. When they had to check on the African business, they always traveled together. Ivan grew up in Transylvania and Africa. When he was grown, he married a beautiful woman named Christina. Ivan was a go getter and made good investments, but he was a little money obsessed. He was a fair man and well respected. Ivan's wife had a slow sickness that was progressing. Because of this she was only able to have one child, a son named Emele. He loved them both dearly but his business took him away from home.

The Dracula family kept their holdings in the gold and diamond mines in Africa. With his parents gone and Ivan the only child, Ivan was the only heir and ran the mining business. So once again Ivan had to leave his family. This trip made him remember stories from his childhood. Ivan had often heard stories from some of the workers' children, of a tribe that didn't age. Many had searched for this fountain of youth but no one had ever found it. While reminiscing on his rounds of the mine, his horse spooked and ran him into the jungle. His horse threw him and took off, leaving Ivan unconscious. When he came to he was in a hut of one of the local tribesmen, the tribesman explained how Ivan was lucky that he had discovered him before the other tribe. Ivan was intrigued as the tribesman told stories of the Houruo tribe. This was the tribe Ivan had heard of as a young boy. He wanted to know where this tribe was. The local tribesman said no one knew where they were but he had seen a couple of them close to his village. They believed the Houruo tribe, led by a witch doctor, used black magic and evil spirits to cure and sustain their youthful bodies.

In hearing the confirmation of those childhood stories Ivan became more intrigued, thinking of his sick wife and how nice it would be to be young again. There were so many things he wanted to do. He became obsessed searching for the Houruo tribe; years went by with little word to his family. Ivan wanted to surprise his wife with a cure. Ivan's son Emele now thirty years old had spent these years tending to his sick mother and running the family business. Feeling abandoned, Emele had grown to hate his father.

Ivan finally found the Houruo tribe. He met with the witch doctor and told him of his sick wife. The doctor said he could cure her. Ivan was so excited he had to return home to tell his wife and son the good news. He did not realize how long he had been gone. He had become an old man.

When Ivan returned home he was saddened to see how sick his wife had become, but he was filled with pride to see what a fine man Emele had grown to be, taking care of his mother and how he had been running the business in his absence, a shrewd trait he had learned from his father.

Emele is six feet tall with a medium yet muscular build. He has black hair kept rather short. His eyes were dark, almost black. They were kind, but could also look right through you. He had a rugged look. His hands were callused, from some hard work, though most of his time had been working from an office or in travels. Emele was well mannered from his wealthy upbringing and wore fine clothes. He especially liked wearing thin long cloaks or capes, a trait he got from his mother. Emele was a bit of a momma's boy, gentle and kind. He was very loving to his mother and accompanied her to many parties in their social settings, until she became too ill to travel. Though many young ladies threw their attentions his way Emele was not the playboy type. He had never been in love but he had had a few girl friends. Though he was admired by many Emele had few friends. He liked the old ways and was interested in his country's history. Emele especially liked the old castle and knew one day he would own one.

Ivan was sorry for not being there but he would make it better now. They would all make the journey to Africa the next day. He told his son all about the tribe who used medicine and magic and how he had found them, describing the location of the tribe and how they were hidden from other tribes that wished them gone. In the morning he would take his wife there and she would be made well. The son wanted to believe his father. They talked more about the location of the tribe.

That night Christina became violently ill, her fever was too high. The doctor was sent for, but there was nothing he could do she was too far gone. This was more than Ivan could take. "This is entirely my fault. I wasted my time looking for something that will never bring the joy I had right here all along."

That night he made his son promise he would never waste his time with such foolish things. "Nothing good will come of it. Enjoy the life you have. Find a good woman, raise a family, take the business, and be happy."

Emele blamed his father for his mother's death. He wanted nothing to do with him. Emele had to get away, he would go to Africa.

Six months later Ivan wrote a letter to his son begging forgiveness. With no word back from Emele, Ivan lost the will to live; he had lost everything, his wife, his son, and his youth.

Emele sank into the business for five years he was obsessed

with building a fortune. He had riches beyond most men's dreams. He bought a huge castle in his home country of Transylvania. He thought he was happy but he had no social life. There will always be time for a family later he told himself. Then one morning while shaving he noticed a wrinkle on his face. Could it be? Was he getting old? Where had time gone? Then he remembered what his father had told him about the Houruo tribe. No, that is a silly notion. But he could not get the idea out of his head. All day this was all he could think about. That night he had dreams about finding the tribe and staying young for a long time.

As the weeks passed he became obsessed with finding the Houruo and talking to the leader. Perhaps he should try. What would it hurt?

The next day he set off for Africa. He would find the Houruo, and he would stay young.

He arrived in Africa and started his search. Not many people would help him find the Houruo. He heard stories of black magic and evil spirits. Other tribesmen told him to stop the search; no good would come of it. It would be best if the Houruo were wiped out.

Emele wondered around the jungles and soon found himself on the trail of the Houruo. Finally he found the village. The Houruo were hiding until they could see he was alone and no threat to them. Then the leader came to Emele. He started talking. Emele had heard this language before. He was not sure of all the words but he understood what was being said.

Emele told the leader of his father and mother and how he had heard stories.

"Some say we are evil and want to kill us." Then he started talking about his life and how old he was. "My father lived to be one hundred and fourty years old. He was strong and fast. He would still be alive today if he hadn't been killed by a wild boar.

I am ninety nine years old."

How could this be? He looked like a man in his thirties.

They continued to talk. The leader was indeed a witch doctor and did use spirits and magic. He told him of a spell his father had used on him when he was around thirty years old. It was a spell that would work on Emele. They came to an arrangement and they would start the spell in the morning. This spell was powerful magic and would take three days to complete. Emele would have some secret wild herbs put into his blood stream.

They had no needles so they cut Emele's arm and blew the mixture into his vein with a feather. The leader danced around him and chanted in a loud voice. Emele must be very still for these three days or the spell would not work.

After one and a half days the Houruo were getting restless. It would be time for the tribe to move on as soon as the spell was complete. They never stayed in one spot too long, for fear of other tribes wanting to kill them. The spell was going as planned. Emele could feel something changing inside him. It was getting dark and he would sleep.

That night he awoke to screams and other loud noises. The Houruo were under attack. Fearing for his life he started running through the jungle. He could not see well but he just ran away from the fire that was burning the huts were he had stayed. His body started feeling weak. What was happening? He was not feeling well. Then he remembered what the leader had said. "He must not move for three days," but it had only been two days. Would the spell not work?

Emele was feeling faint and sat down beneath a tree. His head was spinning. He passed out.

When he awoke he felt pain all over his body. He opened his eyes. It was not quite morning. He could see huge bats all around him. They were biting him. They must have been attracted to the smell of the potion on his skin and in his blood. He could barely move. The bats were biting him more. He could feel his blood draining from his body, but there was nothing he could do. He passed out again.

The next time he awoke it was late afternoon and the sun was shining on his face. It was hot, too hot. He crawled to the dark shade. He was thirsty and hungry. He scraped at the ground and found some grubs. They were not good but it may help him stay alive. He felt sick. Why did he do this? He remembered the words his father had said.

Well I must survive. I need to get back home. Emele hid during the day and traveled by night. He caught some small animals and ate them raw. He was craving raw meat and blood. His senses were heightening, he could see well in the dark and his hearing was excellent. After five more days, Emele slowly made his way back to his home by the mines. One of the workers, a young man who was a loner and befriended by only Emele, found him and carried him inside. He did not look good. He was near death. The worker washed him and cleaned his wounds. The next morning Emele was still alive but in a weakened condition. The blinds were closed and he slept most of the day dreaming of horrible thing, tossing and turning.

The worker that was caring for Emele was preparing a supper when he cut his hand. It was a deep cut and he bandaged it. It was getting dark now and the worker took Emele some food. The worker tried to hold his head up to drink.

What was that smell? It made Emele's heart start pounding. He felt a thirst like he had never felt. The worker's cut was bleeding through the bandage. Emele grabbed the worker's arm and bit him where he was cut. He was sucking the blood and biting into his flesh. He could feel his teeth growing longer and he felt so alive. The worker was yelling for help. Emele threw him on the bed and bit him on the side of the neck. The worker was dead.. "My God what have I done?" It all happened so fast he didn't even know what he was doing. Emele felt as he had never felt before, so alive. It was scarey. What would he say what could he do? He must get rid of the body. He felt sad and welled up with tears. There was nothing he could do for his friend now but bury him in the woods. Emele slipped out into the night and buried his friend being careful no one would see him. He finished the job and went back to his house.

Emele slept the rest of the day that night he awoke again with the thirst. It was controlling him. He must have blood. He crept into the village looking for someone who would not be missed. Then he thought of one of the workers, a mean man whom no one liked, no family. No one would be sad to see him go and no one would miss him. Emele made his way to the man's hut he silently went inside. He saw him lying on a cot. Emele could feel his fangs growing, his eyes turned red. He was on the man in a second holding him down sinking his fangs into his neck. This man was big and strong yet Emele held him with what felt like little effort. Emele could feel this blood flowing through him warming his body. It was such a rush, he felt so alive, so strong. This time he did not feel sad. He took the body to the mine and made it look like an accident. He thrust a rock onto him crushing his head. Emele returned to his home. He heard a scream and ran outside to see what was going on. It was his friend that he had killed the night before. Somehow he had come back. He was holding a young woman and Emele could see his fangs and his eyes. He had become like Emele. When the worker saw Emele, he dropped the woman and charged Emele with his mouth wide open. They struggled. He was strong, but not as strong as Emele. Emele bit his neck and drained the blood from his body one more time. He could not have any witnesses. He caught up to the woman and grabbed her and once again fuels his life by taking hers.

He thinks the situation over. Perhaps they will come back from the dead as he came back from so close to death. He can't have his friend or the young woman coming back like this. From now on he will have to be more careful. Emele cuts the heads off and lay them in the jungle the animals will do the rest.

Emele does not like to kill but it is as if his thirst takes over. When he tries to eat regular food, he does not taste anything and feels unfilled. He gets vicious and loses control. He becomes compelled to drink the blood of a human. He had tried to drink the blood from animals, but it doesn't quench his thirst and he still loses control.

So far he has kept his victims to those he feels society would do better without, but on this night a young man sees Emele grab a local trouble maker and follows him. As he peeks through the trees he sees Emele hold the man while he tries desperately to get away until Emele sinks his fangs into his neck. Within a few seconds the man stops squirming and a few seconds more the lifeless body falls to the ground. Scared the young man turns to run away, stepping on a twig it snaps and Emele hears this. With the speed of a jaguar Emele is on the young man taking him down to the ground. The young man pulls a knife and sinks it into Emele's stomach then he stabs him in the shoulder. Emele is outraged. He feels the pain but it does not slow him down. He pulls the man's head back and bites his neck. Emele has never felt such a rush. He looks at his wounds and watches in amazement as the wounds close and heal. He feels no more pain. It is as if he were never hurt at all. Emele grabs the bodies and takes them deeper into the jungle. He rips the heads from the bodies and walks away.

Emele must take care of the business. Too many questions

are starting to come around about his health. No one seeing him around has made some workers question if Emele is fit to run things or if he is even alive. He will have to make an appearance and let everyone know he is still around and in charge. He holds a meeting and says because of conflicting schedules he will only be seen in the evenings.Any business needing him will be conducted then. This settles the rumors and gets things back on track.

Emele travels back to Transylvania to his castle. He had hired a poor family, the Rhensfields, to watch over the castle and keep things up there for his return at any time.

Gustaf Rhensfield was a slender man. He was never clean shaven, and his curly hair gave him a scruffy look. He was young, but looked older from a hard life of working at a young age. His face was weathered and tanned. He was an excellent horseman. He could make horses do anything, but he gentled them and they trusted him. He was very kind to people and animals. He was a little gullible and excited easily. He was very protective of his family or friends. He would do anything for his wife, Jenny, who he loved more than anything. There was nothing he wouldn't do for her.

Gustaf's wife Jenny was a beautiful young woman. She was known as beautiful Jenny. She had long blonde hair and bright blue eyes. She was five feet five inches tall and very shapely. She was bored with most men, and knew they only wanted to have her as a conquest. Truth be told she could have had any man she wanted, which is just what she got. She wanted Gustaf. She was not fond of the name Gustaf, so she always called him Rhensfield. She was very outgoing. She knew Rhensfield liked her a lot, but she also knew he was too shy to make the first move. Her wealthy parents did not approve of their daughter's choice in Rhensfield. They cut her off financially and disowned her when she married him. Jenny didn't care, she liked working alongside her husband and she didn't mind hard work. She knew Rhensfield would never hurt her. She had been down that road before. She was very loving and was very happy with her husband and their two young children. She was also an excellent cook and enjoyed mixing spices and other ingredients to make new dishes.

Gustaf Rhensfield is very loyal to Dracula for giving him such a good job and letting his family stay in the castle. There is nothing he would not do for Emel. Emele calls Gustaf by his last name Rhensfield, at his request, and Rhensfield calls Emele, Dracula out of respect. With all that has happened things may change. Would Rhensfield be so loyal now? Now he must lay down some important rules for the caretakers as to where and at what time they will be around, so they would not learn his secrets. He tells Rhensfield that they can work about the castle all day but not to disturb his bedroom or his study and they will remain locked. Rhensfield may be called upon all hours of the night as Emele will sleep most of the day do to his new allergy to the sun.

Dracula and Rhensfield have a talk. "I become restless at night and have to get out. Sometimes I may just walk about the courtyard, or I may prefer to go for a stroll in the country. If you hear me, don't bother to get up. If I need you I will let you know."

"You need to be careful out there, especially in the country. There are drifters and thieves out at night." said Rhensfield.

"Oh, you needn't worry about me. My father taught me to defend myself against all manors of men".

"Well you know there are wolves and wild dogs too that can shred a man to pieces."

"Well, I will be careful." He paused a moment then said "I

also must do most of my business at night, so there will be the need to hitch up the carriage once or twice a week. That reminds me; I should probably set up an appointment right away." Emele was thinking about his banker, who loved having rich customers and would do anything to keep them. Even if he thought their demands were odd or demanding. He would just say they were eccentric.

Emele was getting by. Once a week he would stroll around at night and find some drifter or go into town and wait for some poor soul to come out of the tavern. He would always dispose of the body where he was sure no one would find them. He had an old mine in the brushy part of his estate that had burned out years ago. No one had any need to even be remotely close to it. He always made sure to decapitate the bodies before taking them into the mine. He had learned he had to feed every seven days, but more than that and his body would take over and he would become careless.

A month here and it was back to Africa for a month. It was much easier in Africa but he loved Transylvania.

Then one night it happened. Emele was out in the courtyard when a thief surprised him. The man had come to rob the castle. When he saw Emele he pulled his gun and shot him in the chest. The bullet went straight through. It hurt but it also made him mad. Emele's eyes turned red and his fangs grew long. He would end this now. Inside the castle Rhensfield heard the shot. He got up and ran outside. He could see two figures struggling in moonlight. Then he saw Dracula bite the man's neck and seconds later rip his head from his shoulders with his bear hands.

What the hell is going on, he thought to himself. Then still dazed he ask "Dracula, are you alright."

Emele turned around to see Rhensfield standing there stunned. Emele still with red eyes and fangs long was caught off guard. In a split second he was right in front of Rhensfield. He grabbed him by the shoulders. Over the past couple of years he and Rhensfield had become rather close. He was indeed a trusted friend. What should he do? Emele transformed back right in front of Rhensfield. "I need to tell you a story of how this came to be."

Emele told his story to Rhensfield, who just shook his head in disbelief. "I tell you this in confidence, you are my trusted friend. I cannot help the way I am now."

Rhensfield had seen the change with his own eyes, but it was hard to believe. Then he thought of what could happen if he were to talk to someone. My family must be kept safe.

"I can see you have much to think about, but this will be our secret."

"But, Dracula, my family."

"They need not know. My secret must be kept."

Rhensfield had seen the horror in Dracula's face and knew he could have killed him in an instance, but he had refrained. He also knew Dracula's secret could not be told or there would be consequences. His family would be in danger. He could move, but that would bring suspicion and Dracula would find him. There was nothing he could do.

THE TIE THAT BINDS

The following night another thief came to the castle. But this time Emele was out in the country. When Rhensfield heard a noise he figured it was Dracula coming in. Then he heard more noises. Something was wrong. He got up to see a stranger going into his children's room. He silently crept over to the door and tried to surprise the thief. Rhensfield grabbed the man and wrestled him to the ground. The thief had a knife in his hand and managed to cut Rhensfield's arm. The scuffle woke Rhensfield's wife, Jenny. She came to see what was going on. The thief stabbed Rhensfield and he fell to the floor.

The thief turned to Jenny. "Run." she told the children.

The thief tried to grab one as they ran by, but Jenny pushed him down. She turned to her husband. He was moving toward the thief. Jenny tried to help her husband, but the thief grabbed her.

"You're a pretty thing aren't you?" said the thief, still holding his knife. "It would be a shame to cut up that face."

"Leave her alone!" Rhensfield said as he tried to stand.

"Or what?"

Just then Emele came into the room. He was silent but swift. Rhensfield's eyes widened and his head turned as he saw him come in.

The thief seeing this turned around. He saw Emele and pushed Jenny to the floor hard. She bumped her head and fell unconscious.

"You want a fight eh?" said the thief, feeling this would be an easy win.

"Oh. Indeed I do" and with that Emele was on him. He held him by the shoulders lifting him off the ground.

The thief plunged his knife deep into Emele's side and gave it a twist.

Emele felt the pain, but it only angered him further. His eyes were red and his fangs long. He bit the thief's neck hard and deep. Then he pulled the head from the body.

Rhensfield watched in amazement at what had just happened.

"Are you alright?" asked Emele.

"He cut me but I think I'll make it. How about you? I saw him stab you."

Emele lifted his shirt. I think I will be okay. He turned toward Rhensfield so he could watch as the wound closed up and healed right in front of them.

Rhensfield stared in disbelief. "Could he have killed you?"

"I truly don't know."

"We had better tend to your wound." said Emele. Then he turned to Jenny. She would be okay. "It's just a bump on the head. She will be fine with a little rest."

Emele put her on the bed and helped Rhensfield up. He looked at the wounds. "This cut on your arm will heal okay," and he looked at the wound on his side. "The blood is clean and red. You will be alright." and he bandaged him up.

"The children! I forgot about the children."

"Don't worry I hid them in the library on my way in. I will send them up. Now get some rest."

Emele quickly cleaned up the mess and disposed of the body. The sun was on the rise. He sent the children to their father. Jenny was coming to. Rhensfield was happy and felt so grateful. This would be the tie that would bind him with Dracula forever. He would be a loyal and true friend.

Emele and Rhensfield were closer now. Rhensfield seemed to understand Dracula and his problem, so he helped him keep his secret and even helped him dispose of the victims. Emele became a little more daring in his choosing of victims. Granted there were times when the victims did the work for him. There was always someone willing to try to rob a well dressed man on a lonely road or in a dark alley in the dead of night, only to realize the terror of their mistake too late.

As the years passed Emele watched Rhensfield's children grow up and his friends grow older, but he never seemed to age. The spell had worked on that part very well. His body had also been able to heal itself in an instant. He had some close calls.

VAN HELSING

One night an old drunk passed out in the alley awoke just as Dracula was quenching his thirst on another victim. He lay still not moving. Although he was drunk he knew what he had seen.

The next morning he was telling his story to who ever would listen or buy him a beer. No one took it seriously for there was no body in the alley and no signs of a struggle. Still one man, suspecting something had been going on for a while, listened. His name was Van Helsing. Too many people had been disappearing. Too many travelers looking for people who should have came this way.

Van Helsing was a man in his late sixties. He was a widower of many years and he had three children, a daughter and two sons. He was gray haired with a trimmed grey beard. He had been a policeman in many of the small towns around the area. His children had loved to hear his stories about the police investigations and their eyes would light up when he talked about them, but the children were grown now with lives of their own. He had inherited a modest sum of money when his parents died, so he did not need to work. Van Helsing worked because he loved investigating.

Van Helsing was very interested in the drunk's story of how a man could hold another strong man in the air and bite his neck and with his bare hands rip the head completely from his body. Then with movements so fast carry the victim away with little effort. He was gone in a second.

Van Helsing would have to do some investigation. He went down to the alley and after careful examination did find a small trail of blood, but it did not go far too many people had tromped through it. He started asking questions about missing people.

Some had noticed that there seemed to be a few less trouble makers around and that crime had gone down. Most didn't give it too much thought. Perhaps a vigilante was taking matters into his own hands. One way or the other it was still foul play and he would put an end to it.

Van Helsing decided he would scope out the alleys at night and see if he could notice anything suspicious. He wandered the streets for several nights and nothing happened. Then one night he caught a glimpse of a man moving through the alley. The man was dressed in dark clothes and was moving at an incredible speed. Van Helsing could see him grab someone and hold him close to him. He yelled and the dark man disappeared into the night taking the body with him. Van Helsing ran after them but he was not fast enough. He saw a carriage driving away with horses galloping at full speed. Van Helsing went back to the alley and held a lantern close to the spot where he had seen the dark man. There on the ground was something shiny. It was a gold watch. He grabbed it and held it to the light. Perhaps this would be a helpful clue. On the back was a small inscription, "With Love."

The next day Van Helsing was asking around about the watch and sure enough someone said it was theirs. He said a robber with a knife had stolen it just the night before.

"Did you get a good look at him?"

"No, it was dark and he poked me with a knife in the back and told me to give him my watch and money."

Back at the castle Rhensfield was pulling up by the doors. Emele stepped out of the carriage.

"That was a little close huh Dracula?'

"Yes, it was. Perhaps you should go to town and find out if anyone is talking about anything."

"Yes Sir, Dracula, I'll go first thing in the morning soon as I get the horses tended to."

Steve Pierce

"That will be fine Rhensfield. Just don't ask too many questions. We don't want to cause any suspicion."

Rhensfield nodded and drove away. He would get rid of the body, clean the carriage and put the horses away for the night. He drove the carriage out to the old mine and dragged the body deep inside. "That will do." he said to himself. Then he returned to the castle and went to bed. The sun would be up soon. He had better get to sleep.

The next day Rhensfield tended to the horses. Then when they had their fill he hitched them to the wagon and drove to town. He went to the mill to get some feed. If anyone knew any gossip it would be Vernon. He was the owner of the mill and he always seemed to know everything going on in town. "What's up today, Vernon?"

"Well, I tell you, something is going on. Some fellow named Van Helsing is asking folks a lot of questions."

"Oh, yeah. Who is this, Van Helsing, did you say? What kind of questions?'

"Well, word is he's been a policeman and he likes to stir things up and get people all excited. Seems he thinks there's a killer in our midst. He's been asking people if they seen anything strange or noticed anyone disappearing lately. Wait a minute, here he comes now."

Rhensfield turned around to see a man coming up the drive.

"Nice team you have there."

"Thanks."

"I was just asking folks about a fine fast team of horses."

"Are you looking to buy?"

"No, I'm just interested in who might have a fast team. Someone almost got run down last night by a carriage. You wouldn't happen to know anyone like that would you?"

"Well, I bet there are lots of fast horses around here."

Vernon and Rhensfield loaded the grain and Rhensfield drove away.

"Who was that fellow?" asked Van Helsing.

"That was Rhensfield, he works for Mr. Dracula. Rhensfield's a nice guy, but that Dracula is a little different. He does all his business at night. Has some kind of allergy from the sunshine. But, I guess he's okay. Pretty well off, got some big diamond mine in Africa they say. He travels down there every month or two."

"Sounds like an interesting guy." and with that Van Helsing walked away.

Rhensfield returned home and finished his chores, Dracula would be up soon and they would talk about this Van Helsing. The sun was setting.

Dracula came out of his room. "What did you find out today?" he asked.

"Well there's a fellow named Van Helsing, and he's been asking a lot of questions about missing people and strange things. Why, he even asked me about my horses and if they were fast, because someone almost got rundown by a team pulling a carriage."

"Perhaps we should not underestimate this Van Helsing. We must be a little more cautious from now on. We don't want to stir things up. This may be a good time to check on things in Africa."

Emele left for Africa. Life was easier there, no one asking questions, and the animals in the jungle were easily blamed for a few missing people. Still he missed his home. The mines were doing fine. He had been here for almost three months and it was time to head back home.

Emele arrived back in Transylvania in the middle of the night.

He was happy to see Rhensfield and his castle.

"What's new Rhensfield?"

"Things have been going pretty well, but Van Helsing is still asking some questions."

"Maybe tonight I should meet Mr. Van Helsing."

"I don't know if that would be such a good idea, Dracula."

"Well, maybe I can put his mind to rest. Get the carriage ready."

Soon Rhensfield had the horses hitched up and ready. "Are you sure this is a good idea?"

"We'll find out soon enough."

The two men headed to town. Rhensfield pulled the horses around the side of the street. Emele stepped out of the carriage and started walking along the road. Sure enough he saw a man watching and moving closer. It was Van Helsing and he was coming over to Emele.

"It's a bit late for a stroll, wouldn't you say?"

"Nonsense, I love the night air."

"Well, some strange things happen in the middle of the night sometimes." as he stepped up to Emele. "My name is Van Helsing." and he held out his hand.

Emele shook his hand and said, "I am Emele Dracula. How do you do?"

"Dracula, I've heard a little about you. People say you keep strange hours."

"Well, I'm sure some people think of me as strange, but I have grown quite accustomed to the night. I have an allergy to sunlight, so this is how I conduct my life. But what about you? It is an odd time for someone to be walking around."

"Well, I've been doing a little investigating. It seems there are quite a few people missing in the past few years."

"There have been a lot of people going to America"

"Yes, I suppose that could be part of it, or maybe Africa. I hear you do quite well with the mines there."

"I can't complain. It does take a lot of my time though, and it is always good to return home."

"Nice meeting you. Do be careful, a man of your fortune could attract trouble."

"I will be careful. You have a good night."

Emele walked a little further and turned around. "Rhensfield, it is time to go."

Rhensfield turned the carriage around, Emele climbed in and they headed home

Van Helsing was watching, wondering what kind of a man Dracula was. Things have been pretty quite the past few months, he thought to himself. Perhaps the troubles were behind them. He headed home and went to bed.

Van Helsing finds out that Dracula has been in Africa for the past three months and wonders if that is why things have calmed down. No missing people and no one wondering the dark alleys. He shall be watchful of Dracula.

Emele is also wondering if Van Helsing is going to piece things together. He must be very careful not to make any mistakes. He may have to venture a little farther from home for his meals.

So Emele does travel farther away to the next towns and takes victims where he can find them, in the country or the towns. It is getting harder to lure bad people out and he must survive, so his thirst makes him take innocent victims. He does not like this, but what can he do, he needs to feed.

Rhensfield is still his best friend and sometimes feels for the innocent but he could never cross Dracula, too much has bound them together. He remembers a couple of years ago when his daughter was attacked in town, and how she told him how a dark shadowy figure came from nowhere and took her would be assailant from her in a blink of an eye. She had never seen anyone move that fast or that quitely. Rhensfield knew it was Dracula, even though he had never said anything about this encounter.

Van Helsing has ben trying to catch Dracula. He has followed his carriage to the country only to loose him or catch a glimpse of a shadowy figure whisking away yet another victim. But there is never a body to be found. Van Helsing has seen people disappear with his own eyes and he knows that they have had their blood drained by this monster of a man, but never well enough to be sure it was Dracula. Where could all these bodies be? It was driving his crazy.

Van Helsing was digging into Dracula's past. He was finding documents that would make him very old. He was asking more questions, but no one has any answers. He believes there is something wrong here but this is like nothing he has come across before. He is becoming obsessed with this case. He is losing touch with his children, as they grow up fast. Anytime he thinks he has a lead that points to Dracula, somehow there is never enough evidence to make any charges. People are starting to think him mad when he talks of victims whose blood has been drained from the body and the strength someone would have to have to do the things he has seen.

Years go by and he is no closer to any proof than when he started. He has told stories to his children, but he is always careful not to mention Dracula's name. He doesn't want trouble for them.

Emele has had a few runins with Vans Helsing and once he even took a bullet from his gun. He has thought of killing him, but that may really stir up more trouble than this would be worth.

Van Helsing's children have moved out and have started their own lives. He still loves them dearly but has become obsessed with getting proof that Dracula is a monster.

LOVE KNOWS NO BOUNDRIES

Emele still must run his business and has accumulated a vast fortune over the years. His banker, Mr. Ramsey, a proud old Irishman, meets him anytime of night as he is his best customer. On this particular night the banker has asked one of his favorite new employees a very dedicated and loyal worker, to join them in their business meeting. Her name is Constance. She is twenty six years old, a tall slender woman with a nice figure, ample bosom and a tiny waist that curved out to her hips, though she usually wore loose fitting clothes that concealed her shape. She has very light brown wavy hair, shoulder length, usually worn up in a bun. Her eyes are blue, but she gets nervous when anyone looks into them. She is pretty but does not see herself that way and does little to emphasize it. A bit of a loner and a bit shy, she has never really dated anyone. She hopes to be a house wife someday with children, but inside she is a romantic, and longs for the man of her dreams to sweep her off her feet and wisk her away to an exciting life. She works hard at her job and worked hard in school to get a job like this. She is very polite and does not say much unless spoken to.

"Constance, tonight you will meet Mr.Emele Dracula, he is a bit eccentric, has some sort of allergy to the sun, and can only be out and about at night, but he is a wealthy and influential man. He is our number one customer so we will do about anything we can to keep him happy. It will do you good to get to know him."

"Thank you for choosing me to help you tonight, Mr. Ramsey. I am excited to meet Mr. Dracula."

When Emele comes into the bank, he is greeted by the owner Mr. Ramsey. "Mr. Dracula, How are you? It's always a pleasure to see you."

"I'm quite well. I'm glad you could meet me this evening."

"I'm glad to be at your service. What can we do for you?"

"Well, I am in need of a book keeper. Some of my papers need to be put in order and updated.'

"I believe we can handle that for you. I would like you to meet Constance, our new book keeper. She has not been here long but she knows her business."

Emele turns toward Constance. He is quite taken by her. 'How do you do, Constance?'

"It is very nice to meet you, Mr. Dracula."

"Please, call me Emele. Have you been in this area long? I don't believe I've ever seen you before."

"Yes. My mother died when I was very young and Father moved us here. He was a policeman and a bit of a detective as well."

"Shall we get to it?" says Mr. Ramsey.

Emele is lost for a second, "I'm sorry. What did you say?"

"Shall we get down to business?"

"Yes, I would like to go over my last few transactions if you don't mind."

"Of course. Miss Van Helsing, would you please get Mr. Dracula's file of his accounts?"

"I beg your pardon, what did you say her name was?'

"I'm sorry. I thought I introduced Miss Van Helsing."

"Yes, But I did not catch her family name." Suddenly Emele felt sick. Could this be Van Helsing's daughter? He had to get away.

"I'm sorry, but I'm suddenly not feeling well. I hate to cut things short but I need to go"

"That is quite alright. We can reschedule anytime."

And with that Dracula left and had Rhensfield drive him home at once.

When they got to the castle, Rhensfield asked. "Is something wrong, Dracula?"

"I just need to rest." and he went to his room. He lay on his bed and thought about this chance meeting. He tried to fall asleep, but could not get the Van Helsings out of his mind. He tossed and turned for hours. The sun was rising and Emele's thoughts turned to Constance. He could not get her out of his mind. She was all he could think of.

He finally fell asleep, and for the first time since his change, he had a dream. It was of Constance. She was just standing there looking at him, staring as though she could see right through him and see his innermost feelings. It was like she understood him. She called his name, Emele, Emele. What was this strange dream?

When he awoke the next evening, all he could think about was Constance. It made him feel odd. It made him feel, lonely. He had not had such feelings for a long long time. He had to see her again. If only for a glimpse, he had to see her.

He would send Rhensfield to town in the morning to make another appointment with Mr. Ramsey. "Make sure to tell Mr. Ramsey to have Miss Van Helsing there also."

"Sure thing, Dracula." Then he looked back to Dracula, confused. "Did you say Van Helsing?"

"Yes, Miss Constance Van Helsing."

"Van Helsing?" asked Rhensfield again. "She's not old man Van Helsing's daughter, is she?"

"I believe she is."

"Are you sure about this? It sounds like trouble to me."

"Yes, I'm sure."

Rhensfield said "Okay, if you're sure, I'll head there first thing in the morning."

Dracula told Rhensfield he would not need him for the rest of the night.

Rhensfield said goodnight and walked away scratching his head.

Emele walked around in the courtyard, wondering what he might be getting into. Was he doing the right thing he wondered? He walked back and forth in the garden all night until the sun started to rise, then he went to his room. He was sure he wouldn't get much sleep. His mind was buzzing with all kinds of thoughts.

Rhensfield got up and hitched the horses. Then he drove away toward town shaking his head.

Emele dozed off for a bit. When he awoke he was not hungry. He felt something else deep inside, to the very core of his being, and he felt alive.

Rhensfield knocked on Dracula's door. "Mr Ramsey said tonight would be fine, about nine o'clock would be best."

"Hitch up the horses, Rhensfield, We're going to town."

On the way to town, Emele felt like a little boy on his first day of school. He was nervous and excited and full of wonder. His thoughts returned to Constance, "What is the matter with me? Why can't I get you out of my head? Well, soon enough we will see what kind of hold you have on me."

When they pulled up to the bank, Rhensfield climbed down to open the door, but Emele was already out of the carriage and walking up the stairs.

"Good evening Mr. Dracula" said Mr Ramsey as he opened the door. "It's so good to see you again. I hope you're feeling better."

"Yes, I am. I'm sorry for having to leave so abruptly the other night."

"Don't worry about it. These things happen" said Mr. Ramsey. "You remember Miss Van Helsing."

"Good evening Sir" said Constance.

"Please, call me Emele. And I am so glad you were able to join us on such short notice."

"Well, Mr Ramsey insisted. After all we must keep our best customer happy."

They were going over the books, but Emele found himself stealing little glances of Miss Van Helsing.

Emele told them "I have made a mess of my records and have not been doing my bookkeeping the way I should. I could really use some help in that department."

"I'm sure Miss Van Helsing would be glad to help you out. Wouldn't you Constance?"

"Well, I would be glad to take a look if that is alright with you, Mr. Dracula?"

"That would be fine. It would be best if you could come to my castle. How does eight O'clock tomorrow night sound?"

"That would be fine."

"I will send my driver Mr. Rhensfield to pick you up. Let's make it a dinner meeting."

Constance was not so sure about this and she looked at Mr. Ramsey. He winked and shook his head in agreement. "That sounds like a good idea, I will see you then."

Emele left the bank and climbed into the carriage.

"Where to Dracula?" asked Rhensfield.

"I think we will call it a night and just go home."

"Are you sure, you must be hungry."

"Just take me home."

When they arrived at the castle, Rhensfield asked, "Are you feeling alright?"

"I would like to talk to you when you get the horses settled."

"Yes sir Dracula." and Rhensfield hurried in his tasks feeling something was wrong and Dracula needed him.

Rhensfield stood by the door to Emele's study. "Come in

Rhensfield, there is something I need to talk to you about as a trusted friend."

This caught Rhensfield a little off guard but he was here for him. "What is it Dracula?"

"Well, I don't know how exactly to put this, but it seems I have invited a young woman to dinner and to look over some books tomorrow and I'm not sure I can deal with this situation." Emele paused a moment. "It seems I am infatuated with this woman, but I don't trust myself to be alone with her. I'm not sure what will happen."

"Well, Jenny and I can do the cooking and be close by. I could bring you drinks and check on you every little bit. And if there is ever anything you need, you just let me know."

"Thank you, Rhensfield, that helps put my mind at ease. I don't know why but I can't stop thinking about her. She is an accountant at the bank, she is very smart and Mr. Ramsey speaks very highly of her. The one thing that bothers me is her name. Constance Van Helsing."

"Boy, Miss Van Helsing again? I don't know about this, Dracula. This might not be such a good idea."

"I know what you say is true but I have to see her."

"Well, if you're sure. I will be watching things, but be careful."

Rhensfield walks out to retire for the night and Emele sits in his chair thinking things over. "Perhaps this is a mistake." he says to himself. He has been pondering these thoughts back and forth for hours. He looks up and sees it is almost dawn. He will not sleep much today, but he goes to bed.

Emele finally drifts off to sleep and once again he dreams of Constance. They are alone in the study looking at his books. She leans over towards him for a closer look and her neck is right in front of him. He can smell the blood and hear her heart pumping it through her veins. He can see it pulsating. His fangs grow long. He opens his mouth. "Nooooo!" Emele wakes up shivering. He feels his fangs are long. "What am I going to do?"

Rhensfield hears the shout and runs to Dracula's room. "Are you alright? What's going on?"

Emele opens his door. "Rhensfield, what am I going to do?" He tells him his dream.

Rhensfield thinks it over. "I bet you are just hungry, heck you haven't ate anything for almost a week. I think it will be okay you just need to feed."

"Perhaps you are right. That is a good idea, but we must hurry. You will have to pick Miss Van Helsing up very shortly."

With that Emele sets out to find the food he needs.

Jenny is in the kitchen and Rhensfield is on his way to pick up Miss Van Helsing.

Emele returns to the castle and cleans up just as Rhensfield pulls up to the castle doors. He is nervous about his dream but also excited to see Constance. He opens the door. "Welcome, Miss Van Helsing. May I take your cloak?" She hands Emele her cloak. "Come, sit in the dinning room, dinner is almost ready."

He walks her to the dining room and pulls out a chair for her to sit. "Would you care for some wine?"

"That sounds nice." Constance says in a rather nervous voice.

Rhensfield pours the wine and announces dinner will be served right away. He is keeping a close eye on Dracula. He does not want anything to go wrong tonight.

At first the conversation is difficult but as the glass of wine disappears so does the uneasiness. Soon the small talk turns to business and as the meal is concluded.

They go to the study for a look at the books. They are seated next to each other and looking at the same page when Constance leans in to look more closely at the figures. Emele is nervous. He can smell her blood and hear her heart pumping it through her veins and his fangs start to grow.

"I'm sorry," Constance says, "but I believe I see a major mistake here." She turns toward Emele and his fangs quickly return to normal. She notices a strange look on his face. "I don't mean to be rude, I just like solving problems."

Emele pulls himself together quickly and says "That is fine, that's why you're here." He was scared for a moment, but he knew he would not bite her. He would never bite her.

They finished up some of the book work and Emele was asking Constance about herself. "So you have not been in town too long?"

"No, I just moved back to be close to family after college, and haven't really gotten settled in yet. I was hoping I could get a little closer to my brothers and my father, but they are so busy and don't seem to have much time for me anymore. I'm hoping that things will get better. We had sort of grown apart over the years. My brothers are involved in their new lives and Father is in his own little world these days. How about you? Have you lived here your whole life?"

"I have lived here a long time, but with the business in Africa I have to travel a lot."

"I think it would be wonderful to travel."

"I enjoy my life, but it can be a lonely life."

"Surely it doesn't have to be lonely, that seems to be a choice I would think "

"Perhaps I just haven't met the right woman" looking into Constance's eyes. "What about you. Surely a lovely young woman as you must have someone."

"Perhaps I have not met the right man yet either" said Constance looking back into his eyes.

It was getting late. "Well, I think we should call it a night. Could you come back in a couple of days?" asked Emele.

"I think that could be arranged." Constance said with a smile. "How about nine o'clock Thursday evening?"

"Yes, that will work out just fine."

"Should we have dinner again?"Emele asked hopefully.

"That sounds very nice. I will see you then."

"Rhensfield, would you please see Miss Van Helsing home?"

"Sure thing, Dracula." Rhensfield said while heading for the door.

"Let me walk you to the carriage." Emele held out his arm and escorted Constance to the door. "I really enjoyed your company tonight and it was good to get some of the book work caught up. Thank you for helping me out." He handed Constance some money for her help.

"I enjoyed tonight as well. And thank you again for giving me a chance to earn some extra money. My bills seem to be piling up on me. I was lucky to get the job at the bank, but I feel funny taking money from such an elegant host."

"I assure you, you are well worth it" Emele took her hands and gave them a small squeeze. He opened the door and told her "Good night Miss Van Helsing."

Constance smiled back and said "Until Thursday." and walked over to the carriage where Rhensfield held open the door waiting to help her in.

Rhensfield climbed up and hollered "Let's go boys!" and they were off. He was thinking what a nice woman this lady is. She and Dracula seemed to hit it off pretty good.

Constance was thinking to herself, "This evening was fun. It really didn't seem like work at all. Mr. Dracula is quite an interesting man." She didn't know what it was but she was attracted to him, not because of his wealth, or his rugged good looks, it was something else. He was easy to talk to and maybe even a little fun to flirt with.

The carriage pulled up to Constance's house and Rhensfield climbed down, opened the door and helped her out. "I will pick you up Thursday at a little before nine then, Miss Van Helsing."

"I will be ready."

Constance went inside and readied herself for bed. "That was quite an evening." she said to herself. She felt happy. She knew she would sleep well tonight.

Emele was too excited to sleep. He walked around the courtyard until dawn. His mind was in a whirl. He felt so alive. For the first time in his life he truly knew what he wanted. "How could this ever work out? What am I going to do?" He thought for a moment and said "Slow down Emele, you're getting ahead of yourself." The sun was coming up and Emele went to his room. He layed on his bed and shut his eyes while thoughts of Constance danced in his head.

Mr. Van Helsing was still working on his case of Mr. Dracula. He has been nosing around the nearby towns and asking questions about any missing people. Emele has been very careful about his victims and sticking to the country and wondering the roads for vagabonds and thieves. He has also been zigzagging from town to town and leaving no trace of the bodies, Rhensfield makes sure of that.

Van Helsing has heard of a black carriage pulled by two fast black horses in different areas at different times. Unfortunately no one has been close enough to notice anything special about the carriage. "I must watch for a carriage, especially the one Rhensfield drives. Perhaps I could mark it somehow. That would be difficult to put something on that others could see but would not be noticed by Rhensfield or Dracula." He would have to study this a while.

Emele was a little happy now and was looking forward to his evenings with Constance. He made a fake book and would deliberately mess up his book keeping just to have Constance come over and fix his problems, but being a sharp businessman he would always keep track of the real book and knew exactly every transaction. Sometimes Constance would question his records. "How can you run a company making mistakes like this."

This seemed like the perfect time to ask the question Emele had in the back of his mind. "Constance, would you consider being my accountant?"

Constance had secretly hoped an opportunity to work more with Emele would somehow come up, and now here it was. "I would have to think it over." she said not trying to sound too eager. "I do have a very good job at the bank, you know."

"Yes, I do know, and that is why I took the liberty of talking with Mr. Ramsey about this. I hope you don't mind. I asked him if there was any way I could steal you away for a couple of hours a day. I also told him it would not be fair to expect you to be at work early in the morning if you have been helping me in the evenings. I also reminded Mr. Ramsey that I am his best customer and it would be an enormous favor to me personally if he could keep you on at the same salary."

"I don't know what to say. I'm not sure I like you talking to Mr. Ramsey about me behind my back."

"I didn't mean to offend you. I just knew Mr. Ramsey would see things my way. I knew he would love the fact that he did me a huge favor and now I will owe him, even if it means costing him and losing a little time of one of his employees."

"Well, it seems you have really thought this through. Just what, exactly, did Mr. Ramsey think of your grand idea?"

"He loved it. I knew he would."

"Well then, since you have already gone through so much trouble to secure my services, how could I refuse?"

"Thank you. Since you are going out of your way to work for me the least I can do is offer you to dine with me each evening before we start on the books."

"I will take you up on your offer, but be prepared to tell me about yourself over dinner. I like to know a little about who I'm working for."

"Sure, as long as you tell me about yourself also."

The following evening Rhensfield picked up Constance and brought her to the castle. Emele was excited to see her, he met her at the door, "Miss Van Helsing, how nice to see you".

"Nice to see you to, Mr. Dracula, but since we are going to be working together I would feel more comfortable if you called me Constance."

"Very well, Constance, only if you call me Emele."

"That would be fine, Emele."

Rhensfied interrupts "Dinner is ready, whenever you are Dracula" he wasn't sure he had heard him they were to busy staring at each other. "Dinner will be served shortly", he said in a louder voice.

Emele looked at Rhensfield. "That will be fine."

They made small talk during dinner. Constance talked about her education and Emele talked about his business travels. When dinner was finished they went to the study. They started going over the books and the receipts. Things were moving along quickly and they soon finished.

"Well looks like we've done about all we can for the day", sighed Constance.

"Well, its still early we could sit and chat awhile, unless you need to get home?" Emele said looking at Constance.

"Nothing waiting at home, I'm in no hurry to go."

Emele offered his hand to Constance and walked her to the love seat. It was a well cushioned S-shaped chair with seats on both sides and when seated you would look at each other across the divider. They talked for a bit.

"Would you care for some wine?"

"That's sounds nice as long as you're not trying to get me drunk and take advantaged of me" Constance teased.

"I wouldn't want you to get drunk I would just tempt you with my charm" Emele teased back.

They both laughed at their silly thoughts.

"I do enjoy your company. It is nice to have someone to talk to" said Emele.

"I enjoy your company too. It gets a little lonely in my house all alone. The evenings can be long. I'm glad this book keeping came up, it gives me time to get out and dinner is more enjoyable when you share it with someone."

"I would hate to think of you being lonely." Emele said, looking into Constance's eyes. He leaned in closer.

Constance looked into Emele's eyes and leaned towards Emele and closed her eyes, waiting for his kiss. She felt his hands softly on the side of her neck and head. He pulled her towards him and kissed her.

Emele's heart raced as he tasted Constance's lips. He was kissing her deeper and harder and Constance was responding. His excitement was growing. He longed to be with her. He wondered if she felt the same. Kisses don't lie, he thought to himself.

Constance's heart was racing also; she had never felt a passion like this. She wanted more, but she would no permit herself to go any further at this time. She pulled away a bit dazed. "I think it's getting a bit late, perhaps you should take me home." This is not want she wanted, but is what she had to do.

"I'm sorry I didn't mean to be so forceful. I don't want to rush things. I will see you home."

Emele felt awkward, but did not want the evening to end like this. He would ride with her in the carriage.

Emele stepped into the hall and hollered "Rhensfield we are ready to go, I will be accompanying Miss Vanhelsing to her home."

Emele walked Constance to the carriage, opened the door and followed her in. Rhensfield climbed up and they were off.

Emele was sitting across form Constance, he reached across and held her hand and looked into her eyes. "I think I'm falling in love with you. Not an hour goes by that I don't think of you. I know we've only known each other a short time and I don't want to rush things and I hope I haven't scared you off."

"It has been a short time and I am having feelings for you also, feelings I have never felt before, but you haven't scared me off" Constance said in a nervous voice. She enjoyed kissing Emele, but wanted to make sure her feelings were real. She hoped he understood.

"Perhaps we could meet tomorrow just to talk", said Emele.

Constance was glad to hear this. "Maybe I could cook you dinner this time at my house."

Emele was relieved. "That sounds wonderful. I will bring the wine."

Rhensfield stopped the horses. Emele helped Constance out, and walked her to her door. "Until tomorrow." he said.

"Until tomorrow", replied Constance, as she watched Emele walk back to the carriage. She stood in the doorway and watched them drive away. "I am falling in love with you too." She closed the door, readied herself for bed. She laid there thinking about Emele. She wondered if they really were rushing things. It felt so right and she trusted him. Tomorrow she would see what happens. She would feel more comfortable in her own house.

Emele told Rhensfield to let him out before they got to the

castle, he needed to feed. He walked along the road his mind racing with thoughts of Constance. He had fallen in love with her. How could he tell her what he has become? He knew he would have to tell her if he wanted to go any further. Soon he had realized that he had wandered off the road. He was not feeling so hungry perhaps he would just go home. He went into the castle and entered the study. He poured himself a glass of wine and sat in the chair. He sipped the wine, but with Constance gone it had lost its taste. Tomorrow he would take things slow and let Constance make the next move.

Rhensfield knocked on the door. "Are you okay Dracula?"

"Yes. I do feel like talking if you have the time."

Rhensfield opened the door and said, "What's on your mind?"

"It's Constance. I'm falling in love and I think I need to tell her about myself, but I don't know how to do it."

"Are you sure that's a wise thing to do. Maybe you should wait a bit and get to know her a little bit better. It may scare her off. She may not be ready yet."

"Rhensfield, what would I do with out you? You're my best and only friend and I value your opinion. I don't want to lose her and I don't want to live without her."

"Sounds like you got it bad. I hope things work out for you and whatever you do I'll be here for you. I'm just not sure she would understand, but I understand what you're saying."

"Thank you Rhensfield it's nice to have someone I can talk to about anything. I guess I'll see what tomorrow brings. Have a good night Rhensfield."

"See you tomorrow Dracula." Rhensfield leaves and Dracula goes to his bedroom.

That night Constance could not sleep. She kept thinking of Emele, and how she was attracted to him. He had some strange ways, but she liked him. She had had crushes on other men;

most of them didn't know she existed. This was different. This was more than a crush. She knew she was falling in love with him. She was pretty sure he felt the same way. "Maybe he is the one," she heard herself say out loud. She rolled over in bed and hugged her pillow. She imagined her pillow as Emele and held it close. She longed for his touch. She couldn't wait until tomorrow to see him, hold him, and love him. Oh my, yes, and love him.

That day Emele could not sleep. He was restless. His head was spinning of thoughts of Constance. He did not want to live without her. He was in love. A love he had not felt before. His heart warmed as he admitted this to himself. He started thinking of her feminine ways, the way she carried herself, the way she walked, oh god the way she walked, and her body, her beautiful body. He imagined how she might look under her clothing. He was becoming aroused. He had not had this kind of feelings for many years. It felt good, warm, and exciting all at the same time. He could hardly wait to see her tonight.

That evening Constance was getting ready for Emele. She fixed her hair and put on the outfit Emele had said he liked, and how beautiful she looked in it. She would be cooking steak tonight. She had learned Emele liked a good porterhouse, thick and rare. She put candles on the table, but not to many. She felt the low light would be romantic. Constance looked around the room. Yes, it would be perfect.

Back at the castle, it was getting dark. Emele had not gotten any sleep. He was so excited to be going to Constance's house. Her inviting him over was a big surprise. He knew she liked him very much, and this was special. He dressed himself in the suit Constance had said he looked so dashing in.

Jenny brought Emele a bouquet of the prettiest roses she had ever grown, and a bottle of wine he had asked for. She couldn't help noticing how happy and excited he looked. He was quite a handsome man. Though, they had seldom spoken, they held a high regard for each other.

Rhensfield opened the door and hollered, "Dracula, are you ready?"

Emele quickly exited the castle, and they were on their way. They soon reached Constance's house. Emele was out of the carriage before Rhensfield had completely stopped.

Constance heard the knock at the door. "Come in," she said.

Rhensfield hollered to Emele. "I will be waiting down the street."

Emele waved Rhensfield off and went inside. Rhensfield pulled up and tied the horses to a hitching post. He would wait inside the carriage and catch up on some sleep until Dracula needed him.

"Something smells delicious," Emele said as he looked for Constance.

She was coming through the kitchen door. "Dinner is almost ready."

"I brought some wine," he said as he handed the bottle to Constance. "It's the one you said you liked best." He also handed her the flowers.

Constance took the wine and the flowers. "It will go great with the meal I have prepared." Constance put the flowers in a vase and set them on the table. She handed the bottle back to Emele. "Would you mind pouring? Dinner is ready. I will bring it to the dining room."

Emele noticed the low candle light. It pleased him. He poured the wine and stood until Constance came in.

She carried in two plates and set them at opposite ends of the small dining table. "There we go."

"Looks exquisite," Emele said as he pulled the chair out for

Constance.

"Thanks you very much," she said as she sat down.

Emele sat in his chair. After a couple of bites he said, "This meal is wonderful. You are quite a talented cook." Though he was hungering for something more.

"Thank you, I worked very hard on it all day, just for you." Constance teased as she winked at him.

Emele smiled and nodded.

Constance was feeling flirty now and kicked off her shoes and rubbed Emele's leg with her foot under the table. At first it startled him, but he was becoming aroused. The way she was eating, was so sexy. It was driving him wild with passion. They quickly finished their meal, and Emele refilled their wine glasses. He followed Constance to the living room. He sat the glasses on the coffee table and sat next to Constance on the love seat.

Constance leaned over and kissed Emele, and their passion took over. They kissed long and hard holding tight to each other. Their hands were busy feeling each others' bodies. "I love you," she whispered in his ear. She stood up and took his hand, leading him to her bedroom.

Emele knew it was right. He scooped up Constance in his arms, and carried her to the bed. He kissed her hard once more, and said, "I love you." He let her down and they stood by the bed kissing.

Constance nervously undid Emele's shirt and rubbed her hands on his muscular chest.

Emele pulled her blouse up from her skirt, and rubbed his hands around her waist. Her skin felt so soft. He moved his hands up her back. He could tell Constance was nervous as she shivered at his touch. He knew she longed for more by the way she was kissing him. He unbuttoned her blouse and unsnapped her bra, and Constance let them fall to the floor.

Constance reached for Emele's belt and unzipped his pants. Her hands were trembling with nervousness and passion. Emele removed her skirt and looked at her body. She was more beautiful than he had imagined.

Constance pulled back the covers on the bed, and they got into the bed. They kissed and held each other tight. Emele's hands were exploring her body with an urgency he had never known. Constance shivered and pulled Emele on top of her. Emele went slowly, and Constance bit his shoulder as he entered her. It hurt, but the pain soon turned to pleasure. They held each other close as they both moved. "Oh my god," Constance said. "I could never have imagined anything like this."

Emele could hardly speak. His vampire blood pumped through his body like he had never felt before. He had to hold back for fear he might change from the adrenaline rush. He could feel his eyes burn. He pulled his mouth from Constance's lips, because his fangs were growing. He was getting scared. Could he control the urges? He thought about how much he loved her. He tried to hold on to that thought as they made love, but he was still changing. He closed his eyes and held her tight as he pushed his face into the pillow next to Constance as the ecstasy took over. Constance moved instinctively, thrusting her hips upward as they climaxed together. They were exhausted, lying motionless, basking in the afterglow.

Emele could feel himself change back to normal. He raised his head. Opening his eyes he looked at Constance. She was lying there with her eyes shut, still lost in the moment. He softly kissed her cheek. She didn't move, but he heard her say" I love you."

"I love you too," he said. He moved off of her and they cuddled together. He could tell she was falling asleep. He held her for hours as she slept. It felt so good to hold the woman he loved. He never wanted to let go, but it was getting close to sunrise. He slowly pulled his arm from under her neck and sat up.

"Please, don't leave" said Constance. "Stay a little longer."

"As much as I hate to leave, I must. I wish we could stay like this forever."

Constance could see it was almost sunup. "I understand" she said as she sat up and gave Emele one more hug and kiss.

"You're making it hard to leave, but we will be together in a few days" Emele said looking in her eyes, and he kissed her softly one more time.

"A few days can be a lifetime."

Emele dressed himself as Constance put on her robe. She walked him to the door and turned him around and wrapped her arms around his neck and gave him one last goodnight kiss.

Emele opened the door and walked down to the carriage. He looked in and saw Rhensfield sleeping inside. "What a great friend I have" he said to himself as he climbed up to the driver's seat and slowly drove the horses home. When they reached the castle, Emele quickly put the horses away then woke Rhensfield. The sun was coming up as they walked inside.

As they walked Rhensfield noticed how happy Dracula looked. "So, how did your night go?"

Emele couldn't help but smile. "It was the best night of my life."

Rhensfield smiled back. He was happy for his friend.

"What's going on out here?' asked Jenny as she came around the doorway. She looked at Emele and then her husband. They were both just smiling. She could see how happy Emele was. "The sun is coming up. You had better get to bed" and she grabbed Rhensfield's arm and tugged him along toward their room. Emele turned and went to his room. "It is good to see him so happy. I'm glad he has found someone. It's not good to be lonely." Then she shut the door behind them as they went in their bedroom. She looked at her husband. "I love you so much." She put her arms around his neck and gave him a big kiss, and then she pulled the covers back on the bed and slid in. Then she said, "Constance seems like a nice lady, do you think she could be the one to be Mrs. Dracula?"

Rhensfield was taking his clothes off and hanging them over the chair. "I hope so. He needs someone in his life."

"It would be nice to have another woman around this old castle."

Rhensfield sat on the edge of the bed and pulled his socks off. "Yes it would be nice if you had someone to talk to besides the kids."

Jenny leaned over and grabbed Rhensfield and pulled him backwards in the bed and kissed him again.

Rhensfield smiled and kissed her back. "I am truly a blessed man, to have a friend like Dracula and a beautiful, loving wife like you. What did I ever do to deserve you?"

Jenny put her finger over his mouth and said "I'm about to show you" and she pulled the blankets over their heads.

Emele lay on his bed. He had never felt so peaceful. He closed his eyes and fell asleep, hoping to dream of Constance.

Constance was trying to sleep. She knew she would have to get up and go to work shortly. She dosed off and dreamed of going on a trip to Africa with Emele. She dreamed of a fancy wedding. She smiled in her sleep. She woke up and readied herself and walked to work.

A SPECIAL GIFT

While at work, Constance found out she would have to come in early and stay late for the next few weeks. A bad flu strain was going around and some of the workers were getting violently sick. The bank had been meaning to hire a couple of people and this outbreak was really leaving them shorthanded. Mr. Ramsey said "I know the hours will be long and stressful, but look at the bright side, lots of overtime means a big paycheck. Unfortunately you won't be able to help Mr. Dracula with his books. I will let him know you won't be available for a short time." Mr. Ramsey could see the disappointment in Constance's face. "I know Mr. Dracula will be sad to hear this, he has told me what a fine job you are doing for him." Mr. Ramsey smiled and said "I can tell by the way he talks about you that he is well pleased with your work." Then with a more serious look he added "Be careful, I think he might be having feelings for you, the way I see his face light up when he talks about you. We don't want him to be misled."

Constance was disappointed to hear this, but what could she do?

Rhensfield happened to be in town getting supplies. Mr. Ramsey saw him and went over to talk to him. "Mr. Rhensfield, could you hold up for a moment?"

Rhensfield turned his head and saw Mr. Ramsey heading his way. "Oh, sure thing, Mr. Ramsey."

"I hate to have to tell you this. I know Mr. Dracula and Miss Van Helsing have been getting along very well together, but"

Rhensfield excitedly interrupted. 'But what!? What, what's going on?"

"Well, it's nothing bad. It's just I'm very short handed. I have people out, very sick, and I need Miss Van Helsing to be here at the bank. I'm afraid she won't be able to help Mr. Dracula for a couple of weeks."

"A couple of weeks! That is a long time!" Rhensfield said excitedly. "But, there is not much we can do. I will talk to Mr. Dracula. He's not going to like this. I know he really appreciates Miss Van Helsing's help."

"Well, it is just a couple of weeks, I'm sure, Mr. Dracula will understand. If he wants to talk to me he knows where I'm at. He can stop by anytime."

"Ok, I don't know, I will see what he says."

Rhensfield finished up in town and went back to the castle. It was almost dark. He knew Dracula would be up soon. He put away the supplies and went into the castle. Dracula was waking.

"I ran into Mr. Ramsey today, and he said they were really short of help at the bank. A lot of people are sick, so Miss Van Helsing would have to be there extra hours. He doubted if she would have time to help you with your books. He said it maybe a couple of weeks. He said, you could talk to him anytime."

"Well then, a couple of weeks is a long time, but if he needs her help she is happy to be there. There's nothing we can do," said Dracula looking a bit sad.

Rhensfield could see the disappointment in Dracula's face. "Well they say absence makes the heart grow fonder," he said trying to cheer him up.

"Indeed it does, Rhensfield, indeed it does."

Van Helsing was snooping around trying to piece things together. Many people were missing, mostly criminal types as far as he could tell. Maybe some sort of vigilante was at work here. He still had nothing connecting Mr. Dracula to anything, and there were no bodies to prove anyone had been murdered. Crime was down and most people didn't care why. No one seemed to know what happened to these people. Van Helsing knew in his gut Mr. Dracula was not as innocent as he seemed to be. He would do more investigating, maybe even some surveillance around the castle. He was asking more questions in town about Mr. Dracula. Most people knew of him but didn't really know him. All had heard he kept odd hours and he was very rich. Some commented on his youthful appearance, and wondered if he stayed younger looking from not being in the sunlight. They all knew Mr. Rhensfield, as the man who worked for Mr. Dracula. Most people liked Mr. Rhensfield and described him as a kind person, who went out of his way to say hi and visit a little, though he said very little about his boss.

Van Helsing wasn't getting much information. He decided to watch the castle, but he didn't see anything of Mr. Dracula just the Rhensfields doing business as usual. He watched at night, but nothing seemed to be going on at all. The castle would get dark early and nothing until daylight. Perhaps Dracula was not feeling well and needed rest. Unknown to Van Helsing, Dracula had decided it would be a good time to check on things in Africa while Constance was busy with all the extra work there. He had left one evening when Van Helsing was busy talking to people in the pub.

Dracula had been taking care of business for two weeks. It was a good thing he had taken time to go, there was some repair work needed that would have went unchecked. He had to have a talk with his people in charge to make sure things were safe for the workers. He even had to fire one manager who was mean to the workers and stealing diamonds. When he disappeared, people just thought he had just run away.

When business was finished, he went back to Transylvania. It had been over three weeks since he had seen Constance.

Although he had been very busy, time had passed slowly. It seemed like he had been away from Constance for months, now finally he would see her again. Tonight Constance would come over for dinner. All Emele could think about was the last time they were together. He closed his eyes and he could smell her perfume. He could taste her lips, how sweet they were. A smile came to his face as he thought of them making love. Tonight he would give her a special gift. Something he had had for many years. Something that meant a lot to him and he knew would mean a lot to Constance.

Rhensfield had left to pick up Constance and would be back soon. Emele could smell the fine meal Jenny was preparing. "Tonight would be another special evening" he heard himself say outload.

Rhensfield pulled the carriage up to the castle and opened the door, taking her hand as she stepped out. "Boy, I know Dracula is excited about seeing you tonight!" he said excitedly.

"Well, I'm glad to hear that. I haven't heard much from him the last few weeks. I was beginning to think he had forgotten about me." Constance said with a grin.

"Oh, heck no! Dracula could hardly wait for you to come over tonight. You're all he's been talking about."

"You really are his best friend, aren't you?"

"Shucks, me and Dracula go way back."

They walked to the castle door just as Emele was opening it. He just stood there staring at Constance, taking in the beauty of the woman he loved.

"May I come in?" asked Constance, noticing Emele was in a daze.

"Oh, yes, of course. I'm so glad to see you." Emele said as he held his arm out.

Constance took his arm with both hands and held tight. "It is good to see you again. It seemed like a really long time." She said looking at Emele.

"Yes it did. I hope we never have to be apart this long again. I really missed you."

Emele led Constance to the dining room and next to the table. He pulled out a chair for her to sit. Before she could sit down, Emele turned her around and pulled her close pressing his lips against hers, kissing her passionately.

Constance was secretly hoping for something like this to happen. She kissed him back and wrapped her arms around him, squeezing him tightly.

God this feels great he thought as he held her. He was becoming aroused.

Constance could feel his hardness. She was becoming aroused herself. She wanted to take him right there on the table. She pulled her lips from Emele's and whispered in his ear. "I want you."

Just then Jenny brought in the first course of their meal.

"Perfect timing huh?" said Constance with a tone of disappointment.

Emele was disappointed too. "Well it looks like she worked very hard to please us. She has been cooking all afternoon. We can't hurt her feelings." Then with a smile he added. "There will always be time for dessert." And he winked at Constance.

Constance gave Emele a coy wink back.

They sat down and enjoyed the wonderful meal and drank the sweet wine. The evening was going great. When they finished their meal, Emele poured Constance one more glass of wine and sat on the chair next to her. He reached in his pocket and pulled out a small wooden box and placed it in Constance's hand. "It is something my mother gave to me and I have cherished it for many years. Now I want you to have it because I cherish you."

Constance opened the box; knowing whatever was inside was a very special gift. It was a red rock. Constance was a little confused.

"It's an uncut diamond. My mother told me it was a rare blood diamond and it would be magnificent if properly cut and polished I could have the work done for you if you want."

Constance was speechless. She was tearing up. "I don't know what to say. I mean, no, of course not. It is perfect just the way it is." Then she thought a moment and added. "It makes me think of how I must have seemed to you when you first met me. You saw the brilliance I could be. I would like it made into a necklace so I can wear it close to my heart."

Then she stood up, kissed Emele and whispered in his ear. "I want you now more than ever."

This was all Emele needed to hear. He picked her up in his arms and carried her to his bedroom, kicked the door open and laid her gently on the bed.

Constance said nothing. She just stared into Emele's eyes with a look of unsatisfied hunger. She stood up and removed her clothes. She was naked, standing right in front of him. She reached over and unbuttoned his shirt, undid his pants, and pulled off his underwear. Then she pushed him down on the bed. She was not nervous this time. She climbed on top of him and started kissing him;

He sat up holding Constance tight. She wrapped her legs around his waist and guided him in. They were both rocking with a slow steady motion.

Emele could hear her heart beating wildly and smell her aroused blood, as it coursed through her body. The urge to bite her was strong. He had to fight this urge he was losing. His fangs were growing. His eyes burned as they turned red. He moved his mouth from Constance's and leaned his head back slightly.

He could see her eyes closed as her head softly moved up and down with the rhythm they had created. He was careful with his touch as his nails grew sharp. He didn't want to scratch her. He was full vampire now. He could not let her see him this way. He started to tremble from his fight within.

Constance felt his body trembling and she held him tight, thinking he was about to erupt from the passion. She held her eyes closed tightly as she climaxed.

Emele couldn't take much more. Then he turned his thoughts away from his fear of biting her to how much he loved her and how much she loved him. He climaxed and quickly changed back to himself. The vampire desires satisfied. Her love had helped him control his thirst.

Constance reached up and touched Emele's face then ran her fingers through his hair. It felt so good, so relaxing. His heart was happy.

Constance's eyes were open now and Emele stared deeply into them. He could see the love in them. He leaned forward and kissed her squeezing her tight against him, and kissed her once more.

Constance moved to the side of Emele, facing him, and he rolled over facing her.

"Wouldn't it be great to feel like this all the time, not having a care in the world?" asked Constance.

Emele nodded. "Yes it would." But how could he ever feel that, no cares at all. He was saddened thinking about his life. He loved Constance more than anything, but would she love him if she knew his terrible secret?

Constance saw the look on Emele's face. "Is something wrong?"

Emele snapped out of it. "No, I guess my mind was wandering."

"I suppose a businessman like you has a lot on his mind.

Traveling to Africa must be exciting. I always wondered what it would be like to travel."

Emele was enjoying just talking. "It's nice, but lonely."

"I would love to go to Africa." Constance hinted.

"Perhaps you could join me the next time I have to go there."

"Perhaps I could." Constance closed her eyes for a moment and imagined herself standing next to Emele holding each other in the star filled night on the open deck of a ship. She smiled.

When she opened her eyes Emele was staring at her. "Looks like someone else was daydreaming" he said.

"More of a night dream."

"Well have you ever dreamed about America?" asked Emele. "I have always thought it would be a nice place to live."

"Surely a man with your business knowledge could live anywhere he wanted."

"Well I suppose if a businessman had the right partner, he could do almost anything."

"Are you looking for a partner?" asked Constance in a more serious tone.

"Maybe. It would be a lonely country where you didn't know anyone." Emele paused a moment then asked. "Do you think you could ever just pack up and leave like that. Just move away on a moment's notice?"

"It would depend on who asked and how he asked me." Constance rolled over to let him think about what she had just said.

Emele smiled and softly poked Constance in the back.

Constance jumped and rolled back over to face Emele. She got on top of him and held his arms down on the bed. "You want to play rough?"

Emele quickly flipped her over and held her on her back with her arms pinned against the bed. He just sat there on her with a crooked little smile as he held her.

Constance struggled a little then said. "Perhaps I have met my match."

Emele felt Constance struggle once more and he let her flip him over. "Perhaps I've met mine." He said as she pinned him down.

Constance leaned down and said "I think you have." And she gave him a quick little peck on the cheek, and they both laughed.

It was getting late now and Constance was thinking the night could not get any better. She had given him some food for thought. "Well it's getting late. We don't want the neighbors talking."

Emele wanted her to stay the night, but he knew she would be getting tired. "Well, maybe we had better get you home."

SOMEONE IS WATCHING

Van Helsing was snooping around Dracula's castle. He saw a figure come out the door closely followed by another. He was too far away to get a good look, but he was sure it was a woman. Then he saw them move in close and hold each other and kiss. Then they got in the carriage and it started off. "Perhaps Dracula has a lady friend, a lover." He said to himself. He wanted to get a closer look but the carriage was too fast. He would wait to see what happened when the carriage returned. He sat down leaning against a tree and waited.

When they reached Constance's house, Emele walked her to the door and they kissed goodnight. Constance went inside and Emele went back to the carriage. He looked up at Rhensfield and said. "Let's go for a little ride on the old road."

"Yes sir" he said and he turned the horses around and headed to the old road.

The moon was full and Van Helsing could see the carriage turn on the old path of a road that was not used a lot anymore. "That's interesting" he said to himself and he started running toward the carriage. He was just starting to get close when he saw the carriage come to a stop. Then he saw two men standing by the horses. It looked like they had guns. He watched and listened as he could hear them yelling to get down and open the door. Rhensfield got down, opened the door and ran to the woods for cover. Van Helsing could hear one man say let him go. Then he heard them yell for Dracula to get out of the carriage. He saw Dracula step slowly out of the carriage to the ground. Then a shot rang out and he saw Dracula fall over. He watched as one of the men kneeled down to go through Dracula's pockets. He watched as Dracula's arms reached up grabbing the man by his head and pulled him close. He saw the man squirm a bit then go limp. He probably stabbed him. Dracula stood up while holding the man's limp body. Van Helsing watched in horror as he thought he saw the head be ripped from the body by Dracula's bare hands, and then simply toss them aside. He saw the other man come out of the carriage and shoot at Dracula. Dracula was close, to close for the man to have missed. He heard another shoot ring out and Dracula grabbed him and pulled him close. He saw Dracula pull him to his mouth and it looked like he was biting him. The man squirmed and managed to get off another shot, before going limp. Then again he saw Dracula rip the head from the body but this time he threw them in the carriage. Then he saw Rhensfield come back to the carriage and pick up the other head and throw it in, while Dracula grabbed the body and easily picked it up with one hand and toss it in the carriage like it was nothing. Then Rhensfield climbed up to the driver's seat and drove away. Then Dracula started walking toward the castle.

Van Helsing made his way to where the carriage had stopped. He looked around on the ground, straining his eyes, looking for blood. He saw nothing. He knew the ground should be red from blood, and he knew he saw the heads ripped off. Had Dracula bit them and drank their blood? He followed the carriage as he watched it turn down an old path. He was going over the events in his mind. From what he saw, Dracula and Rhensfield were being robbed and were simply defending themselves. Had the robbers missed their shots? Dracula seemed to be doing fine. In fact he seemed to prefer walking instead of riding the carriage home.

Van Helsing watched as the carriage slowed down and turned on an old rock path. It went a little farther then it stopped. He watched as Rhensfield got down and pulled the heads and bodies from the carriage. He dropped the bodies down a hole and put the heads in a bag, then went in the hole himself. After a couple of minutes, Rhensfield came out of the hole and drove the horses toward the castle.

Van Helsing waited for a bit then walked over to the hole. It was an old mine shaft. He remembered coal mines in the area, most of which were now closed or collapsed. Although the sun was coming up it was still dark, too dark to see in the hole. Van Helsing looked around and made a torch from a stick and some grass he tightly wrapped around the stick. He entered the mine shaft and was soon almost overcome from a rancid smell. He choked back the vomit and continued deeper. When he held the torch high he saw bodies, lots of bodies. Some were piled up next to holes ready to be buried. He saw mounds of fresh dirt, probably covering hundreds of bodies. He turned to leave when he saw another tunnel, when looking closer, he saw rotting corpses full of maggots and rats chewing off the flesh. He was overcome by the smell and sight of the decaying bodies. He fell to his knees and vomited violently. He started back to the entrance. He stopped for a minute to look closely at the bodies. He held the torch close to the neck of one body. It looked like teeth bite s in the neck skin. He looked at some of the other bodies. Some were too torn to tell much, but there were definitely deep bite holes in some of the necks. Could it be that Dracula had killed these people biting into their jugular vein and drank their blood? Why would he do that and why tear the heads from the bodies? He saw no point in that. Dracula had to be some kind of sick monster to do these things.

Van Helsing had seen enough. He crawled out of the mine and rolled over on his side. The fresh air was so good to breathe in. He laid there for a moment and gathered his composure. He thought about what he had just seen. Dracula was a murderer of what might be well over a thousand people, and it didn't matter

Steve Pierce

if he lured them out. He was a cold blooded killer, a monster, and Van Helsing would deal with him shortly. Van Helsing had seen the strength of Dracula when he tossed the bodies easily into the carriage and how he had held on to the robbers while he killed them. He also wondered about the gunshots. This Dracula was a force to be reckoned with. Van Helsing would have to catch him off guard. Maybe next weekend if his lady friend was there, this would be a distraction. Van Helsing would wait.

SECRETS REVEALED

The next week was turmoil for Emele. He wanted to ask Constance to marry him and move away to America, but how could he do this when she didn't know his secret? Could she still love him if she knew? He hated this dilemma but it was one he had to face. He could get through anything with her by his side, but without her he wasn't sure he could live.

Rhensfield came and knocked on Dracula's door. He could tell his friend was in great distress. "Dracula are you okay? Is there anything you want to talk about? I'm a good listener."

"Yes, Rhensfield. I would truly like your advice on something that is bothering me." Dracula said as he opened the door. "Perhaps we could talk in the study."

"You bet, Dracula, I could tell there was something bothering you."

They went to the study. "Would you like a drink?" Emele asked. "I know I could sure use one."

Rhensfield didn't know what was bothering his friend but he knew it was something big. He saw how nervous Dracula was. "Sure." He answered. "Make it a strong one."

"You're right. I think scotch sounds good." He poured the drinks and handed one to Rhensfield. They both sat in chairs next to the desk. "Rhensfield, you are my best friend and I value your opinion. The thing is I really love Constance. I don't want to live without her. I have thought of asking her to be my wife and going to America, where no one would know anything about me."

"Sounds like you have it all figured out."

"I wish it were that simple. I know she loves me, but she doesn't know about me."

"Look, Dracula, I knew you before I really knew you. Once I understood your problem. I accepted you for you. I think once she understands you're a good person with a problem, she'll come around."

"I know I should have told her my secret before things got this far, but I must tell her before we go any farther. I don't want to lose her, but I can't keep this from her any longer."

Rhensfield thought just a moment then said. "Well, maybe the next time you see her you should talk to her. They saw love conquers all. Constance does love you. I know that. I think it will work out. Just sit her down and explain it to her nice and slow."

Dracula nodded in agreement. "You may be right. I will tell her my story. Thank you Rhensfield, for everything." He got up and patted Rhensfield on the back. They finished their drinks and went their separate ways.

Constance was to come to the castle for dinner that Friday night. Emele was nervous. He had sent Rhensfield to pick her up. When Rhensfield got to her house he walked her to the carriage and said, "Dracula needs to have a very serious talk with you. You need to just sit down and listen. He's my best friend and I don't want to see him hurt."

Constance could see the intense look on his face. She knew he was serious. "I love Emele. I would never do anything to hurt him."

"I know you love him, so please just hear him out. Just sit down and listen."

Constance was confused. "Okay, I will." She said trying to put him at ease. What was he talking about and why was he so worked up? She was thinking Emele might pop the question and ask her to go to America with him. She was excited and nothing would change her mind, besides she had something to tell Emele herself.

When they reached the castle, Emele met them at the door. He took Constance's hand and led her to the study. He shut the door and just looked at her for a minute.

Constance could tell he was really nervous about something, but asking someone to marry you and move to another country could be a little scary.

Emele sat Constance down. "I need to talk to you about something very important. I need to tell you something about myself. Something I would change in a minute if I could. Something I would change for you, Constance."

"What are you talking about?"

"I love you Constance. I want you to marry me and move to America with me."

Constance interrupts, "Yes I will marry you and go anywhere with you! I have been in love with you for quite some time now. You're all I think about."

"Wait, I, you don't know what I've become. Long ago I wanted to live young forever and I did something I never should have done. It changed me, and now I. I don't know how to tell you this."

"Whatever it is, we can work through this. I love you."

"Constance, I love you more than anything, but I've become a monster."

Constance was bewildered. "What are you talking about? Are you trying to hurt me?"

"No, no! Hurting you is the last thing I would ever do. I swear this on my life. I love you but this is hard for me to say, because I'm afraid I will lose you forever and I couldn't live with that."

A noise came from the front door. Someone was yelling and cursing.

"Rhensfield! What's going on?" yelled Emele.

"I'll take care of it Dracula" Rhensfield yelled back.

"Emele, I don't know what you're trying to say, but it doesn't matter. We can see this through" said Constance looking very excited now. "I have something to tell you also."

"Where is that Bastard?" came a voice from the hall.

"Dracula look out" yelled Rhensfield as the study door burst open.

Van Helsing was in the doorway. "You murderer! You monster."

Then he saw Constance. "What the hell is going on here? What are you doing with my daughter?"

Constance was really confused now. "Father? What are you doing?"

"Constance, this man is a monster. He has killed hundreds of people. He drinks their blood. I have seen the bodies drained and beheaded."

"What are you talking about?" Constance looked at her father, and then she looked at Emele. "Emele?"

"I will kill this murderous bastard and do the world some good." Van Helsing said as he reached in his coat pocket.

"Constance, I was trying to tell you." Emele said his voice trembling, worried about what was happening.

Van Helsing pulled a gun.

Emele could not see. He was facing Constance.

"Father! NO!"

BANG, BANG, BANG. Three shots went into Emele's back. He turned around fast. He could not control his anger of being shot along with the thought of losing Constance. His eyes were red like fire. His fangs were longer than ever and his nails were long and sharp. In a second he had Van Helsing by the throat and lifted him off the ground. He was ready to kill. His chest was heaving as the blood ran from the bullet holes in his back.

"Now, You die!" Emele said pushing Van Helsing's head to the side fully exposing his neck. He opened his mouth wide ready to bite deep and hard.

"Emele!" sobbed Constance. "He's my father."

Emele fought his vampire instincts back with every ounce of his being. When he regained his composure he looked over at Constance. Seeing her face like that was more than he could bear. His heart was pounding, his mind racing. All he could think was I'm losing her, the most important thing in his life. That look of disbelief and horror in her face said it all. He dropped Van Helsing to the floor. He started walking toward Constance. "Constance?"

Constance was in shock. She didn't look at Emele. She just backed up a little.

Emele's heart was breaking. He had never felt so alone. "I love you, but the look on your face says it all. I'm a monster. You can't even look at me. I tried to change more than you will ever know."

Rhensfield came in. He had been listening not knowing what to do. "Dracula is a good man. He saved my whole family from murderers. He's my best friend. I know it's hard to understand, but if you could just let him explain."

"He's said too much already." Van Helsing said as he slowly stood up. "He's a cold calculating murderer, a demon I tell you."

Rhensfield looked at Emele. He could see his best friend's heart breaking. He grabbed Van Helsing and tried to pull him to the door.

"Constance, I love you. I can't live without you. My heart is breaking for I know I'm losing you" Emele said as he took another step toward Constance. He was crying.

Constance was still in shock. Her face showed no emotion. "I don't know, I can't think." She did look up at Emele.

Van Helsing broke free from Rhensfield's grip. He ran to the fireplace and grabbed a poker. He turned to Dracula, who was still looking at Constance's eyes, hoping to see a glimmer of love.

"Dracula look out!!" Rhensfield yelled as he tried to stop Van Helsing.

Emele tried to turn around to see what was happening, but Van Helsing plunged the poker through his back with all his might piercing his heart.

Emele could feel the pain as Van Helsing pushed on the poker again, driving it clear through his chest. He had never felt such pain. Was it the poker piercing his heart or just his heart breaking? He looked at Constance. "I will always love you." He reached a hand toward Constance and fell to his knees. The blood ran from his body making a dark red pile on the floor.

Rhensfield threw Van Helsing back. He tried to pull the poker from Emele's chest. "It's going to be alright, Dracula, just as soon as I get this damned thing out of you. You'll see." Rhensfield's eyes were tearing up; he really wasn't sure this time.

"Leave me be Rhensfield."

"But Dracula."

"Leave me be!" Dracula sat back and looked at Constance. He could feel his life slipping away.

Van Helsing just sat there. He was sure Dracula was dying. Emele felt himself getting older as the blood ran from his body. With the last of his strength he grabbed the poker and pulled it from his chest and dropped it to the floor. "I love you Constance, I will always love you." He said as his hair turned gray and his body shriveled, and then he fell over.

Constance was so confused. A moment ago she was so excited to be with Emele, marry him and move to America with him. How could things change so much so fast?

"Good riddance!" said Van Helsing. He walked over to Constance. "Let's go home."

"I need a moment alone." said Constance.

"I'll be outside. Hurry up. We're done here."

Constance watched as her father walked out. "Rhensfield, could you give me a moment?"

Rhensfield slowly walked out of the room.

Constance looked around trying to take in what had happened. Then she stepped over to Emele. It had all happened so fast. She looked at Emele on the floor. The blood had stopped running. He laid motionless on the floor a withered old man. She had loved him. She felt tears welling up inside. She let them flow and she cried hard. She reached down and touched Emele's hand.

He mouthed I love you.

Constance ran from the room crying.

Her father said "Let's go home, it's been a long day."

Walking past her father, she walked over to Rhensfield. "Would you take me home, please?" She couldn't stand to be with her father right now.

Rhensfield was still teary eyed. "Anything for you, Constance." She got in the carriage and Rhensfield headed the horses on the way. It was the longest ride she had ever taken. Her mind ached. So many emotions. Her whole life had been turned upside down. What would she do? Where would she go? She couldn't even think straight. She just wanted to get away. Rhensfield pulled the horses up to Constance's house and helped her out of the carriage. "Anything I can do for you?"

Constance just walked toward her house not saying anything. Rhensfield went back to the castle.

Van Helsing had walked home.

The next morning Van Helsing walked to his daughter's house and knocked on the door. "Constance, are you alright?" No answer. Again he knocked louder. "Constance, are you okay?" He tried the door. It was unlocked. He opened it and walked in. He looked around and hollered for Constance. There was no answer and he didn't find her anywhere. He walked back to the door to leave, when he saw a note on the table that was folded with the word Father on it. He picked it up and unfolded it and began to read.

"Dear Father, so much has happened. If we had been closer, I'm sure I would have told you about Emele. I was deeply in love with him. I still have all these feelings to deal with. I don't know what to do, but I can't deal with this here. Maybe a new place will help me. I can't go on living here. Please try to understand, and don't try to find me, but do pray for me. Constance."

Van Helsing slowly walked out of the house and shut the door. "If only I…" He folded the paper up and put it in his pocket and started walking home. "She'll come to her senses." He told himself. "She'll be back."

But Constance would not be back. She took a few belongings and was going to get away. She didn't know what else to do. She made her way to the shipyard and bought passage to America.

As she stood on the ship she watched the land disappear. Then she moved to the front of the ship and looked out over the ocean. "This is just what I need, a fresh start for myself," she said to herself as she rubbed her hands over her lower stomach, "and for you."

She wasn't sure what lie ahead for her, but she would raise this child in a different country where no one knew her or Emele.

Back at the castle Rhensfield and Jenny followed the wishes of their friend. Dracula was buried in an oak casket in an empty storage room of the lower level of the castle. It was a small ceremony, just a few friends that Dracula had done business with.

Rhensfield had tried to get in touch with Constance, but his attempts were futile. She had vanished. He asked around town, but no one seemed to know anything. He even asked Mr. Van Helsing, but he just said he didn't want him bothering him or his daughter, and if it were up to him he'd be in jail. Rhensfield was hopeful Constance would be back soon, and he could talk to her in a few days.

Jenny had thought it strange that Dracula never seemed to age and she asked her husband "How old was Mr. Dracula?"

"I'm not really sure" he answered, although he knew Dracula was older than they were, he wasn't about to tell his wife. It was hard enough for him to believe how his body had aged right before he died. Rhensfield had not let anyone see Dracula's body, and he meant to keep that a secret.

Emele's will was read. Half of the estate was to go to the Rhensfields, and the rest was to be put in an account under Rhenfield's supervision as to who would receive part or all of it. Dracula had told Rhensfield his wishes to make sure Constance was taken care of if anything happened to him. The Rhensfields could live in the castle as long as they wished, but it was not to be sold.

Rhensfield knew Dracula and Constance had been intimate but in her absence he didn't know what to do. He wondered if she would have gone to America. He would do what he could to find her and keep the account growing.

MOVING ON

The trip across the ocean seemed to take forever. Constance's mind ached from all that had happened. She wondered if she had done the right thing, leaving so suddenly, leaving her family and the few friends she had from work. Everything was in such a whirl. It all happened so fast. She never really had time to think things through. She just left. She thought about Emele, and her heart sank low. She was in love with him. Why did this have to happen? Why does it hurt so badly? Even after seeing him change into some sort of monster. He was trying to tell her something heavy on his mind and heavy in his heart. She could see it in his eyes.

She remembered how his eyes went from sad to full rage after being shot, and how fast they went to disbelief of knowing she had seen his secret before he could explain. She just stood there petrified while his heart broke, not hearing his story. A tear came to her eye as she thought of how she stepped back and couldn't even take his hand when he was dying. The tears came fast now and she cried hard. She wasn't sure what he would have told her about himself, but she knew he loved her. She knew she still loved him, and now he was gone. He was gone.

The ship finally reached America. Constance and the other passengers were herded to the immigration office. She sat quietly for what seemed like hours. Finally her turn came. She was led to a desk and seated. She had to answer all kinds of questions about where she was from, what she did there, why she left, and why she came here. Of course she couldn't tell them the real truth. After filling out many papers, they gave her some papers and told her to keep them in a safe place. She needed to find a place to live and find a job, and report back to them on her progress.

Constance hit the streets, looking for a place to live. Soon she found a cheap apartment, it was small but it would do. Now she had to find a job. She bought a local paper and checked the classifieds. She was hoping to get work at a bank, but that was probably too much to hope for. She applied for a few secretary jobs and for a couple of jobs in some smaller shops in town. One of the businesses asked her to come back for an interview. It was an accounting office. They hired her as a secretary and receptionist. She was hoping after a while to become an accountant there.

She told people her husband had been killed in an accident and it was too painful to stay there with no family or close friends, so she came here, a dream of her husband's as well as her's.

She enjoyed her job. The people were nice to work with. After a couple of months she had insurance benefits. She was feeling good and was basically happy. She often thought of Emele when she was at her apartment alone. He was her first real love and it still hurt.

She found a medical clinic and a doctor. Months went by and her due date was coming close. One night she fell asleep and had a dream about her baby. It was a boy. When she looked at him as the doctor held him up for her to see, he opened his eyes and mouth to cry, his eyes were red and he had fangs. Constance shuttered and woke up to a terrible pain. It was a contraction. She was scared. She had bought a used car a couple of months ago, and she drove herself to the hospital. When she got to the hospital, she was taken to a birthing room. Her contractions were close together now. She was in a lot of pain, but her mind was worried. "What if the baby looked like Emele?" she asked herself. When the contractions came even closer together, all she could think of was pushing.

The doctor came in and coached her as one of the nurses held

71

her hand. "She's ready" said the doctor. "Push when you feel the contraction. Take a deep breath and push!"

The nurse was busy reassuring Constance, but she was in such pain she wasn't listening. She just wanted to push and be done, and see her baby, a normal healthy baby. She screamed and pushed hard.

"Good, one more good push should do it" said the doctor.

Constance took a deep breath and pushed with all her might as the baby was born. She felt the relief and exhaustion as she fell back in the bed.

The doctor cut the cord and held the baby up for Constance to see. "It's a girl, a healthy baby girl."

Constance looked at her baby. "She's beautiful."

The nurse took the baby and started cleaning her up. "She is a beautiful baby girl" she said as she handed the baby to Constance. "Have you got a name picked out for her?"

Constance looked at her baby. She had a lot of thick black hair. She was the most beautiful baby she had ever seen. "Yes. Her name is Emelia."

"That's a beautiful name" said the nurse.

Constance fed Emelia. She was so full of love and happiness again.

After a few days Constance and Emelia were released from the hospital. Constance took Emelia to her apartment. She had bought several items for the baby and her coworkers had thrown her a shower, so she had almost everything she needed. She was ready to be a new mommy.

She was allowed three months paid maternity leave. She loved being home caring for her little Emelia. She would sometime just hold her and stare at her and think how much she looked like Emele. She would sing her lullabies and rock her in the rocking chair.

She still missed Emele and thought how happy and full of pride he would have been to know he had a daughter.

The time was going fast. Little Emelia was growing and doing fine. Constance would be going back to work soon and she had to find a baby sitter or a day care.

Constance found a sitter and in a few days went back to work.

A few weeks later she met a man at work. He was a good looking man, sandy brown hair, a smaller but muscular body, and a rugged face. You would not have guessed it to look at him, but he was a chef, and he owned his own restaurant in town. His name was Edward Johnson and he needed a bookkeeper. The bookkeeping was taking too much time and he didn't get to cook and visit with the customers like he used to.

Constance had become an accountant and was to do his bookkeeping. They met often and one day Edward asked Constance to join him for dinner. Constance liked Edward, so she agreed. They had a really nice time.

They continued dating and fell in love with each other. Edward loved little Emelia, and Constance could tell he would be a wonderful husband and father by the way he treated them.

One special night Edward asked Constance to marry him and she accepted. Soon they were married. It was a beautiful wedding, small with just a few friends. Edward's parents had been killed in an auto accident a few years ago, and he had no other relatives he was close to. Constance was a beautiful bride and Edward looked so happy as Constance walked down the aisle toward him.

Soon Constance quit the accounting firm and worked in their restaurant keeping books and waiting or cooking or whatever was needed. She was happy helping her husband, and everyone at the restaurant liked her.

The restaurant was doing well and making good money.

Though they were not married long, Edward and Constance decided to have children right away. Soon Constance became pregnant and gave birth to a girl. They called her Sarah after Edward's mother.

Emelia was only eighteen months old when Sarah was born, but she was excited to have a baby sis-sis. She would stand next to her crib and stare at her. Constance could tell they would be close as they grew up.

Soon Constance became pregnant again and had another baby girl. They called her Claudia, after Constance's mother.

Time went quickly now and the girls were growing fast. Edward was a wonderful husband and father, but sometimes when Constance looked at Emelia, with her dark eyes and hair, she couldn't help but think of Emele and it would make her a little sad. Edward had adopted Emelia to be a legal guardian, and they never told her he wasn't her biological father.

Ten years into the marriage, Edward had days he didn't feel quite right. After a few days in a row of feeling like this he went to see a doctor. After many tests, the doctor told him it was a rare form of cancer, and there was not much they could do for him. Some patients had a little relief from a dryer climate.

Edward had talked to Constance about moving to Las Vegas to open a steak house, and now this might be the right time to make the move. They talked and agreed to give it a try.

Edward wanted to get things going as soon as possible. He would fly out and look for a place. Shortly after arriving he found the perfect location. The building needed some work, but it was definitely the one. Edward called Constance to tell her about it. Constance could tell by the excitement in his voice that he had found the right place. She did not need to see it, she told him to go for it.

One of Edward's cooks had told him if he ever wanted to sell his restaurant to give him a chance to buy it. They talked and agreed on a price. Edward bought the new place and got a crew working on some remodeling.

Next, they needed a home. Edward found a nice house, so Constance and the girls flew out to see it. It was perfect with plenty of room and in a good neighborhood and not too far from the restaurant.

Edward would stay there while Constance and the girls would finish their school year and sell the house.

The school year ended and the house was sold. The movers came a loaded everything in a big truck. Constance and the girls would drive the car to their new house. They were all excited about the big move. There was not a dull moment while Constance drove. The girls asked so many questions; Constance finally had to make them lie back and try to sleep.

Soon they were sleeping. Constance looked at them in the rear view mirror. She could see Emelia and Sarah leaning on each other. They were so close, a couple of tomboys. Then she looked at Claudia. She was more of a girly girl, more like Constance, and that was fine. They all played together and actually got along most of the time.

As she drove in the silence she thought about Edward. She prayed he would be okay. She knew Edward, and though he had talked about moving before she knew his urgency was to get things settled for her and the girls. Hopefully they would have a long life together and watch their girls grow.

The move went well. Everyone got settled in. The girls each had their own room. Soon school started and the girls made a few new friends, but they remained very close. After school the girls would come to the restaurant and stay in a special part Edward had designed for his family. It had a living room with a television and a dining table. It also had a big bed room with two queen size beds. The girls had fun playing and sleeping in the same bed.

Constance and Edward were working on the final decorations of the restaurant. They looked around, it was perfect. They would have their grand opening that weekend.

Edward sat Constance down at the center table and pulled a bottle of Champaign from an ice bucket under the table. He popped the cork and the Champaign sprayed out. He poured two glasses and handed one to Constance and said "A toast. To my loving wife, for having faith in me and making all my dreams come true." They clanked their glasses and drank. They made love right there on the floor in the middle of the restaurant.

The grand opening went better than expected and the restaurant was soon a success. Constance kept the books and cooked when she had time. She also waited tables and cleaned. Edward cooked and from time to time would visit with the customers.

Things went well for about five years. The girls were all in their teens and growing into beautiful young ladies. The steak house was doing well. With his illness always on his mind, Edward had worked hard to pay things off early. They even had a nice savings account.

Edward had not mentioned his symptoms coming back, and did his best to hide it from Constance. He had not gotten good news from his doctor. He didn't want Constance or the girls to worry about him, but he would have to tell her soon.

Constance had been worried about Edward. She had noticed a change and suspected his illness might be progressing. She had questioned him directly, but she knew he wasn't telling her everything. She knew he didn't want them to be worried about him, or have them hovering over him feeling helpless, but now it was time to talk.

Edward came home that night looking very tired. Constance

could tell he had a lot on his mind. He asked if the girls were in bed and he was told they were in bed asleep. He sat down on the sofa next to Constance. He was at a loss for words, but knew he had to tell her. Constance looked him in the eyes and could see he was uneasy about what he wanted to say. She wanted to cry, but she had to be strong for him and she held back her tears.

He told her his illness had progressed with a vengeance and he had tried to hide it because there was nothing to be done. He wanted to live as normal as he could for as long as he could. He didn't want to tell her, but he hoped she understood. He also didn't want the girls to worry or be all sad around him. He loved them so much. He still didn't want to tell them but he only had a few weeks left.

Constance couldn't hold her tears back any longer. She hugged Edward close and squeezed him tight. Then she wiped her tears and they talked more. They decided to tell the girls Daddy was sick again. Constance would make sure they gave him lots of hugs and kisses. It would be hard to act normal and they were sure the girls would pick up something was wrong. If they asked her a question, she would answer it the best she could.

The weeks went by slow and fast. It was difficult. Edward was in the hospital now and the end was near. Constance knew the girls were pretending for their daddy, but now it was time to talk to them. She was gentle in explaining things to them. Daddy would not come home from the hospital this time. She told them they had to be strong. Daddy didn't want to see sad faces. He wanted to be able to say how proud of them he was and how much he loved them, and to say goodbye, and tell them to watch out for each other and take care of their mother.

That last day at the hospital was the hardest day of their young lives. The girls didn't want to cry, but they all ended up crying. They knew it would be the last time they would see their daddy.

They all exchanged long hugs and kisses. Edward talked to each of them for a minute alone. Then he talked to all of them together. He knew they would pull together and get through this. They were close. They said their goodbyes and the girls went out to a private waiting room. Constance stayed with Edward and held him. He whispered he loved her and to watch for opportunist, with her good looks and trusting nature, she would never see them coming. She promised him and hugged him and told him she loved him too. Then his heart monitor went off and he was gone. She slowly walked to the girls and they all walked slowly to the car holding hands and crying. No one said anything all the way home. They somberly walked to the house and all sat together on the sofa. They fell asleep right there holding each other's hands.

The funeral was huge. Edward was well liked and many people showed their condolences with flowers and cards.

Edward had done a great job of setting things up for his family. Constance would never have to work unless she wanted to, but he knew she liked working because she enjoyed it. They decided his life insurance would be put in trusts for the girls.

The next few months were hard. They all missed Edward. At first the girls would all go in Emelia's room and sit on her bed talking about their dad and then talking about their mom. These talks became less about their dad and more about their mom. They worried about her. They tried to make her happy and usually at least one of them was around her. Constance worried about them too. She was deeply touched at how they did their best to have one of them around her. They had done a good job raising them, and teaching them the importance of family.

Constance returned to the restaurant to keep busy. She hired a couple of new people to fill in Edward's place. She never realized how much he did, but she knew he never considered it work because he enjoyed it so much.

Over the next couple of years Emelia and Sarah were helping in the restaurant, cleaning and doing other work. Claudia would help a little, but she was not old enough to work a lot. When Emelia graduated from high school she wanted to work there. Constance wanted her to go to college, but she knew this was what she wanted. She started out bussing tables, but soon she was waiting table and working as the cashier. Emelia liked waiting table the best. She liked talking to the people.

One night Constance heard Claudia mumbling in her bed. When she went to her room, she saw her shivering, soaked with sweat. Constance shook her gently. "Are you alright?" Claudia's eyes were rolled back in her head. Constance was scared. "Emelia" she hollered. "Emelia!"

Emelia and Sarah both came running to Constance's voice.

"What's going on?" Sarah asked as they entered the bedroom.

They could see Claudia did not look well and the look on their mother's face.

"I'll call 911" Emelia said as she dashed for the phone. She made the call and was assured the ambulance was on its way. "The ambulance is on its way" she said as she came back to the bedroom.

Sarah had gotten a cool washcloth and handed it to Constance who held it on Claudia's forehead.

They all stood staring at each other silently hoping the ambulance would get there, not knowing what else to do.

When the ambulance arrived they started an I.V. for dehydration. She was stable as they took her to the hospital. Constance rode in the ambulance while Emelia and Sarah followed in the car.

When they got to the hospital the doctors examined Claudia

and ran some blood tests. Constance and the girls went to the front desk to give them Claudia's information to get her admitted. When they finished, they went to Claudia's room.

Claudia was sleeping.

The doctor entered the room and said Claudia was not really showing any signs of anything other than dehydration. They would keep her overnight with an IV to replenish her and wait for more results from the blood tests. He said she needed to rest tonight, so they should go home and get some rest as well and they could come back in the morning. The hospital would call if anything changed.

Constance said she would stay in the room with Claudia. Emelia and Sarah were to go home and come back in the morning.

The girls said goodnight and goodbye, giving their mother hugs and kisses, and told Constance to call if there was any change or if they found out anything. The girls left the hospital and drove home. They were worried about their sister, but both tried to talk about other things to keep their minds from thinking bad thought.

Constance sat in a chair next to Claudia. Thoughts came of Edward waking up in a cold sweat before he became ill. She remembered this and couldn't help wondering if perhaps Claudia was getting what Edward had. She tried not to think about this, but as she looked at Claudia lying there, she couldn't help it.

Constance had a restless sleep that night, worrying about her Claudia. The night seemed to last forever.

When morning arrived a nurse came in and took Claudia's vitals. Claudia was still tired and slept right through it. "Everything is looking good." she said looking at Constance.

Constance tried to smile as best she could. It sounded good, but she still worried.

Soon the doctor came in. He examined Claudia and said, "The

blood tests are normal and I don't find any symptoms to warrant keeping her here. I will discharge her. Just keep an eye on her and make sure she gets plenty of rest and drinks plenty of fluids over the next few days. I think she will be fine. Maybe she just overdid it or got too much sun."

Emelia and Sarah were just coming in the room as the doctor was leaving. "What's the deal?" asked Sarah.

"Well it seems our little sun child needs to relax and recoup for a couple of days" answered Constance, trying to hide her concerns. "The doctor seems to think she just overdid it."

Claudia was awake and giggled at "sun child".

"She's been released, so we can go." Constance said looking at Claudia. Seeing the old gleam back in her eyes, she knew Claudia was back to her old self.

With that said Sarah jumped on the bed next to Claudia and started tickling her. "You little faker! You had us all really worried. Now let's get you home, you little turd."

They went home and things went well for about a month. Then Claudia had a similar expirience. She was once again rushed to the hospital. This time her white blood cell count was up, but she still showed no other symptoms. She was prescribed an anti-biotic and sent home. Over the next week Claudia felt better and things went back to normal.

Steve Pierce

THE AWAKENING

One night after work Emelia was walking home. It was a dark night, but the air was cool and it felt good to walk. A car was coming up behind her so she stepped to the side of the road. The car slowed down and went by then stopped and backed up. When the car got along side Emelia a voice asked, "Do you need a lift?"

Emelia could not see a face when she looked in the car it was too dark. "No, I'm not going very far. Thanks anyway."

"A pretty girl like you shouldn't be out alone at night,"

"It's alright I'm almost home."

The car drove on by and turned the corner up the street. Emelia kept walking. She heard footsteps coming from behind her. She looked around and saw a man jogging toward her. She stepped over a bit and kept walking. Then WHAM! Emelia went down in the grass from a hard shove. The man quickly jumped on her before she could get up. He held her down and started punching her in the face.

Emelia's heart was pounding. What was happening?

The man tore her shirt and pulled at her skirt. He reached under her skirt and ripped her panties off. He was trying to spread her legs with his knees.

Emelia tried to hold her legs together, but her attacker was too strong. He forced her arms above her head and held them with one hand. With the other he punched her in the face again.

It hurt so bad. Blood was running over her face. She tried to struggle free and got one arm loose. She clawed at his face as he unzipped his pants. She was trying to scream but nothing would come out.

He punched her face again and pushed his erection to her. She

82

felt herself rip as he entered her and the blood flow lubricating as he plunged deeper. She went numb. She wanted to cry. She felt so helpless, sad, weak, and discouraged. Then suddenly as her emotions peaked, she felt a rage grow from inside, consuming her to her core. Her body was as if it were on fire. Her eyes opened wide and she saw clear, through the blood in her eyes. She pulled her arms free and pushed the shoulders of her attacker back. What was happening? She was not scared anymore; she was just angry, very angry. Her eyes saw perfectly in the dark. Her heart was racing so fast she thought it would explode. She felt her teeth grow long and before she knew what was happening she sank her fangs deep in his neck. She tasted his blood and her body went crazy. She grabbed his head to twist it and used such force he was decapitated. She held the head in her hands for a second and dropped it then pushed the body off of her and to the side. She stood up. She felt weak for a moment. She almost threw up. She couldn't think. She was dazed. What had just happened?

Emelia slowly gathered herself. She looked around. It had all happened so fast. She should go home and call the police. But what had happened? What would the police see? How did a small woman fight off an attacker with such force? She looked at the body with the head ripped off. She started to panic. She looked around and saw the car the man had been driving. She bent down to drag the body by the legs. She was surprised at her strength, as she easily picked it up and carried it to the car. She threw it in and went back and grabbed the head. "Disgusting" she said as she threw it in the car. She sat in the car and drove out to the desert. She pulled up behind some rocks and pushed the body and head out of the car. She drove back a few blocks from her house and quickly ran home.

She reached the house and unlocked the door and quietly

went in, hoping no one would see her. She did not turn on any lights. She could still see amazingly well in the dark. As she crept through the kitchen, she noticed a paper on the table. It was a note for her. "Emelia, had to take Claudia to the hospital. Sarah is with us. Love, Mom"

Emelia started to cry. She worried about her sister. She also knew the stress her mother was going through. She would talk to them in the morning. Right now she needed to tend to herself and clean up and get some rest.

She went to the bathroom and looked at herself in the mirror. "Oh my god!" she said as she saw how swollen and bloody her face was. Blood was caked in her hair and on her face and neck. She had cuts around her eyes and her lips were cut and bruised. Her clothes were torn and covered in blood as well.

She took off her clothes and put them in the trash bag. Then she turned on the shower and got in. The hot water felt good as it ran down her body. The water ran red for a long time as she slowly washed her body. She stood in the shower just letting the water run over her for a while after she was clean.

She started feeling better. She turned off the water and carefully wiped the towel over her face softly pressing it to the cuts around her eyes. She expected it to hurt, but it did not. She touched the towel to her lips and carefully pressed, it did not hurt either. Then she wrapped it around her hair. She slowly dried the rest of herself off with a second towel. She stepped out of the shower and looked again in the mirror. She could not believe what she saw. Her face was still a bit swollen but her cuts were faint scars. "What the?" She opened her eyes wider. It was true. She felt her lower body. There was no blood and she was not sore. "Weird." She said in disbelief.

Emelia heard the door opening downstairs. "I can't deal with them right now; I'll talk to them in the morning." She quickly and quietly put on her pajamas and silently went to her bedroom and crawled under the blankets.

Emelia had just pulled the covers up when there was a soft knock at her door.

"Emelia, are you awake?"

It was Sarah. "Yeah, come on in; just don't turn on the light, okay."

Sarah opened the door, walked over to Emelia's bed and sat down.

"Another bad night?" asked Emelia.

"Yes. We were really worried about Claudia, but once we got to the hospital she started feeling better and they sent her home with us. She is supposed to go back in the morning."

"I really worry about her and Mom. I wish I would have been here to go with you guys."

"I worry about them too. Mom thinks it might be what Dad had."

"Let's hope not."

Sarah looked at Emelia. "Are you alright? You look different."

"Yes, I'm fine."

Sarah stared at Emelia. "Are you sure?"

Emelia couldn't lie to Sarah. "Something happened tonight."

"What do you mean something happened?"

"Well, you have to promise not to tell Mom. Okay?"

Sarah knew Emelia wouldn't say another word unless she promised. "Okay."

"I was attacked tonight."

"What do you mean attacked?" Sarah said rather loudly in a worried voice.

"Shhh! Mom can't hear this, okay. I was walking home and some guy attacked me." Emelia could see the scared look on Sarah's face. "A man ran up behind me and knocked me down and tried to rape me."

"Oh my god! Are you sure you're okay? What happened?"

"Well, he was punching me and tearing my clothes, but somehow I got away."

"Wow you were lucky! How did you get away?"

"I went crazy and fought back and..."

"And what?"

"I killed him."

"Oh my god! You killed him?"

"Shhh! Yes I killed him. Then I panicked and took his body out to the desert and dumped it away from the road."

"Are you sure he was dead?"

"Trust me, he's dead," Emelia said as she pictured the headless body.

"Sounds like he got what he deserved."

"Yeah."

Sarah looked confused. "Why did you hide the body? It was self dense. We should call the police."

"No. You can never tell anyone this. I don't think Mom could handle the added stress of the cops hounding me or knowing I was attacked. She worries enough the way it is."

"You're probably right." Sarah paused a moment looking bewildered, then asked "How did you kill him?"

"I don't know what happened, I just went crazy." Emelia knew she could not tell her the total truth about what had happened. She was not sure herself. "I got a huge adrenaline rush. I twisted his head and his neck broke."

"Wow, that's wild, but good. I mean he could have killed you."

"I know."

Silence filled the room for a moment, neither one knowing what to say.

"Well, I better let you get some rest. I'm glad you're okay. I love you, Emelia." said Sarah as she leaned over and hugged her.

"I love you too" Emelia said as she hugged Sarah back.

Sarah left the room closing the door behind her.

Emelia closed her eyes, but she was not tired. It was the first time she could really think about what had happened. What had happened? She ran it over in her mind. "What did I do?" she said out loud to herself as she remembered biting the man's neck. She ran her tongue over her teeth. She also remembered how good the warm blood tasted. She was disgusted by her thoughts. "Teeth can't grow like that. What happened to me?" She pondered at the strength she had felt and how powerful it was. She did like that part. Finally around five o'clock she fell asleep.

At eight o'clock that morning Constance was making breakfast. Sarah and Claudia were sitting at the table. "Where is Emelia? Constance asked looking at Sarah.

"She's probably still sleeping. I talked to her a little last night. She was worried about us and had trouble sleeping." Sarah replied.

"Do you want me to wake her up, Mother?" asked Claudia.

Constance thought a moment then answered "Yes, tell her breakfast is ready."

Claudia started toward Emelia's room.

"Wait, I'll go with you." said Sarah as she got up from the table.

They went to Emelia's room. Claudia opened the door. Seeing Emelia sleeping there she hollered "Wake up sleepy head."

Emelia opened her eyes, looked at Claudia and Sarah standing in the doorway and pulled the covers over her head and rolled over.

"Hey, Mom wants us all to have breakfast together." Claudia said as she jumped on Emelia to give her a hug.

"Easy" said Sarah, knowing Emelia had had a rough night.

"Alright, I'm getting up." Emelia said as she sat up. "Get off of me and I'll be down in a minute."

Sarah and Claudia went back downstairs to the table. "She's on her way down" said Claudia.

Emelia got up, looked at her face in the mirror. There was not even a scar. She felt great, a little tired, but great. She got dressed and went downstairs.

"Good morning, Mother," said Emelia as she came up behind Constance and hugged her.

"Good morning," said Constance and she turned around to hug her back. She looked at Emelia, "Are you okay? You look different... in a good way."

Emelia shrugged her shoulders. "I'm a bit tired, had a rough night, but I feel fine."

"I don't know, you just have a different look about you."

Claudia looked at Emelia. "Well, I think she looks fine. Can we eat now?"

Constance sat down at the table joining her daughters. She had said enough, but something didn't feel quite right.

They all chit chatted while eating, but Emelia did not eat much. She had a lot on her mind and she really wasn't that hungry.

They finished their meal and cleared the table.

"We need to get you to the hospital," Constance said to Claudia.

"I would like to go with you," said Emelia.

"Maybe we could have an early lunch," said Sarah.

"We just finished breakfast," said Claudia.

"So, I think that's a good idea," said Constance. She loved it when she could be with her girls. She worried about Claudia. As she looked at Emelia, she worried about her too.

While on the ride to the hospital, Emelia thought the sun was really bright. She put on her sun glasses, but the sun still seemed really bright. When Constance turned a corner, the sun shined through the window on Emelia's arm and legs. It was hot. It almost burned. She scooted over in the car out of the sunlight. She was tired. She leaned back and fell asleep. She started to dream. She dreamed she was soaking in a warm bath. It felt so good. She was thirsty and put her mouth down to take a sip of the water. It tasted so good, but it wasn't water. She felt her teeth with her tongue. She had long fangs. She opened her eyes and looked. The tub was full of blood. She was startled. She screamed and kicked out waking herself up.

"Hey," said Sarah. "What's going on?"

"I guess I dosed off and had a freaky dream," said Emelia breathing hard.

Constance looked at Emelia in her rear view mirror. "Are you okay?"

Emelia could see Constance staring at her in the mirror. "I'm fine. I just had a freaky dream."

Constance put her attentions back on the road. She pulled in the hospital entrance and parked the car.

As they got out of the car Emelia could feel the hot sun on her skin. She looked at Claudia and Sarah, "Race you," she said as she ran to the front doors. The girls ran behind her but she was fast and reached the doors way before them.

"Gee, I didn't know you could run so fast," said Claudia.

Constance watched shaking her head. "When will they grow up?"

Emelia stood there looking through the shaded window, smiling and waving.

Constance stared at Emelia, thinking how much she took after Emele, looking more like him every year. It was time to tell her the truth. She would do it. A tear came to her eye as she thought how proud Emele would have been of his daughter. She walked in the lobby and they waited for Claudia's name to be called.

Soon they heard "Claudia Johnson" from a nurse standing in the hallway. They all followed her to a room. "The doctor will be in soon. Sit in the chair and I'll draw some blood." The nurse swabbed Claudia's arm and pierced her skin with the needle hitting the vein the first try. "There we go," she said as the blood started to run in the vial.

Claudia looked away, but Emelia watched the blood flow. Her stomach growled loudly. She sucked in her stomach hard to stop the noise. She felt weird. She felt... hungry. She could smell the blood with every breath she took. She was embarrassed and turned away as her stomach growled loudly again. Emelia walked out to the lobby where Sarah was reading a magazine.

"What's going on?" asked Sarah as she looked up from her magazine.

"They were just drawing some blood for more tests. They should be out in a minute," answered Emelia as she sat down next to Sarah.

Soon Claudia and Constance came out to the lobby. "Well, that's it for today," said Constance. "Let's go home."

On the way home, Emelia sat in the middle of the car avoiding the sun. When they got home, Emelia said "I'm not feeling quite so good. I think I need a nap."

"When you wake up I would like to talk to you," said Constance as she gave her a hug.

"Sounds good," Emelia said and she went up to her room. The sun was shining brightly through the windows so she shut the curtains, then she lie down and covered up and soon fell asleep. When she woke up it was dark outside. Emelia stretched and stood up, made her bed and went down the steps. She felt great, better than she could remember. She was singing as she went around the doorway to the living room.

"Hey, sleepyhead, that must have been some nap. You look vibrant," said Constance. "The girls went out to a movie. Do you have time for that talk now?"

Emelia looked a little puzzled. "Okay, sure. What's this about?"

Constance sat on the couch and patted the seat next to her. Emelia sat down and looked at her mother.

"This is hard. Maybe I should have told you this before or maybe I shouldn't be telling you now at all, but either way you need to know," Constance said as she looked nervously at Emelia.

"You're starting to scare me. What is it?"

"Well, about twenty some years ago, I lived in Transylvania. I had just started a new job at a bank. I was very shy and didn't make friend easily. I had never really had a boyfriend, at least no one serious. My boss was impressed with my work so one night he asked me to work late and meet one of his special clients."

Emelia didn't know where this story was going, but she was intrigued. Her mother had never talked much about her past.

"When I first met him, I thought he was a bit odd. My boss had told me he was eccentric. But he was such a handsome man and I was instantly attracted to him. I worked with him a few more times at the bank. Then he asked my boss if he could hire me part time as an accountant. He said he needed some help with his bookkeeping. He had some sort of allergy to the sun so we had to work in the evening. He invited me to have dinner before we started. He started flirting with me."

"Oh, Mother!" exclaimed Emelia. "Then what happened?"

"Well, I flirted back. It was so easy for me to talk to him. I felt comfortable around him. Over time I fell in love with him."

"Did he fall in love with you too?"

"Yes. I think he was going to ask me to marry him and go to America."

"So what happened?" Emelia asked excitedly.

"We were intimate... and I became pregnant." Constance eyes started to fill with tears. "We were to meet for something important he wanted to talk to me about. I think he was going to pop the question and I was going to tell him I was pregnant. But before we could meet he was killed in an accident. In shock and disbelief I took a trip to America and that's where I had you."

"Edward wasn't my father?"

"Edward loved you as if you were his own, but Emele Dracula was your real father and I never got a chance to tell him." Constance pulled a necklace from her pocket. "Emele gave this to me and now I think you should have it."

Emelia was still a little shocked at the news, but she held out her hand to take the necklace. "That's different," she said as she looked at the stone.

"It's an uncut blood diamond. Emele told me it would be brilliant if I had it cut and polished. But I loved it the way it was. It's yours now so if you want it done that's okay."

"Mom, are you sure you want me to have it? It must mean a lot to you."

"Yes it does, but lately I see so much of Emele in you, I want you to have it. When you were born with your dark hair and eyes, you reminded me so much of him I named you Emelia."

Emelia turned around and let Constance put the necklace around her neck. "It is so beautiful. I will keep it as it is." Emelia turned back around to face Constance. "What was he like?" She had so many questions to ask.

They talked for over an hour. Constance told her everything except the truth about their last night. She told her Emele was a bit old fashioned and how he loved the old ways. He loved his castle and his horses and carriage and about the special bond he had with the man that worked for him. "Now you know a little more of your history and why you look a little different than your sisters. I will leave it up to you if you want to tell them. You girls are so beautiful." She gave Emelia a big hug.

"That's because there is some of you in all of us, Mom," as she hugged her back. "Thanks for telling me. It's kind of weird knowing I had a dad I'll never met. But Edward was a great dad and I miss him a lot?"

"So do I, Honey. So do I."

Emelia was changing, feeling a bit different. She could not take the sunlight. She took the late shift at the restaurant. She worked from nine P.M. until five A.M.

It had only been a week since her attack and she was feeling hungry, really hungry. She took a break and ate some food, but this time it did not taste that good and she was still really hungry. She went back to work. A young couple came in and was seated in Emelia's station. She took menus and introduced herself. When she came back to take their order, she was distracted. She could hear their hearts beating. She looked at the man's neck and could see and hear the blood pumping through his veins. She looked at the young woman. She had a low cut dress showing lots of skin, little straps that barely covered any shoulder. Her hair was pulled back in a long beautiful ponytail. Her neck was long. Emelia could feel her fangs growing.

"Could we have another minute or two? I can't decide what I want yet;" asked the young woman.

"Sure." Emelia was happy to hear this. "I'll be back in a couple." She quickly went to the restroom. No one else was in there. She splashed water on her face and looked in the mirror. "Get a grip!" she said to herself. She dried her face and looked back in the mirror. She looked fine, normal, no fangs. Was she imagining things? "Huh" as she shrugged her shoulders. Then she went back to the young couple. "Are you ready to order now?"

"Yes, I'll have the T-Bone, rare with a baked potato, just butter, and a garden salad with French dressing on the side," said the young woman.

"And for the gentleman?' Emelia could hear their hearts beating. She could smell their blood. Her stomach growled loudly.

"Sounds like you could use a steak yourself," joked the young man. "I'll have the New York strip, medium, French fries and a Caesar salad."

"Very good," said Emelia trying to hide her nervousness. "I'll get these going right away."

She dropped the orders off to the kitchen and ran back to the restroom. She locked the door and went to the sink. She splashed water on her face.

"Missy, are you alright?" came a voice from behind her.

Emelia was startled. She didn't think anyone was in here. She quickly turned around baring her fangs mouth wide open.

The lady behind her was old and when Emelia snarled at her, she fell down.

"Oh my god," Emelia said as she stepped close to help the woman up. Her fangs were gone. "I don't know why I did that. Are you okay?"

"I guess you startled me as much as I startled you."

Emelia took the woman's arm to help her up. Suddenly she felt her fangs grow long. Her fingernails grew fast digging in to the woman's arm.

The old woman screamed from the pain and as she did she looked at Emelia's face. She was terrified.

Emelia covered the woman's mouth to stifle the scream. She

could smell the blood dripping from the woman's arm. She was full vampire now. She tried to hold back, but the urge was too great. Her hunger was too strong. It was useless. She had to feed. Her mind went crazy trying to fight it off. Before she could think of what to do, she was biting the old woman's neck, drinking her blood, draining her life.

The woman was dead. Her life drained. Emelia now realized what she had done. This was not a bad woman. She was probably a wife, a mother, a grandmother, and now she was dead. Emelia cried for the life of the woman she had just taken. She was sad, but her body was so happy and satisfied. Then her mind cleared. She had to act fast. She needed to clean up and get rid of the body.

She washed her hands and face. Then she looked at the body. There was no blood on the floor. She had not wasted a drop. She picked up the body and sat it on a toilet and shut the stall door. Then she opened the door and looked out. The hall was clear. She quickly grabbed the body and took it out the back door and placed it in the dumpster. She moved some garbage bags around and covered up the body. That would do for now. The dumpster would not be emptied until the following day. It would be light soon. Emelia's shift was over. She needed to get home. She would deal with this better tomorrow.

Emelia got in her car and drove home. While her mind was thinking about the terrible thing she had done, her body felt so alive, so rejuvenated. She pulled in the driveway, parked the car and went in the house. Constance was in the kitchen. Emelia rolled her eyes. "Oh great'" she said under her breath. She did not feel like talking right now.

"How was your night?" asked Constance as Emelia tried to sneak by.

Emelia turned around and trudged over to Constance. "It was

okay, but I'm really tired."

Constance looked shocked. "Well, you certainly don't show it. You're almost beaming. If I didn't know better, I'd say you met someone."

"No, Mother. I just had a rough night.

"Do you want to talk about it?"

"No, just some rude customers." Emelia smiled. "There was a guy who was really cute." She knew this would settle her mother down.

"I knew it. Tell me about him."

"Not much to tell. He was with a girl, but I caught him looking at me a few times across the room."

"With you working the night shift, I don't see much of you."

"I know. Maybe we can talk this weekend."

"Okay. I'll let you get to bed." Constance leaned in and kissed her on her forehead. "Good night." She hugged her. "Wow, you feel really tight. Are you sure you're okay?"

Emelia hugged Constance back. "Yes, Mother. I just need some sleep. Good night."

Emelia got ready for bed. She was having all kinds of feelings. She was confused about what was going on. She felt remorse when she thought about the old woman, but she felt so great she couldn't be sad. Her body tingled when she remembered how sweet the blood was. She tried to focus on what had happened. She thought about the young couple. She remembered the excitement and fear of almost losing control when she smelled their blood while it coursed through their veins. She wished she could remember more of what happened with the old woman. All she knew was she lost control. Her hunger took over. What if it happens again?

She put on her pajamas and crawled in bed. She would likely not sleep well tonight with all the thoughts running through her mind. After a while she did fall asleep. And when she woke up it was time to get ready for work. She got ready and drove to work.

When she got to the restaurant she started working. Her thoughts soon turned to the body in the dumpster out back. She would sneak out when it got slow usually between three and five A.M. She would put the body in her car trunk and drive it out to the desert.

Work was going well. It was about two in the morning. Emelia dropped an order off to the kitchen. She heard a noise outside and went out to check on it. She saw garbage bags on the ground around the dumpster. She quickly looked in the dumpster. The body was gone. She started to panic. She heard a noise from behind her. When she turned around, she saw an old woman standing there looking bewildered. It looked like the woman from last night. Emelia got closer. She could see the woman had fangs and claws. She was staring at Emelia. Emelia felt a confrontation coming. She started growing fangs and claws herself. The old woman lunged at her with mouth open, fangs long, claws sharp. She grabbed Emelia and was trying to bite her. Emelia fought back pushing her head away. The woman was strong and ferocious, but Emelia shoved her back to the ground. The woman lunged at Emelia again and Emelia grabbed her. She forced her down and wrapped her legs around the old woman's waist. The old woman bit Emelia's arm. Emelia dug her claws into the woman's neck and tore her head loose from the body. The woman was dead. Emelia had to work fast. The fight had made noise and surely someone would come to check the commotion. Emelia put the head in a bag and put the body in the dumpster. She would pull her car around and pick them up.

She went back inside as another worker was coming to check the noise. "A couple of kids were goofing around out back. I chased them off." Emelia said to the worker. Then she told the night manager she was not feeling well and needed to go home. She pulled her car around to the back. She loaded the body and the head in her trunk. Then she drove out to the desert and buried them in the sand. Then she drove home.

Emelia crept through the house and into her bedroom. She started to think about her attacker and wondered if he had changed any. It was still a while until sunup. She silently went back through the house to her car. She drove to the spot she had put the body of her attacker. She walked around the rocks. The body was gone. She opened her eyes wider and could see perfectly in the dark. Several yards away she could see tracks and a few bones scattered here and there showing signs of animals at work. She felt relief knowing he had not changed.

Had the old woman left, Emelia would have never known she changed. She would have just wondered what happened to the body, not knowing she had come back like her.

Emelia's vampire instincts were starting to kick in and she understood the need to decapitate any victim of hers, lest they come back like her. She also knew if they did come back they would try to kill her first. She thought about her attack. It had been eight days after her attack that she lost control to the hunger. She didn't like losing control. She didn't like killing innocent people either. She remembered all the signs. Her stomach growling when she saw blood the next day and being able to smell and hear blood moving through someone's veins. She knew it would happen again. Maybe next time she could choose the victim and make it someone more deserving. There were lots of people who had done terrible things.

She drove back home and went to bed. She tried to sleep but had a restless night.

That night she went to work. While working she caught herself wondering if any of her customers were truly bad. For the most part they seemed nice. Sure an occasional rude person or a few drunken friends trying to party still, over breakfast, or now and then you got a couple of guys being rowdy, and the guys who like hitting on their waitress. But most tipped well and seemed decent. When she thought about tips and guys hitting on her she realized how both had increased greatly since her attack. She remembered Claudia saying how she had gotten sexy almost overnight, and teasingly calling her, "the seductress" when she had gotten ready to go out on the town with Sarah that weekend after her attack.

Emelia had always thought of herself as pretty maybe even sexy, but had she become seductive?

"Hey, how about some service," came a call from one of her tables.

Emelia was startled and came back to reality. She went about her job, still paying more attention to what she thought of the types of people that came in the restaurant. When Emelia's shift was over she went home.

Constance was up cooking some bacon and eggs. "Hey you how about some breakfast?"

"Sounds good," said Emelia.

Claudia came around the corner, "Sounds great and smells even better."

Sarah was making her way down the stairs. They all sat down at the table.

"Hey sleepy you about missed out," said Claudia as she grabbed a handful of bacon.

They all chatted as they ate. Emelia looked tired now. Claudia went over to the window and opened the blinds. "This will wake you up."

Emelia felt the hot sun on her skin and squinted her eyes. "Wow, that's bright." She backed her chair away from the sunlight. "Well, I'm bushed. I'm going to bed. Good night or day whatever. I'm tired."

They all laughed and said good night to Emelia as she headed up to her room.

As she lay there trying to go to sleep she thought maybe it was time to get her own place. She would miss her mother and sisters, but she could see things getting difficult. Questions like, why does the sunshine bother you and why do you sleep all day? Not to mention what might happen if someone cut themselves or if she just lost control. She couldn't live with that. Yes, it was time to move out. Maybe even get a new job. Somewhere she could find the right kind of people. Her life had changed and she must change with it.

Over the next couple of days Emelia found a small house. It would be hard to tell her mother she was moving out and it would be harder to tell her she would not be working at the restaurant when she found a new job.

The next night she did not work. She called a taxi and told him to take her to a strip club. At first he didn't want to take her. He said if she was looking for work he knew some nice respectable places that paid well. Emelia told him "I don't want a lot of people to see me, Ok?"

He said "I know a place, but the cliental is not so nice."

"Let's check it out and I'll be the judge." Emelia said as her heart beat a little faster.

The taxi stopped at a rundown place on the outskirts of town. "Watch yourself" the driver said as Emelia got out and paid him.

"I will, thank you." She looked around, and then went inside; found a table near the corner with not much light. She sat down and studied the crowd and the dancers. It was definitely a rough crowd. Most of the customers were drunk. The girls weren't bad looking but didn't put on much of a show. They just sort of stripped and waited for someone to give them money. They didn't really dance at all.

Perhaps she could add a little flare to this place and take out some of the riffraff.

It had been seven days since she had fed, and she could feel the hunger getting stronger. She saw one of the customers getting physical with one of the dancers. A bouncer came over and grabbed him. The man was trying to fight with the bouncer, but the bouncer obviously knew his business. He threw the guy outside and told him to go sleep it off.

Emelia went out the back to see what he was up to. She watched from the shadows as he went to his car. He was not getting in, but reaching under the seat. He stood up and shut the car door. He had a gun in his hand. Emelia looked around no one was visible. The man was heading back to the club. Emelia knew this was trouble and could feel an adrenalin rush and was filled with excitement at the thought of taking out the bad guy. She could feel her fangs growing and see her claws.

Emelia silently ran very fast and grabbed the guy before he knew what was happening. She forced him down and bit hard into his neck. The warm blood felt good in her mouth and she could taste the alcohol on her tongue. The man raised his arm and before Emelia noticed it she felt a sharp pain in her side as she heard a shot ring out. She was scared. She quickly forced his arm to the ground without releasing her bite. He was not moving. She still felt the pain but had to move fast before someone investigated the gun fire. The music in the club was loud and no one paid enough attention to notice the sound of the shot.

Emelia quickly dragged the body to the dumpster, cut the head from the body, and covered it with trash in the dumpster.

Should she see a doctor? Her side was still bleeding. She went back in the club to the restroom. She checked to see if anyone was in the stalls. They were empty. She locked the door and lifted her shirt. The blood had stopped running. She pressed on the bullet hole. It did not hurt. She remembered how fast her other injuries had healed from her attack. She would have to be careful, she may have been lucky tonight.

Emelia tore off the bottom part of her shirt that was bloody and cleaned herself off. When she finished the bullet hole was gone. With the lower part of her shirt torn off it exposed her midriff and showed how shapely her figure was.

After having fed she was feeling confident and it showed as she left the restroom. The owner noticed her right away as cat calls came from customers. He was quick to offer her a job.

Emelia was a bit flattered and told him she would think about it.

The owner gave her a card and said he could tell she had something special. She would draw a crowd.

Emelia called a cab and went home.

As she lay in her bed she wondered what it would be like to strip in front of people. Could she really do it? The hours would be great and she would not have to go far to find a meal to satisfy her hunger. Emelia thought about the kind of music she would play and what kind of seductive dance she would do. She would give it a try. What would she tell her mother? She would just say she found a new job.

A NEW ERA

In the past twenty one years back at the castle Rhensfield was making his rounds, making sure everything was okay. He went to the basement where his friend was buried. He went in the room and sat down by the grave. "I sure do miss you, Dracula. It seems like it has been a really long time." It had only been a couple of years. "I'm sorry I let you down. I haven't been able to find Constance. Someone said she may have gone to America. Gosh, I wouldn't know where to begin to find her if she did. I know you loved her very much. I wish things could have been different." A tear came to Rhensfield's eye and he wiped it away. He stood up and turned to walk out, then he paused a moment. He listened close, cocking his head a little. He thought he heard something. It sounded like a faint heartbeat, pump, pump; pump, pump. He listened harder. He heard nothing. He shook his head as he walked out. "This old castle makes some weird noises sometimes." The sound though very faint, continued.

Rhensfield would keep a vigil on the place, and he did. It had been over twenty years. Rhensfield and Jenny were close to eighty now. They lived in the castle and were visited by their children and grandchildren. Rhensfield often visited Dracula's grave and would sit and talk about the old days and how he missed his friend.

Rhensfield had been sick for a while and Jenny had pneumonia and was fighting it off for several days, but she was losing. The children were called.

Rhensfield was holding her in his arms while they exchanged words of love. Jenny knew she was dying. She looked in Rhensfield's eyes. "I know my time is done, but I love you and I will be waiting in Heaven when you are done with your life here."

Rhensfield held Jenny close and kissed her softly. "I love you too, and we will be together again soon."

She smiled and was gone. Rhensfield cried, but he knew she was in a better place. "It would have been nice if you could have seen the kids one more time." He knew this would be the last time he would see them. He knew he would not live long without her.

The children came and mourned their mother. It was a beautiful funeral. Jenny had always wanted to be buried in the old cemetery behind the castle. She had always kept it up with flowers, and when the sun shone through the trees, she imagined it looked like heaven.

They kids stayed a couple of days and tried to talk their dad into coming home with them, but Rhensfield wouldn't hear of it. "I will finish my days here," he told them. They knew he would not last long after talking to his doctor, who said he would probably not survive a trip to their home.

They said their final goodbyes and went back to their homes. Rhensfield went back to the castle and went to bed. It had been a long day and he fell asleep fast.

Down in the basement of the castle the ground over Dracula's grave started to shake. The earth pushed up and a frail hand made its way through. Then another frail hand made its way through. Both hands struggled to push the dirt to the sides. Then a head popped up and shoulders followed. A frail grey haired man with clothes half rotted lifted himself up and took a deep breath. It was Emele. He was weak and needed to feed. He took another deep breath and coughed out dust from his lungs from the long slumber he had had. He lifted himself up and took another breath. "Rhensfield!" he yelled. "Rhensfield" he yelled once more. No answer. He slowly uncovered the rest of his body. He stood up. His legs were trembling from nonuse for so long. He took a step, then another. It felt so good to move again.

Something had summoned him from the grave. What was it? Something was wrong, maybe someone in trouble. Someone close to him maybe. What was it? "Rhensfield!' he yelled again.

Emele remembered everything that had happened that night like it was yesterday. His heart felt heavy. How long had it been? Was Rhensfield still around, and what about Constance, sweet Constance? What had happened to her?

Rhensfield was dreaming. He dreamed that Dracula was calling him. He awoke and listened. He heard nothing, but he would go check it out. He slowly made his way to the room his friend was buried in. He listened at the door. He could hear heavy breathing and coughing. He slowly opened the door. He saw a tattered old man. "Hey!" he said.

As the old man turned around he recognized Rhensfield. He was older but it was him. "Rhensfield, it is good to see you, old friend."

Rhensfield could hardly believe his eyes. "Dracula?" he questioned.

Emele nodded.

"But how?" Rhensfield asked with a puzzled look on his face. "You, you were dead."

"I don't know..... It is like it all happened yesterday. But looking at you and myself, I can see it has been a long time."

Rhensfield stepped closer. "I guess it's been about twenty years."

"It was as if I was sleeping and someone called to me, waking me up. Then I pushed and pulled myself free. But I am weak, and old, and hungry. I don't think I will last long." He paused a minute then asked "What of Constance?" A tear came to his eye.

"Oh boy, Dracula. I don't know. When it all happened she was stunned, maybe in shock. She asked me if I would take her home. I did, and I told her I'd check on her in the morning. When I went back the next morning, she was gone. She didn't tell anyone. She just left. Some of the people at the bank said she talked about America. I tried to find her. I even went to see her dad, old man Van Helsing, but he wouldn't even talk to me. He just said if it were up to him I'd be in jail."

"How is Mr. Van Helsing? Alive and well?" asked Emele.

"For an old guy he gets around really good, a lot better than me."

"Perhaps I should visit Mr. Van Helsing."

"I don't know Dracula, you look pretty weak."

The two sat for a while as Rhensfield told him about the last twenty years. He had sold the diamond mine in Africa, because he could not oversee it. He talked about his children and how they had grown up and moved on with families of their own.

Emele could see how time had passed by and how aged Rhensfield had become. He noticed a tear come to his eye as Rhensfield told him about Jenny. "She was my life, Dracula. I know I don't have long myself. That's okay though. I will be with her again." Rhensfield looked deep into Dracula's eyes. "She was my soul mate. I know Constance is your soul mate. You have to find her, Dracula. I bet if anyone could find her, you could."

"Look at me Rhensfield. I'm too weak to catch anyone. I need to feed, but I'm too weak. Was I summoned from the grave just to die again?"

The two looked at each other. Both saw frail bodies that were not long for this world.

Rhensfield smiled. "Dracula, you're my best and only true friend. I will give you strength to go out and find your true love."

Emele was puzzled. "What are you talking about?"

"Take my blood and strengthen yourself. Go out there and

find Constance."

Emele just stared in disbelief at what he just heard.

"It's okay. You have risked your life for me and my family. You could have been killed. I remember long ago when we were attacked in the castle. I will never forget that or hearing my daughter tell me how someone saved her life, someone who moved fast from the shadows. Though I never thanked you, I knew it was you. Now I can help you. I have missed talking to you. You gave me and my family more than I could ever have asked for. I would die for you."

Emele was very touched to hear these things, but he would not take his friend's life.

Rhensfield had seen Dracula try not to feed and fight the hunger. He also saw him lose control when he waited too long. He got up and walked slowly over to Dracula, pulled a pocket knife from his pocket and cut his neck, just a bit so the blood would ooze just a little. "Just bury me next to Jenny."

Emele could smell the blood as his senses heightened. He could feel his fangs growing. His eyes turned red and his fingernails grew long. He looked at Rhensfield. "Please, don't do this. Get away from me."

Rhensfield tilted his neck. "Go find Constance. I know you can do it. I just hope you will be as happy as I've been all these years."

Emele couldn't help himself. He stood up, trembling, not from weakness but from his will fighting against his hunger.

Rhensfield stepped closer to Dracula. "Goodbye my old friend."

Emele could feel his heart pounding out of his chest. He could not hold back any more. He grabbed Rhensfield by his arms and bit hard into his neck. Within seconds he was drained dry. Emele was getting younger and stronger fast. Still holding his friend, he looked at his lifeless body. "AAAAHHH." He cried out as tears filled his eyes. He gently sat down, holding Rhensfield in his arms. He sat there for an hour knowing what he had done and what he had still yet to do. Finally he took a deep breath and quickly severed the head of his friend.

Rhensfield had bought two caskets when Jenny had died. Emele placed his friend in the casket and buried him in the grave next to Jenny. He put flowers on the grave. "I will miss you, my friend."

Emele slowly walked back to the castle. He cleaned himself up and wrapped a towel around himself. He went to his old room. It was as he had left it all those years ago. He opened the closet and put on some clothes. He fluffed the dust from the covers and lay down on the bed. It had been the longest night of his life. The sun was coming up.

That night, Emele reacquainted himself with his castle. He walked through all the rooms. He looked in his secret hiding place. It still held all the gold and diamonds he had stored there. He was still a very rich man, but how could he say he had come back from the grave. He still looked as young as he was twenty years ago. He remembered the account that had been set aside for Constance, in case she returned, although it was not specified who would receive the money. That was it; he would be his own son.

He found addresses for Rhensfield's family and sent letters of sympathy to them from Emele Dracula II. He explained how he had just come from Africa to find his father, how he had met their father, and learned of Emele's death, and how Rhensfield had died in his sleep the next night.

The next day Emele woke early and called the bank to talk to Mr. Ramsey. He set up an appointment with Mr. Ramsey to talk about the Dracula estate.

The next night Emele went to the bank. When he saw Mr. Ramsey, he recognized him right away. "Mr. Ramsey, I presume?" He held out his hand to him. He was older, but it was him.

Mr. Ramsey held out his hand as he looked up at Emele's face. Then with a shocked look and disbelief he said. "Emele Dracula?"

"I'm sorry. I get that a lot. I'm Emele Dracula II. People say I'm the spitting image of my father, Emele Dracula."

Mr. Ramsey rubbed his eyes. "I can't believe the resemblance. If I didn't know your father died twenty years ago, I'd swear you were him."

"This is why I'm here. I am from Africa. A few months ago my mother, on her death bed, told me I was the son of Emele Dracula. She made me promise I would find him and let him know he had a son. She had always told me my father had died before I was born. I must admit I was excited to meet him. Well, I finally arrived only to meet Mr. Rhensfield and find out my father had died about twenty years ago. I was saddened to learn this, but Mr. Rhensfield told me a lot about him, including the story about a woman Mr. Dracula had been very close to. He also told me there was an estate of some value I should claim. Mr. Rhensfield told me he was not doing very well, but he would come to the bank to talk to you, but that night he passed away in his sleep."

"I had heard Mr. Rhensfield was in poor health. Well, that is quite a story. I'm sorry to hear of all your misfortune. The Dracula estate is quite a sizable one. I knew your father well, but I never knew he had a son." Mr. Ramsey leaned back in his chair, scratched his balding head and thought for a moment. "The bank would need some sort of proof."

"I'm sorry I don't know what to say." Emele was becoming

worried. "My mother didn't have any record of my birth. She said I was born at home with a midwife." Emele thought a moment, and then said. "I do have a ring my mother gave me. She said it had my father's crest on it."

Mr. Ramey was still as sharp as a tack. "I remember Mr. Dracula's crest. Let me see that ring." He looked at it, he was sure it was exactly like the one he saw Mr. Dracula wear all those years. "I knew Mr. Rhensfield. He was not the kind of man to lie. He and your father were very close. I think they would have done anything for one another, so I'm sure if he knew about your mother, well, with your looks and the ring. That's enough proof for me. Let me get the paperwork lined up and we can take care of this in a few days."

"I'm sorry; one thing I inherited from my father was an allergy to the sun. Would it be possible to do this in the evening?"

"Of course. Are you staying at the castle? I can send word when I get the paperwork done."

"Yes, I am staying at the castle. I have some business to do here." Emele looked at Mr. Ramsey. "I was also hoping you could help me out with something else."

"I will do what I can."

"Do you remember a Miss Van Helsing? Mr. Rhensfield told me she used to work for you."

Mr. Ramsey thought for a moment. "Ah, yes. She worked for me about twenty years ago."

"I was told she was a friend of my father. Do you know if she is still around? I would like to talk to her."

"Yes she was a friend of your father. She used to work for him as an accountant. I believe they were more than just friends. You should have seen the way they looked at each other. But when your father died, she just disappeared. She was such a nice young lady, but she just left. I don't think her father even knew where she went."

"I would really like to find her and talk to her about my father."

"You might ask some of the other workers, but twenty years is a long time. They may not even remember her."

Emele shook Mr. Ramsey's hand and thanked him for his help. Then he left and his thoughts turned to Mr. Van Helsing. "I think I will have a chat with Mr. Van Helsing." He said to himself. Emele's eyes turned red as he thought about what Van Helsing had done to him.

He made his way through the town to Van Helsing's house. He peeped through the window to see if anyone was home. Then he saw Van Helsing sitting in a chair all alone reading a paper. He went to the door and knocked. When the door opened he pushed his way through knocking Van Helsing to the floor. Emele picked him up by his neck. Staring at him he asked, "Do you remember me?" Emele's eyes were red his fangs growing. He could see the terror in Van Helsing's eyes as he remembered.

"You're dead! I killed you, you murderess bastard!"

Emele squeezed his neck, slightly choking him. "You took my life and you took my love." He lifted Van Helsing off the ground. "Where is she?"

Van Helsing struggled to get free, but Emele's grip was too tight. "I wouldn't tell you if I knew." He coughed out.

Emele threw him across the room.

Van Helsing sat up coughing. "You're a monster. I don't know how you are alive, but I will take care of that." And he grabbed a poker from the fireplace.

Emele walked slowly to Van Helsing. "I will teach you what it is like to die and come back."

Van Helsing stood up and raised the poker and charged Emele. "Die." He said as he drove the poker toward Emele's chest.

Emele moved to the side as the poker stuck in his shoulder.

Not phased he grabbed Van Helsing and dug his fingernails in to his shoulders. "Where is Constance?"

Van Helsing was in pain. His eyes were watering and his face wincing.

Again he asked. "Where is Constance?" He dug his nails in deeper.

"I don't know." Van Helsing said as he tried to move his arms, but the pain was too much.

Emele lifted Van Helsing up tilted his neck and plunged his fangs deep into his throat. Then he dropped him to the floor. "Now we wait."

Emele pulled the curtains shut, and started looking through a desk in the study. There he found a note Constance had written to her father. Now he knew Van Helsing did not know where Constance had gone. The sun would be up soon. Emele sat in a chair, but he was too wound up to sleep.

He thought of Constance. Where would she have gone? Was she married? Did she have a family? It did not matter. He would find her. If she was happy, he would just see her. Knowing she was happy would be enough.

He rumaged around through the house until the sun went down and Van Helsing started twitching. He rolled over and screamed from the hunger. His body was changing. His body was turning to vampire, and he wanted blood, Emele's blood. He stood up and turned toward Emele. "What have you done to me?" His eyes were burning and his fangs growing. He growled and charged Emele.

"Oh, you want to feed. Maybe I should leave you this way." Emele turned vampire instantly. "No, we are not finished yet." Emele grabbed Van Helsing. "Now you know what it is like."

Van Helsing was fighting to get free, clawing and trying to bite Emele, but he was no match for him.

Emele looked him in the eyes and opened his mouth wide exposing his fangs fully. He bit Van Helsing hard again in the neck and watched as he was dying. He stopped just short of killing him. Then he lowered him to the ground sitting him on his knees. He stood with his feet beside Van Helsing's body squeezing his sides tight with his legs, then gripped the sides of his head and pulled upward. He could feel the muscles stretching. He looked in Van Helsings eyes and watched the terror as he knew he was about to die. He pulled more. Then the spine snapped as the vertebrae separated. He heard the tendons snap as the muscles pulled free and the last bit of blood ran from the head as it came loose.

He picked up the body and sat it in the chair. Then he put the head back on the neck and pushed it down so it sat atop where it belonged.

Emele looked around the house. He went back to the desk and opened every drawer, looking for any clue that might help him find Constance. He found nothing. He went to the bedroom. On the night stand he saw a couple of small framed pictures. One was of a young Van Helsing with a woman, probably his wife Emele thought. He could see some resemblance to Constance. Another picture showed two young men looking much like their father. Then his eye caught the picture of Constance. It had to be taken about the time he met her. He remembered the love he longed for, her touch, her kiss. His heart ached. "I will find you" he told himself as he kissed her picture and put it in his pocket. He searched the whole house but no clues of where Constance might be.

He went back to the living room and waited a few hours until around three o'clock. Then he placed some newspapers around the body and set the house on fire. He slipped out the backdoor and went home to the castle. Emele would lay low for a couple of days, before he would venture out again.

News of the fire and death of Van Helsing reached his sons, and they were soon in town to mourn their father. The brothers were both hoping the other had heard from their sister, Constance. They would have liked to been joined by her in their time of sorrow, but with no word from her for over twenty years, she could be dead as well. Arrangements were made and the funeral took place a couple of days later.

Steven, the younger son, had talked to the funeral home director about his father. The director had told him it was a strange thing, their father's body had been badly burned but his neck had been disjointed and there was very little blood in the internal organs. The police said there no signs of a break in or struggle, and nothing seemed out of place, no valuables missing. The fire looked like he had fallen asleep in his chair and his pipe had fallen on the dropped newspapers starting the fire.

Steven remembered his father had told his brother and him a story of a monstrous man who killed people by biting the necks, drinking their blood and decapitating the body of his victims. Steven had thought his father was just spinning a yarn, a wild tale, but the father had sworn it to be true and added he had killed the man. Now, Steven did not know what to believe. With no suspects and the police not investigating, the issue would disappear. The sons and their families went back to their own lives, but the thoughts about those murders and their own father's suspicious death stayed in the back of their minds.

After lying low for a few days, Emele went in to town. He stopped at a couple of people's homes that had worked with Constance at the bank. One lady could not remember Constance at all. Another lady remembered working with Constance at the bank. The lady said she and her husband had been to Florida for a wedding of a cousin, and when they returned, Constance asked her a lot of questions about America. Then a few weeks later Constance just didn't come to work. The lady said she tried to talk to Constance's father, but he didn't want to talk about it, some sort of falling out between them. He just said he didn't know where she was. She told him to let her know if he heard from her.

Emele was certain Constance had gone to America. He would travel there as soon as he got things taken care of here. Where would he start? The United States was a big place?

A few months later Emele's finances were back in his control, and he had someone lined up to care for the castle and garden. He bought a night flight ticket to New York. It was an international flight that would fly nonstop toward the sunset so the plane would land in the night time. He would feed and get some luggage and be ready to go.

This was Emele's first flight, and it was a little scary, but he would endure anything to find Constance.

Emele made it to New York. He didn't know where to start. He was all alone in a world that had changed so much from his. He would need a place to stay, a place with some privacy. He picked up his bags and walked to a hotel near the airport, one he had overheard another passenger talk about. It was almost sunup. He checked in for three days, went to his room and tried to get some sleep. It had been a long night.

The next night Emele found a house for sale. It was expensive but secluded. It was furnished. It was perfect. He made a deal and bought the house. He was settled in the next night.

A FRIEND IN NEED

Emele needed to feed, so he walked down to the old part of the city. He would glance down the dark alleys looking for the right person. As he walked along he heard sounds coming from the next alley. When he looked down the alley, he saw two men beating up a third in the shadows. They were killing him the hard way, one man punching bare fisted and the other brandishing a baseball bat. They had him on the ground now still kicking and hitting him with the bat. Emele could tell he wouldn't last much longer.

As Emele approached the men, the one holding the bat said, "Back off Pops. Just turn around and mind your own business."

"What's the problem here gentlemen?" asked Emele.

"It's none of your concern. Just turn around and be on your way" said the other man as he pulled a skinning knife from under the back of his shirt and started slowly walking toward Emele.

Emele kept walking toward them. "And if I make it my concern?"

"Then you can only blame yourself" said the man as he stepped toward Emele, and he tossed the knife to his other hand.

Emele started changing fast and quickly grabbed the man, who plunged the knife deep in Emele's side. Emele picked him up and bit his neck deep, drank the blood, then threw the body against the alley wall as it still twitched. He removed the knife from his side and dropped it to the ground.

The other man stood frozen in disbelief of what he had just seen. He was trapped in an alley with only one way out; through the man he had just watched kill his partner. He was truly terrified and was trembling. The adrenalin rushed through his body as his brain told him to run. He yelled and charged Emele holding the

116

bat high.

Emele could smell the man's fear and adrenalin in his blood.

The man swung the bat hard at Emele's head, but Emele caught it in his hand and pushed the man to the ground. Then he grabbed the bat with both hands and snapped it like a twig and tossed the pieces aside. The man was shaking and put his hands up to defend himself. Emele grabbed the man by his left arm and pulled his body close. He tilted the man's head to the side with his left hand and bit his neck and drank then dropped the body. Then he ripped the heads from the bodies and wrapped them in some plastic from a dumpster in the alley and put the bodies under the garbage.

Emele turned his attention to the man on the ground. He kneeled down beside him. The man was still breathing, but he was unconscious.

He was a tall fellow, six feet two inches in height. He was young, maybe twenty one or two. He had dark hair that was to his shoulders. Emele could not see his eyes but they were dark and deep. His five o'clock shadow was dark and thick. He looked like he might be Italian. He had a muscular build, wide at the shoulders with strong arms. His hands were callused, so he has known hard work. With his face bloodied and swelled from the beating he had taken, he did not show it now, but he was a handsome man. Emele imagined he must have been caught off guard for the men to get him down. His knuckles were bruised, so he had obviously gotten in a few punches. He looked like he could take care of himself.

Emele picked him up and carried him home. He didn't know why but he felt a kinship to the young man. Emele put him on a bed in one of the bedrooms down the hall from his own. He cleaned his wounds and left him to rest.

After two days, the young man started mumbling and stirring.

When Emele saw him moving, he asked. "How are you doing?"

"I feel like I've been hit by a Mac truck," the man said. Then he opened his eyes a little. "Where am I?" Looking at Emele, he asked "and who are you?"

"I am Emele Dracula. You are in my home. I saved your life. Some men were trying to beat you to death."

"That part I remember. You're not a cop are you?"

"No, but I need some answers from you, starting with your name."

"Giovanni, Michael Giovanni."

"Well, Mr. Giovanni, why were those men trying to kill you?"

"It's a long story."

"I've got all night."

"Well, it started about a year ago. My family disowned me. Cut me off without a dime. So, I hitchhiked here and fell in with the wrong crowd." Michael didn't know why, but he felt at ease talking to Emele. "I didn't know they had Mob connections, but I found out the hard way, when I tried to cut out the middle man from one of their deals. So obviously, they had to teach me and others a lesson at my expense, not to mess with them. If you hadn't come along, I'd be a dead man."

"Sounds like you've known trouble. Have you learned your lesson?" asked Emele, as he looked him intensely in the eye.

Michael got a big grin on his face. "Trouble seems to find me some times, and you would think I would, but you just never know."

"Well, I have known trouble myself. But right now I'm looking for someone who can help me."

Michael never even flinched; He just nodded his head like he understood perfectly what Emele was talking about. "Well, I'm your man."

Emele smiled, "You get some rest, and we'll talk more later. I have an errand to run. I'll be back in a few minutes," and he left the house.

Emele sneaked around to the window, where he could watch Michael, to see what he would do in his absents.

Michael got up and started walking around the house. He was going through some of Emele's things. He came across a box. When he opened it, he was surprised to find it full of money. He started to count it. "Whew," he whistled. Then he put the money back and closed the box, and finished looking through his dresser. He found Emele's passport, and looked it over good. Then he put it back. Then he walked to the kitchen and opened the refrigerator. He made a sandwich and grabbed a beer. Then he went to the living room and turned on the television and sat on the sofa and ate his supper.

Emele watched a while longer then went back in his house. The test was over and he felt a little more trusting of Michael. It was getting late, almost sunrise. He would see how everything went while he slept. Tomorrow he would put him to another test. For now he would say goodnight and go to his room.

The next evening, Emele got up and looked for Michael. He was in the bed sleeping. Emele would let him sleep for now, but if he wasn't up soon, he would wake him.

Emele went to the kitchen and poured himself a scotch on the rocks. He sat down at the table and waited. Soon he heard Michael stirring around.

"Hello, Mr. Dracula," Michael said as he came through the doorway seeing Emele sitting at the table. "That drink looks good."

Emele got up and poured Michael a scotch on the rocks and handed it to him.

"Thanks," he said. "So, what's on for tonight?"

"Tonight we need to talk" Emele said. "I get the feeling you are a bit of a shady character, that is alright, because I feel I can trust you, and I feel you trust me."

"Of course I trust you, you saved my life."

"Mr. Giovani."

Michael interrupts. "Look as long as we're talking, you might as well know. My name is Michael Giovani, but friends call me Gieves."

"Okay, Gieves. I'm new here. I grew up in a different time and place, an old country with horse and carriage. I liked that. I had a trusted friend as my driver. I'm sad to say he is no longer with me. " He paused a moment then continued. "Now it seems I am in need of a driver, and you are in need of a job. Can you drive an automobile?"

"I can drive anything, well maybe not a horse and carriage. If the pay is good, I'm your man."

"On another note, I have an allergy to sunlight. It burns my skin. As a result, I do my business at night. Unfortunately, a lot of places are not open in the evening, so I could use someone to run errands and find some information for me in the daytime and be my driver at night. I would pay you well, but I would need one thing, complete loyalty."

"You treat me good, I treat you good."

"I'm looking for someone, a woman."

"Sounds like trouble to me."

"And, I need to tell you something else about myself." Emele said uneasily. "I went through a change many years ago. I had been looking for a tribe in Africa, known for their longevity. I found them and the chief put me through an ordeal for the transformation, but before it was completed the ceremony was interrupted by neighboring tribes hell-bent on killing these people, for their black magic and evil ways. The tribe was massacred and I fled for my life. This interruption with other complications caused some side effects."He paused a moment, then looking intensely at Michael asked, "Do you frighten easily?"

Gieves did not have any idea of what was coming. He was confused but answered, "No, not really." He was puzzled but wanting to hear more, waiting in anticipation as his heart beat a little bit faster to contemplate what Dracula considered frightening.

"I really can't explain it to you so you would understand, so I will show you." Emele said, confident his secret would be safe with Gieves, but he was also prepared to take further action if this did not go well. "I will explain more in a moment."

Emele started to change. His fingernails were growing long and sharp. His eyes turned red. He held his mouth shut for a minute as he watched Gieves' face show disbelief at what he was seeing. Then Emele opened his mouth wide showing him his long fangs.

He sensed Gieves was about ready to move. "I won't hurt you. If I wanted to hurt you, you'd be dead already." Then Emele moved around Gieves, from one side to the other and back to front very quickly, standing in front of him he grabbed him by the throat with one hand and lifted him off the ground, holding him in the air for a minute.

Gieves' eyes were opened wide in dismay at what had happened. He put his hands on Emele's hand trying to pull it from his throat, but it was useless. Gieves now knew Emele was not lying about how he could have killed him easily if he had wanted to. He was amazed at the strength Emele possessed. He was relieved when Emele sat him back down and changed back.

Emele told him how he needed blood, human blood, at least once every seven days or the hunger would take over and he would lose control. He said he had tried to drink animal blood but it didn't work. He still had the hunger. If he let it go too long he might kill anyone. He tried to pick victims who were criminals or evil people that had no morals or respect for other human beings. Over the years he had seen people do despicable things to others. He also told him how important it was to decapitate the body afterward.

Gieves was full of questions, but he was too rattled to ask.

"I'm sure you have questions. You've taken in quite a bit. I will answer them later. Right now I need to tell you why I am here. Twenty years ago I fell in love with a woman and I had plans to marry her and bring her to America, but there was a fight and I was left for dead. To the world I was dead. I was slowly recovering in my grave, when someone called to me. That is why I need your help."

Gieves raised his eyebrows and said "You need my help?"

"Yes, I need a driver who can take me places that knows this town. I will protect you and you protect me."

Gieves had a good feeling about this, maybe because Emele saved his life, maybe because Emele told him his story, maybe because he was a sap to help someone find his true love, or maybe , just maybe because deep down he needed someone too. "When do we start?" he asked.

"Tomorrow we will buy a car, a big car. Do you know where we can get one?"

Gieves got a big grin on his face. He had always wanted to drive a big black Limousine. "A man of your stature should ride in style. I know a place that will sell you what you need. They are open late, so we can go in the evening."

The next evening they went to the dealership. Since Emele didn't know anything about cars, he let Gieves do the talking.

The salesman showed them a nice car with leather seats and

a powerful engine. Emele liked the looks of it. It was a really nice car.

The windows were darkly tinted. The salesman said they would keep the sunlight out. Emele wondered if he would be able to ride in the back of the car in the daylight. The car was very luxurious. It had very comfortable plush leather seats on all four sides forming a square with two open spots for the doors. It had a bar that folded down from the back of the front seat, with a small refrigerator and storage for glasses and bottles. The car was well insulated and very quiet. The window in between the driver and passengers could raise or lower, and was darkly tinted, so the driver could not see through it, and it kept the sound and light out. It was finished with some wood interior, that had designs burned into it that reminded Emele of the crest of his carriage. He liked it very much.

The salesman told them to take it for a test drive.

The car had a powerful engine that responded quickly. Gieves liked the way it handled. For a longer car it cornered very well. It was fun to drive.

Emele sat in the back. It was a very smooth ride. Emele was impressed. "How do you like it, Gieves?" He asked, although he didn't have to ask, the smile on Gieves' face showed his feelings.

"It's great."

When they returned, Gieves and the dealer talked for a while haggling on a price. Finally a deal was reached and the car was bought. One of the stipulations was it had to be ready right away for them to drive home. After a short wait the car was detailed and ready. Gieves drove Emele home.

Now that they had transportation, Emele could start his search.

Steve Pierce

A SISTER'S LOVE

Over the past few months Emelia was getting used to her new life. She was fast becoming the favorite dancer at The Club. She was drawing the crowds. Her prowess kept the guys wanting more. She was well liked by most of the other dancers. The couple of mean girls that worked there were intimidated by her and became more civil to the girls when she was around. The owner was impressed with the way she handled herself on and off the stage. She would dress up in little costumes that were fantasies for the customers, and the music she picked always seemed to liven up the place. She made a lot of money and she was saving most of it. Her boss was making more money, and he didn't want to lose her. He told her not to mention it to anyone, but he was going to pay her more than the other girls. He even told her she could be kind of the assistant manager. She would have the power to hire new girls and help make up the schedules for the dancers. He said he valued her opinion about making changes to the decor of the place.

She had also gotten used to her feeding schedule. She found a couple of places close to the club, where drug dealers and pimps hung out. She even scoped out the papers to watch for pedophiles and murderers who were out on bail. When they disappeared, people just thought they fled to another state. While she didn't like killing she pictured herself as a bit of a vigilante, making the streets a little safer, and she was.

She really couldn't talk a lot about her life to anyone. She really didn't have a close friend. She missed her family, but she found herself avoiding them. Although she loved them very much and missed them, she felt different around them and didn't want to get into a deep conversation about her life. She didn't like lying. So she made up reasons to stay away.

Sarah had noticed how Emelia had changed over the past several months. Now Emelia seemed distant since she moved out, and she didn't visit much anymore. She had become more of a loner and they all noticed she seemed to avoid the family. Sarah missed her. They had been so close growing up. She would go visit her.

Sarah did go to visit Emelia that evening. She reached her house and knocked on the door.

Emelia opened the door. "Hey, Sarah, I was just getting ready for work."

"I was hoping you had time to talk a bit. We never see each other anymore."

Emelia could see the sad look in Sarah's eyes. She missed her terribly, but how could she talk to her about her life now and what had happened to her. It probably wouldn't hurt to chat a little. "Well I guess we could talk for a little bit."

Sarah's face lit up. Emelia opened the door wide and her and Sarah went to the living room and sat on the couch.

"So what's going on? We haven't talked for such a long time" said Sarah.

Emelia didn't want to go into lengthy details about her life, but she answered, "Wow, it has been a long time. So much has changed."

"You haven't been around the house much. Mom is worried about you."

"I know I haven't been around much. Working nights and sleeping days doesn't leave much time. I do miss everyone. Time just gets away."

"Claudia would like to see her big sister more."

"I talked to Mom on the phone the other day and she said she didn't seem to get any better, just kind of staying the same. I've been meaning to drop by."

Sarah sensed Emelia didn't want to talk about family. "You look good. How is your job going?"

"You know how we used to dream of being dancers?"

"Yeah."

"Well don't tell Mom, but I dance on stage." Emelia was a little embarrassed and it was hard to tell her sister this. She also worried what Sarah would think of her. She took a deep breath and said "I'm a stripper. I dance and take my clothes off." After saying this, she was a little relieved.

Sarah could see her uneasiness. "Wow, I mean, I bet you're good at it. You always were a good dancer. You had those seductive moves."

They uneasiness was gone. They both laughed, remembering how they used to dance in front of the mirror.

"Well, I don't want to brag, but I do have quite the following" joked Emelia.

"I'll just bet you do. I'd love to see your show sometime."

"Well come on down. I'd even let you give it a shot."

"Maybe I will" Sarah laughed.

"I really don't know how to tell Mom what I do. I know she would ask me."

"I think Mom has an idea. She told me a while ago she was worried about you doing that job. When I asked her what job? She said a nosey jealous neighbor asked her how Emelia liked stripping at that club."

"Wow, what else did Mom say? I suppose she was disappointed."

"Not really. She said she knew it was hard to find work sometimes. As long as it pays the bills and she's happy, that's the main thing."

"Well I guess Mom's a little more understanding than I

thought." She paused a moment then asked. "How are you doing? What's going on with you?"

"Well, I was thinking of moving out to my own place, but I don't think I could afford much of a place. I was hoping maybe you might want a roommate."

This caught Emelia off guard and for a minute she didn't know what to say. "I keep odd hours. I don't know if it would work out so well."

"I have a confession to make. I'm not a waitress. About three months ago I quit working at the restaurant, and took a job at a strip club."

Emelia could hardly believe her ears.

Sarah continued. "I like stripping, but my boss is a big jerk. He comes up behind me when I'm putting on my makeup and touches my shoulders or starts rubbing my neck. I tell him it makes me nervous and not to do it. He says that is why he needs to do it, to relax me. I don't mind when guys I'm dancing for touch me, but he creeps me out. The other girls say if I put out he will leave me alone and move on to the next new girl. He's such a pervert. I was hoping to quit and maybe get a job at the club you work at."

"Sounds like your boss needs to be taught a lesson. I'm sure you could get on at the club. My boss has me do a lot of the hiring and other work as well. I'm kind of like the assistant manager, I guess."

Emelia had fun talking to Sarah. She really missed her. She missed their friendship. But could she keep her secret life a secret and hide her condition from her sister if they worked and lived together? She thought a minute and decided it would be worth the risk. If worse came to worse, Sarah might be the one person she could talk to about this. It might actually be a relief. "I'm always looking for new talent, if you're serious."

"Sounds great!" Sarah said excitedly.

"If you need a place to live, we can try that too. It would be fun to have my old roomy back."

"Great!" Sarah said with a smile.

"Whoa, I need to get going. Why don't you come down to the club and check it out."

"Okay, sounds good. Let's go."

Emelia quickly got ready and they drove to the club.

When they reached the club, Emelia said "I know it looks a little rough on the outside, but it's better on the inside."

As they walked in the crowd came to life and started whooping and hollering at the sight of Emelia. "You weren't kidding; you do have quite a following."

"They can get a little rowdy, but they're okay. Just be on your guard, some guys drink a little too much and think it's alright to grab your ass as you walk by. They don't mess with me, but they hassle the new girls when I'm not around.

They made their way through the crowd to Emelia's dressing room.

Emelia got ready to go on stage. "I'll go on in a minute and then work the crowd, and I'll be the last one on stage just before we close. I like to stick around and make sure the girls get to their cars and on their way home. So feel free to roam around and mingle, I'll meet you back here after my first set."

Sarah wondered why Emelia would hang around so late. 'Why do you wait for the girls to leave?"

"Sometimes they get hassled and guys just keep them from leaving by standing in front of their car, saying hey, come party with us. You know it's usually harmless but the girls just want to get home."

"What about you. Don't you worry about breaking things up?"

"Don't worry about me. I can take care of myself." She winks at Sarah and says "Trust me."

Emelia looked at her watch next to the mirror. "Well it's showtime."

Sarah left the room and found a place to stand not far from the stage but off to the side. She had a good view of the stage and the crowd.

The spot lights centered on the doorway at the back of the stage. Emelia came walking out in high heeled, black leather boot, slowly swinging her hips from side to side, then pausing a moment at the fan as it blew her hair and her frilly negligee exposing her black lacey bra that was trimmed in red lace and her short black shorts that had red ribbon laced on the sides that held them together. She twisted her hips slightly bending just a bit and pouting her lips, fueling the seductiveness of the mood.

Sarah watched in awe as the crowd became mesmerized by her sister. She had never seen an audience so captivated.

The music started and Emelia danced across the stage to the pole, swinging and dancing to the rhythm of the music as the crowd came to life.

Sarah's jaw dropped. She couldn't believe what a seductive dance routine Emelia had. "She has definitely learned some new moves" she said to herself.

Emelia danced around the stage then crawled across the floor back to the pole, pulled herself up and spun around a few times. Then she walked around the stage as men put dollars in her garter. After she made the round, she stepped to the center edge of the stage, put one leg on the chair of a young man watching, and swung her hip out and said "Untie me big boy."

The young man nervously unlaced the ribbon and pulled it free. Emelia held her shorts in place and turned her other hip to the young man, and he unlaced the other ribbon. Emelia pulled her leg back up and got center stage and let the shorts fall exposing her black thong. She grabbed the pole and bent backwards. She reached behind her back, undid her bra and threw it to the crowd. Then she crawled across the stage slowly like a tiger sneaking up on its prey. When she reached the edge of the stage, she stood up and ran to the pole and climbed to the top. She swung around several times until her feet reached the floor. Then she put her arms up high and slowly ran them over her body, following her curves until she came to her thong. She quickly slid her thong off, and kicked it to the side. The lights dimmed and the crowd applauded as she walked to the doorway.

Sarah went back to Emelia's dressing room. "That was incredible!" she exclaimed.

"Thanks" Emelia replied. "You're next."

Sarah shook her head. "No way, I can't follow that."

"Oh, it will be fine. The crowd is just pumped now. Let's see your act." Emeila looked at Sarah, "I know you want to. I'll introduce you"

Sarah agreed. She was feeling pumped herself. She quickly got ready, putting on heavy makeup and a skimpy outfit. She put on ruffled panties, a short fluffy red skirt and a white button shirt, that fit tight pushing her breasts up and overflowing from her bra. She put her hair into two pigtails and was ready.

Emelia put her clothes on and walked on stage. "Well," she said "you guys are in for a real treat. My sister, Sarah is her and she is going to perform for you."

The crowd watched and applauded as Sarah came on stage. The music started and she did her routine.

When she finished, Emelia asked the crowd, "Well, what do you think, should we keep her?"

The crowd whistled and hollered. "I'll take that as a yes."

Emelia and Sarah went back to her dressing room. "Hey,

Sarah, you really won them over. That was quite a routine."

"Thanks, you were right the crowd was easy. You really had them pumped."

Emelia and Sarah talked more until it was time for Emeila to wrap up the show and close the place down. Then they drove to Emelia's house and Sarah spent the night.

Sarah moved in the next night. Emelia was actually excited to have her living and working with her. It was so nice to have someone to talk to, and Sarah knew not to get too personal with the questions. She knew Emelia would open up and talk when the time was right.

Things were going well and the weeks went by fast.

One night after closing Emelia needed to feed. She sent Sarah home, and locked up the club and started walking. Several people were still out and about. She decided to take the long way to find a victim at one of her hunting spots.

Sarah decided to take the scenic route. She had a lot on her mind and just felt like driving. Before she knew it, she was in the bad part of town. She decided to turn around and get out of there. She had heard of gang violence in that area. She whipped her car around and the front tire went off the road and went into a hole. When she pulled it back the tire popped loose from the rim. "Oh great," she said to herself. She looked around. It actually seemed pretty dead not much traffic. She put on her emergency lights and opened the trunk. She got out the jack, lug wrench, and spare tire. She was just tightening up the last lug nut when a car came by. The car slowed down, and as they passed she could see several guys in the car. The car slowed down and turned around. Sarah put the tire and jack in the trunk, but held on to the lug wrench, jumped in the car and speed away. The other car swerved as it came close to Sarah's car almost forcing her off the road. She pulled back on the road and drove toward the club. The other car turned around and chased her. Pulling along side of her car, they forced her car off the road making her stop.

Emelia heard the commotion and saw Sarah's car being surrounded by gang members. She ran toward her. She heard glass break and saw them pulling Sarah through the window screaming.

When Emelia reached them, they were holding her down punching her and tearing at her clothes.

Emelia went wild. Her claws were long and her fangs were huge. The adrenalin coursing through body was giving her extra strength. She grabbed the first guy with her claws, ripping out his neck, and tossed him aside. She picked up the next guy and slammed him hard on the pavement. Another guy pulled a gun and shot Emelia twice while she pulled one of the attackers from her sister. She was too mad to deal with the pain right now. She quickly snapped the neck of the man she held and charged the shooter. She opened her mouth wide and drove her fangs deep in his neck almost biting it in two. She felt a knife stabbing into her side. She turned around and saw the last man. His eyes were wide. He was scared, but ready to fight. She picked him up by his neck with one hand so fast that he lost the grip on his knife leaving it buried deep in Emelia's side. She pulled him close and bit him draining the blood and life from his body. The man she had slammed to the pavement was crawling toward Sarah. Emelia grabbed his leg as he reached for Sarah. She twisted his leg so fast the bone shattered. The man screamed from the pain as the bone tore through his muscle and skin, protruding outward. She pulled him closer and picked him up by his neck and squeezed his throat, crushing his windpipe. He was dead, and she dropped him to the ground.

Sarah was covered with blood and in shock. She was helpless

and couldn't move, but she had witnessed everything.

Emelia picked up Sarah and quickly checked her wounds. They were mostly superficial. She put her in the car. "We need to get you to a hospital." She looked at the bodies and car. "Damn it" she said. She looked back at Sarah. "Are you okay?

Sarah nodded wide eyed back to Emelia.

"I'll just be a minute. I have to set things up." With lightning speed she threw all the bodies in the car tearing the heads from the ones she had bitten, and tore the gas line loose. She got in the car with Sarah and drove the car back onto the road. She pulled a lighter from the glove box and opened the door. She lit the lighter and held it down close to the ground touching it to the gas that was running from the tank and floored the car. The fire followed the gas to the tank and the car exploded as they drove away.

Emelia was worried about her sister. She was driving fast.

"Slow down" said Sarah. "I don't want to go to the hospital."

"But you're hurt" Emelia siad.

"Not as much as you." Sarah said as she pointed to the knife still stuck in Emelia's side. "What's going on?"

Emelia looked down where Sarah was pointing. Seeing the knife she said "Oh, yeah. I had forgotten this." And she reached down and pulled it out.

Sarah watched in amazement and saw the knife wound close and heal in a matter of seconds. "What's going on?" Sarah asked again.

"You're in shock. You'll feel better when we get you to the hospital."

"I'm not going anywhere until you tell me what happened back there. I've never seen anything like that."

"We need to get you to the hospital" demanded Emelia.

"You don't think they will ask you questions about what

happened, or call the police to check things out."

Emelia thought about what her sister was saying. She was right. "Well, I'll take you home, but you do as I say."

Sarah nodded.

They sat quiet for a moment just driving. Then Sarah started to cry.

Emelia reached over and gave Sarah a hug. "It's alright now. It's over."

"Those guys were going to rape and kill me, I know it."

Emelia squeezed her a little tighter.

Sarah continued. "No. There was nothing I could do. I tried to fight, but it was useless. They just grabbed my arm and took my lug wrench and threw it down, and pulled me out like I was nothing." Sarah cried hard now. "They would have killed me if you hadn't shown up. There was nothing I could do."

Emelia pulled the car over. "Listen, you are okay now. You're safe. Got it?"

Sarah choked back her tears. "I'm okay. Just get me home." She just wanted to feel safe in their home.

Emelia drove them home quickly. She helped Sarah to the house and got her in the shower. "A long hot shower will help fix you up, then straight to bed. You need rest."

"Would you stay in here while I shower?"

"Sure."

Sarah took a long hot shower, and put on her robe. Then she sat in the bathroom while Emelia got ready for bed.

Emelia went to her bedroom and Sarah went to hers.

Soon there was a knock at Emelia's bedroom door. "Emelia, are you awake?"

Emelia opened the door. "Yeah. What's wrong?" she said seeing a terrified look on her face.

"I'm scared. Can I sleep in your room tonight?'

"Sure, come on in."

Sarah went in and climbed under the covers. It reminded Emelia of when they were young and Sarah would wake from a bad dream.

Emelia shut the light off and got into bed. The sun would be up soon. She reached over and hugged Sarah. "Good night Sarah. Now get some rest."

"I can't rest. I'm scared....And what was going on with you. You looked so different. Your eyes were red! And you moved so fast and you were so powerful. I never saw anything like that. You saved my life." Sarah exclaimed almost out of breath.

Emelia had a vision of Sarah lying there raped and murdered. She didn't ever want to have a vision like that again. "I couldn't stand it if anything happened to you, but you are fine now and you need to calm down."

"I can't calm down. I need to know what happened to you. I mean you were shot and stabbed and, and, and it didn't even slow you down."

Emelia wasn't sure how to tell Sarah what had happened. How could she explain what Sarah had seen? She would have to tell her the truth. Would Sarah be able to accept her the way she was. Sarah was scared, but she was not scared of her. She was in the same bed holding on tight. Perhaps she would understand. If anyone would it would surely be Sarah. She would tell her the truth. "Do you remember back when I told you I was attacked?"

"Sure."

"Well, that night when I was being attacked I changed. I don't know how or why, but I changed. I told you I killed him by breaking his neck."

Sarah was all ears now and concentrating intensely on what Emelia was saying. "I remember."

"That wasn't the truth. I was scared and felt helpless and mad, and something changed inside me. My teeth grew and I bit his neck and drank his blood then I was so disgusted, I tried to turn his head away from me and I twisted with such force, his head tore loose from his body."

Emelia went on with her story and told her all about the old lady in the restaurant bathroom and what had happened after that. She told her her life's story from the day of her attack to what had just happened. When she finished she looked at Sarah. She had just listened to everything she said without interrupting.

Sarah could tell how hard it was for Emelia to tell her story and how worried she was that she might lose her family if they knew. She also knew the time Emelia was talking about and she remembered how Emelia had changed to a night person and how she became more seductive after that night. And it made sense why she wanted to be alone once a week and why she alway told everyone not to worry, she could take care of herself. She reached her arms around Emelia and gave her a big hug. "It's alright. You're my sister and I love you."

Emelia was relieved to hear this. It felt good to finally talk to someone about her life. She felt a little happier now. "Let's get to sleep. I think we will both sleep like logs today."

Sarah wouldn't be able to sleep. She felt safe next to Emelia, but she still felt helpless. She lay there thinking about how Emelia had moved so fast, so strong and so brutal against the gang members. She thought of how she didn't even realize there was a knife sticking in her side, and how fast she healed when she pulled it out. Emelia had told her she knew she wasn't destructible, but she had been through a lot. Finally Sarah whispered, "Emelia, are you still awake?"

"Yes, what is it?"

"You said if you bite someone they come back like you, right?"

"Well it happened the first time, and she tried to kill me."

"What if you knew the person you bit or if they were close to you?"

"I don't know, my instincts tell me not to let that happen again. That is why I only feed on bad people and decapitate them, so they don't come back."

"Do you think you could reason with them if you knew them?"

"Well the old woman caught me off guard. I didn't have time to think a lot about what to do."

"Well, seeing you in action was like nothing I've ever seen, or even imagined. Right now I feel so...frail and helpless. I hate it! I want to be strong like you" said Sarah looking deeply at Emelia.

This caught Emelia by surprise. For a moment she was dumbfounded. Then she looked at Sarah, who was still staring at her waiting for a response. "I don't know what to say to this. It's a different lifestyle. I'm not sure you would like it."

"All I know is I hate what happened to me, and I hate feeling like this."

"It may seem impressive, but it can be hell. Killing is not fun. I have to tell myself I'm helping save good people in order to do it. I get sad every time I think about that old woman. She was probably someone's mom, grandma, or wife. I wouldn't wish that on anyone. I tried to curb my appetite with animal blood, but it didn't satisfy my hunger and I almost lost control again. I still don't know what caused me to change. All I can think of is maybe the guy that attacked me had something that reacted in me, changing me fast. He never bit me and I changed right away. He wasn't strong like me. I had no trouble getting him off me after I changed. I've never done drugs and we can't ask him anything. Besides I'm not sure you could kill someone."

"After what I've been through, I'm sure I could" said Sarah seriously. "I listened to your story and I wasn't scared or appalled.

I admired you. Taking out the bad guy or girl"

Sometimes Emelia had wondered what it would be like to have someone like her, to talk to without worrying what you might let slip, or maybe have someone to hunt with, to have your back. Emelia smiled a little smile, and then seriously asked "Are you sure?"

"I've never been more sure about anything."

"I'm not sure about what will happen. The first old woman I bit was the only one that I didn't cut the head from. It may have been a fluke." Emelia pondered a moment. "Maybe we could do a test somehow."

"That's a good idea."

"We could take out a baddie and restrain him and see what happens. We should do a test run to double check this theory. I couldn't live with myself if you didn't come back."

They would do a test to make sure. Emelia had someone in mind, Greg. He was a loner who sold drugs. He had been in and out of jail several times for domestic abuse. He always managed to get set free, because the women were too afraid to testify against him. Emelia knew this because it happened to one of the girls she worked with recently. Emelia knew where he liked to hang out. They would set their trap for him and wait until the time was right

Sarah would distract him and get him alone, and then Emelia would bite him and put his body in the trunk. They would chain him up in an old abandoned warehouse Eemelia knew about. Then they would test the theory and wait for the change.

The next night after work Emelia and Sarah drove to the spot Greg liked to hang out to sell drugs. As they got close Emelia said "That's him over there. Let me out here, then drive slowly toward him and tell him you need some cocaine to get you through the night."

Sarah was nervous, which worked to her advantage by making her look like she needed a fix. She drove slowly up to Greg and he walked over to the car. He bent down by the window, looking in the car and at Sarah. "What's the matter? Having a long night?"

Sarah was a little scared, even though she knew Emelia was ready to strike. "Yeah, I need something to get me through it" she said looking a bit fidgety. "Do you have any cocaine?"

"I think I can handle that if you have the cash" he said with a smile.

Sarah pulled a couple of twenties from her pocket and held it out to him. He pulled a small bag from his pants pocket and dropped it in Sarah's lap as he took the money.

Emelia made sure there were no witnesses. Then with lightning speed she was behind him pulling his head back, biting his neck deep. He was caught off guard and didn't have time to fight. He was gone quickly, and Sarah popped the trunk and Emelia threw the body in, and they drove away.

They drove to the warehouse. It was an old building that had the windows boarded up, and had not been in use for a long time. Emelia broke a small chain and opened an overhead door and they drove inside. Then she got the body and Sarah grabbed the chains. They sat him down and chained his body to a railing bolted to the wall. The sun was coming up, but the warehouse was dark. The girls lit some candles, so Sarah could see. Sarah would keep watch first and Emelia would take over after a few hours.

Everything was calm. After a few hours, Sarah woke Emelia and she took over the watch so Sarah could get some sleep. It was a long day, but finally the sun started to disappear. Both girls were awake now, and waiting for the victim to stir,

Nothing was happening as the girls waited. Then about two

o'clock the chain made a little jingle.

"Stay back Sarah!" said Emelia as she changed.

They both watched as he started to move. He rolled around a bit, growling as his body went through the change. He grew sharp fingernails and licked his tongue over his fangs as they grew. He stood up slowly as his eyes turned red focusing on Emelia. He lunged toward her, pulling the chains tight.

"Hey, settle down. I just want to talk to you" said Emelia as she felt a confrontation coming.

Sarah was scared and moved back farther, drawing Greg's attention to her.

Emelia stepped into his line of vision to Sarah. "I need to talk to you."

"No!" was all he said as he lunged hard once more toward Emelia. He was becoming agitated by the chains. He swung his clawed hands wildly at Emelia and jerked hard on the chains.

"I'm not sure this was such a good idea" said Sarah.

This turned Greg's hungered attention back to Sarah, and he lunged hard at her, as he did some of the bolts in the railing pulled loose from the wall. Emelia grabbed him ready to give him a killing bite. As her fangs dug in his neck he spun around knocking her head into a steel beam hard, causing her to lose her grip. She fell from him, stunned for a second, which was long enough for him to grab her and bite her neck.

Sarah grabbed a two by four and hit Greg on top of his head. He let loose of Emelia and grabbed Sarah's leg. She fell down dropping the two by four. He pulled her toward him, ready to bite.

Emelia was in a weakened condition, but she had to save her sister. She used all her strength to pull herself up and grab Greg's head. She twisted with all her might as he was sinking his fangs into Sarah's throat. His head tore loose pulling a big piece of tissue from Sarah's neck. Emelia threw the head aside and looked at Sarah.

Sarah reached her hand up to cover the wound, but the blood was spurting out to fast and she lost consciousness as Emelia picked her up in her arms. She didn't know what to do. She tried to stop the bleeding but it was too late. The blood slowed down to a trickle. Emelia knew this wasn't good. She started to cry as she shook Sarah. "Sarah! Sarah!" Emelia fell to her knees still holding her sister. "What have I done?" she screamed.

She sat there crying holding her sister's lifeless body close, wondering what to do. It wasn't supposed to be like this. What could she do? Sarah was dead. Would she come back? Was that bite enough to change her, or had she simply bled to death. If she did come back could Emelia control her? Would she listen to her and be reasoned with?

Emelia had to think positive no matter how hard it was. "Sarah will come back and she will listen to me, because she knows me and trusts me. I'm her sister not some stranger off the street, and we are close. Sarah wasn't some low life thug strung out on drugs. It was going to be alright" she said trying to reassure herself.

It would be a long day. Emeila had work to do. She took Greg's body and head out of the room to the car and put them in the trunk. Then she chained Sarah's body to the pillar and held her head on her lap. She sat still for the rest of the night. She knew she would not get much rest, but she had to try. She would need her strength and wits about her when Sarah came back.

The day seemed to drag on forever. Emelia tried to sleep, and she did doze off from time to time, but it was not a restful sleep.

When dusk came she was ready, hoping Sarah would come back. A few hours went by and Sarah wasn't changing. What if she didn't come back? No, she had to think positive. Sarah would wake up and Emelia would be ready. She sat there holding Sarah's head on her lap, stroking her hair with her fingers and looking at the wound on her neck. It was not healing. It was after three o'clock now and Emelia was starting to get a bad feeling.

Emelia bent her head down and kissed Sarah's forehead and hugged her tight. "Come on Sis, it can't end like this" she said starting to cry.

Emelia was holding her tight when she heard the chain jingle. She looked down at the wound. It was healing. It was healing fast, really fast. She could hear Sarah's heart beating faintly, and she listened as it grew stronger. Sarah started moving. Emelia could see her changing, but she was not afraid. Emelia was changing as well. She scooted back behind Sarah and held her with her legs wrapped around her waist with her arms pinned against her side, facing forward.

Sarah started growling.

Emnelia tightened her grip and said "Sarah, it's me, Emelia." She put her face next to Sarah's and said again "Sarah, it's me, your sister Emelia." She looked at Sarah and could see her open her mouth and feeling her new found fangs with her tongue. Her claws were growing as well and she tried to scratch Emelia.

Emelia squeezed her tighter and heard a rib crack. She felt Sarah wince from the pain. She said "Sarah, it's me Emelia. Don't struggle. I don't want to hurt you, but you have to listen. You have to control the hunger. Listen to me! You have to control your hunger. I will help you, but you have to listen to me."

Sarah eased up a little. "Emelia?"

"Yes Sarah, it's your sister Emelia." Emelia sighed in relief. "You have to listen to me, okay?"

Sarah nodded.

"Can you control your hunger?"

"I don't know. I'm so hungry. All I can think about is biting you and tasting your sweet blood that I can smell and hear pumping through your body.'

"I know it's hard but you have to fight it. Then I will let you loose so we can get you the blood you need. You have to control it? Don't let it control you. You are strong enough to do this. I know you are."

"I'm trying" Sarah said as she concentrated hard. "I can do it, but can we hurry? I'm so hungry."

Emelia slowly loosened her grip on Sarah, She was not struggling. Emelia let loose and stood up. She reached for Sarah's hand and helped her up. "Let's get going. The sun will be up soon enough."

They ran and got in the car. Emelia drove to a drug dealer's hangout.

"Hurry, Emelia. It's getting bad."

"Hang on Sis, we're almost there."

Emelia saw a man walking down the street. There was no one else around. "I hope he's not a nice guy" she said as she pulled the car closer. She recognized him. He was a bad guy.

Sarah jumped out and had the man down in a second biting his neck deep, satisfying her thirst. He struggled, but he was no match for Sarah. She held him still until he faded away. Her hunger quenched, she loosened her grip and opened her mouth, releasing his neck form her fangs.

"Now comes the hard part. You have to remove the head from the body. We don't want him looking for us, do we? We need to hurry."

Sarah remembered seeing Emelia use her claws to do the trick. She plunged her clawed hand through the man's neck. "Oh, gross" she said as she felt the muscles tearing and heard tendons snapping.

"It gets easier" promised Emelia. "Now let's get this body in the trunk and get home."

Emelia grabbed the body and threw it in the trunk next to Greg. "Bring the head."

Sarah picked up the head and put it in the trunk.

"Wow! I feel so, so great. It's incredible! I feel so alive, so powerful." She picked up Emelia and hugged her tight.

"Easy Sis, we need to get going."

Sarah put Emelia down and they got in the car and drove.

"We can bury these guys tonight. We need to get home and keep this car in the shade."

Sarah was so excited she felt such a rush. "I never imagined how this would feel. It's indescribable. I feel so powerful."

"Just remember, it comes at a price" said Emelia. "You will need blood, and we have to be careful. We need to be choosy who we take. We don't want to hurt innocent people. We want to help get rid of the bad people."

Sarah nodded in agreement.

"We also have to make sure we take care of the bodies." Emelia looked at Sarah intensely. "This is the most important thing. You have to remove the head and dispose of the body the right way. We can't draw attention of any kind. It will be enough just with people disappearing."

Sarah looked at Emelia. "I understand. I know how serious this is." Then she got a little smirk. "But I can't help being excited. I can't imagine ever feeling helpless again." She reached over and gave Emelia a little hug. "Thanks, Sis. I know this was a tough choice for you to make."

Emelia smiled at Sarah. "I'm glad. I wish I could have talked to someone about what happened to me. It would have been nice to know what was happening and what was going to happen." She felt tears welling up, but held them back.

The sun was coming up as the girls entered the house. "Wow!

That sun is hot today" said Sarah as she felt the sunshine on her skin.

"Yeah, it can burn your skin quick if you're not careful. It's one of the downsides now. No more suntans" said Emelia.

Sarah had so many questions she wanted to ask Emelia, but she could tell Emelia was really tired. She would ask her later. She said "Goodnight, or good day, or whatever" then she giggled.

"I still say goodnight. It won't seem like the next day until I go to bed and get some sleep. And it's been a long day." Emelia said as she gave Sarah a hug, then she added. "Do you want to sleep in my room? I remember having some weird dreams after I changed."

"Thanks. That might be a good idea. I'll try not to keep you awake."

The girls went to bed. They would have a busy night. They were both scheduled to work and they had to bury the bodies in the desert.

Emelia slept like a rock, but Sarah had a restless night. She tossed and turned dreaming. She dreamed she was in a fancy restaurant. She was dressed in a white frilly dress, sitting in the dark corner sipping red wine. It tasted so good as it slowly ran out the glass and into her mouth, teasing her taste buds as it rolled over her tongue. She smiled from the pleasure it gave her. Then a waitress came to check on her. The waitress screamed and ran. Sarah looked around, the lights were bright and everyone was staring at her. The table cloth was red from the wine that had spilled from the bottle that lay on its side, the wine still flowing. Sarah watched in horror as the wine turned to blood running thicker. She looked at the glass she was holding. It was filled with blood. She dropped the glass and it shattering as it hit the table, sending the blood splashing on her white dress and her face. Sarah felt her fangs growing and she opened her mouth wide. People started running and screaming. Sarah sat up with a jolt, breathing hard. She looked around the room. The windows were closed with heavy dark curtains blocking any sunlight that might try to light the room, making it as dark as a moonless night. Sarah could see perfectly in the dark now. Getting her bearings of where she was she relaxed. It was only a dream. She shuttered and lie back down in the bed. She was covered with sweat. She looked at Emelia, her back toward her sleeping soundly. She had not been disturbed by her startled awakening.

Sarah slid silently out of bed and walked to the bathroom. She looked at herself in the mirror. She wasn't covered with sweat, it was blood! Her negligee was covered with blood! Where did it come from? She looked at her body. She didn't have any wounds, but her fangs were long and she tasted blood. She ran back to the bedroom. She pulled Emelia's shoulder to turn her over and wake her up. As Emelia was turned over Sarah saw her opened eyes and blood on the pillow. She saw fang wounds on her sister's neck and a tiny trail of blood that had run from them. "Emelia!" She screamed out loud, waking herself up for real this time.

"Sarah, what's wrong?" asked Emelia.

Sarah was shivering. "What's happening?" she asked looking very disoriented.

"I think you were dreaming."

Sarah took a deep breath. She looked at Emelis. "You're okay!" she said as she hugged her holding her tight.

Emelia could see the tears in Sarah's eyes when she looked up at her. "What's going on?"

"Oh my gosh! I just had the most horrible nightmare" she said looking at Emelia. She gave her another hug. "I'm so glad you're okay."

146

Emelia hugged her back. "That must have been some dream."

Sarah told Emelia about her dream and how she thought she was awake, only to be awakened by her own screams. Then Emelia told Sarah about the weird dreams she had had. The girls continued to talk until sundown. Emelia was answering Sarah's questions as good as she could. They also decided it might be a good idea to hunt together for a while. Emelia would show Sarah the places she knew the really bad criminals hung out.

In some of her spare time, Sarah liked to hang out around the strip. She was very interested in mob involvement in the drug and prostitution rings. She would talk to some of the working girls and find out if they worked on their own or if they worked for someone, and if they did work for someone were they treated right. She found out there were several girls that were forced to work the streets, who would like to get out of the business and several girls who were routinely beaten by bad men. There were also some who had worked on their own but had been forced to work for people who took most of the money they made and did not treat them very well. Some were also too scared to talk and became uneasy when Sarah tried to talk to them.

Emelia would listen to Sarah's ideas, but it would be tuff to take on the mob, because they usually hung out in groups and were usually armed, but they did take them down when they got the chance.

It was easier to get rid of the pimps that worked alone. They were usually checking out the streets for new talent, and Sarah and Emelia would easily catch their eye as they hung out on the street. The pimps would pick up girls and make them promises of big money, but they would always take most of it themselves and say it was for their protection, but they made a deadly mistake when they picked up Sarah or Emelia.

Things were going good for the sisters. Sarah was becoming a

Steve Pierce

favorite at the club, not quite as popular as Emelia, but her fans were growing. Emelia was glad to have someone like her to talk to and hang out with.

CONSTANCE'S REQUEST

Things were not going so well for Claudia. She was getting sick more often. She was diagnosed with the same cancer her father had. Treatment was not very successful, and in fact usually made her feel worse. There was not a lot of hope. It just seemed like nothing worked for her.

Constance would cry a lot when she was by herself, never letting any of the girls see her like this. She had to stay positive and strong for Claudia.

Emelia and Sarah would visit them two or three times a month, sometimes together and sometimes on their own. They liked seeing their mom and sister, but they felt uneasy when the conversation turned to how they were doing. They were sad to see how sick Claudia was becoming, but they were glad seeing how happy she was to see them. They felt a little guilty about not coming around so much and swore they would try to visit more. Over the next few months they did.

Over the past year, Constance had suspected Emelia of changing into what Emele was. She was never around in the daylight. She didn't eat much when she came over and Constance knew she worked at night. She hoped she didn't kill anyone but deep down she knew better. She could tell Emelia became uneasy when she asked her personal questions. It was time for a serious talk.

One night when Emelia came over to visit, Constance asked her what had happened.

Emelia was uneasy, but she told her mother the truth. She told her about the rape and how it changed her. How she grew fangs and long fingernails and strength and a hunger for blood, human blood. She started crying when she told her she couldn't help it.

She said she tried not to feed but she lost control and preyed on an innocent old woman. She also told her how she found out the hard way she had to rip the head from the body or the victims came back like her. So now she only fed on bad people and tried to make the world a better place. She also told her how she had saved lives by killing murderous people in the act.

Constance tried to keep calm listening to Emelia's story. She had some questions, but did not want to interrupt her.

Emelia also told her about the night she saved Sarah from the gang members, and how helpless Sarah felt after that. She took a deep breath and said, "I wasn't sure it was the right thing to do, but Sarah was so scared. I knew she would never feel safe again, so we did a test on one of the victims to see if they would come back like me. If things went well, I was going to bite her so she could be like me. Things got out of hand and Sarah was bitten, so now Sarah is like me."

Constance had noticed Sarah had become more like Emelia. She had suspected it for a few months, but she never said anything until now. "I thought Sarah had changed, but I had to know how first."

Constance paused a moment. She needed to talk with Emelia and she wasn't sure how to ask her the question she needed to ask. "I don't know how to ask this. It was not an easy decision. I still don't know if it's the right thing to do, but I'm at my wits end."

Emelia wasn't sure what was coming, but her mother definitely had her attention.

"You know Claudia has been sick for such a long time. At times I would think she was going to bet better, but I was just fooling myself. She would feel better once in a while, but it always came back worse." Constance started to tear up. This was extremely hard for her to talk about.

Emelia reached over and put her arm around Constance. "I know, Mom. I know how hard it is for me to see her and know how sick she is. I know it has to be a lot harder for you to see it every day. I should have been here more for Claudia and for you. I'm sorry."

"It's alright. I knew you had a lot going on in your life too. Claudia didn't want me to say anything to you or Sarah because she didn't want you to worry about her. But now the doctors told me Claudia's options have run out and she only has two months at best." Constance broke down crying. "I can't stand the thought of losing her." Constance wiped her tears. "I don't know if this is right or wrong, but I have to ask you to do something for me."

"I don't want to lose her either. I would do anything for you or for Claudia. You know that!"

Constance took Emelia's hands and looked her in the eyes. "I want you to bite Claudia." She could hardly believe the words she was saying.

"Mother, are you sure?" Emelia said looking back in her mother's eyes. "I'm not sure Claudia would want this. Things will be so different. I can't picture her killing anyone."

"I had a deep talk with her, and she is unsure, but if we don't do something soon it will be too late. I need you to do this for me." Constance's look was intense.

"Are you sure?"

"Just do it... Take her under your wing and teach her what she needs to know."

Emelia nodded. "Okay, Mother. I'm not sure it will work as sick as she is, but we will try."

They stood up. Emelia kissed her mother and said goodbye.

Emelia drove home and waited for Sarah to get home from work.

Emelia was in deep thought when Sarah came in, and she

151

could sense something was up. "What's going on, Emelia?"

"I went to visit Mother tonight and we had quite a talk. It seems she knows a little about what I've become. I don't know how, but she does. She also said she thought you were like me."

Sarah was shocked to hear this, but she didn't want to interrupt.

"I told her my story, and then I told her yours. I had to. After I told her this, she told me about Claudia. Our suspicions are right. She is not getting better as Claudia told us. In fact, Mom said the doctors have run out of options and they told her she only has two months at best."

"Oh, god! I mean I know we wondered, but just hearing it. It's still a shock" Sarah said fighting back her tears. "I just refused to think about that."

Emelia couldn't hold out any more. "Mom asked me to bite her, and I said I would. I told her I wasn't sure it would work as sick as she is."

Sarah sat silent for a minute thinking. "It might work. It probably would have been better a while ago, before she became so weak."

"The thought had crossed my mind, but with her being so sick, I just didn't know, and I just can't picture our little sister killing anyone. I'm not sure she would want this."

"Does Claudia know the plan?"

"Mom said she talked to her about it, but she wasn't sure. I told Mom we would both be over tonight to talk to her about it. Hopefully she will want to try it."

"What if she doesn't?"

"I know she will be scared, but she has to be scared already. I think with both of us there she will come around."

Sarah nodded in agreement.

The two sisters went to bed as the sun was rising.

When Emelia and Sarah arrived at Constance's house she met

them at the door. She had been crying.

"Are you sure you don't want to be here, Mother?" asked Emelia. "I'm still not sure it will work. This could be it" she said as she held back her tears.

"I don't know.... Maybe I should be in the house."

"I think that is a good idea" said Sarah as she reached for Constance's hands. "How is she holding up?"

"Not so good. She is weak, but she smiled when I told her you girls were coming to talk to her."

Constance went to the kitchen and sat at the table with a cup of coffee. She still wondered if this was the thing to do.

Emelia and Sarah went to Claudia's room.

"How you doing kiddo?" asked Emeila.

"Not so good, but better now that you guys are here" answered Claudia as her face lit up with a little smile.

"We came to talk to you" said Sarah.

"Mother said you were coming to talk to me about something important."

"Wow, I don't know how to start this" Emelia said nervously. "I went through some sort of change about a year and a half ago. I don't really know what happened. I was attacked and it triggered something. My senses got heightened and I became fast and strong. Unfortunately there is a down side. I craved and needed blood, human blood. I couldn't help myself. I changed, I grew long fingernails and fangs. I killed an innocent old woman. As I drank her blood my body felt so alive. Since then I've learned I need to feed every seven days to control the hunger, feeding on those who have no respect for the lives of others, mean, vindictive people."

Claudia's eyes were huge. She couldn't believe what she was hearing.

Emelia continued. "I can't stand the sun. It burns my skin, so

I have to lead a night life."

Sarah butted in. "If you get bitten, you will be like Emelia. That's what happened to me. I wanted to be strong like her, so we were going to do a test."

Emelia interrupted. "If I bite someone, they come back like me. We were going to do a test to make sure we could reason with the person, because they may just want to kill me because the hunger is so strong. The test went wrong and Sarah got bit. Anyway, we couldn't reason with the guy, but the bond is strong in our family, so I could reason with Sarah."

"It's great and I feel so alive" said Sarah.

Emelia looked at Claudia and said "Mom, Sarah and I don't want to lose you. Mom told me what the doctors said. I know it isn't good. We decided it would be worth a shot for you to be like Sarah and me.... But it is up to you. I'm not sure this will work, because you are very weak. If you want to try this we will do it. It has to be your decision." She paused a moment then asked "What do you think?"

Claudia looked at Sarah, then at Emelia. "I remember back about a year and a half ago. You changed almost overnight. I noticed a new look you got without even trying. I remember the boys staring at you almost in a trance. You were so sexy."

Emelia remembered when Claudia called her the seductive one, and a little smile came to her face.

Claudia continued. "I remember several months ago I saw Sarah change in the same way. I was secretly hoping I would too. I was hoping it was hereditary. I've been waiting, but nothing. Now I know. I feel like I haven't really lived. I've been sick for so long.... I guess I'm saying yes. Let's go for it."

Sarah was excited. "Good. Our baby sister will be one of us!"

Emelia was excited too. "We will hope for the best. It will be like you almost die, but then you will wake up, and you will want to feed. The hunger will be strong. We will have to restrain you until we can reason with you. Then we will help you feed."

"I just want you to know, if this doesn't work, it was my choice. I know I'm sick and weak. So don't blame yourselves."

The girls all held each other in a group hug. Then Emelia changed. Sarah changed and held Claudia.

Constance was wondering how it was going in there, so she silently walked over to Claudia's room. The door was ajar and Constance couldn't help herself. She peeked through just as Emelia was opening her mouth wide with long white fangs. Both girls had long fingernails and Constance saw the fear in Claudia's eyes as Sarah held her tight, waiting for what was coming next. She watched in horror as Emelia sank her fangs into her neck, and she pictured Emele holding her father ready to do the same. She wanted to close her eyes or look away, but she was helpless, frozen in the moment. This was her baby. What had she done? She almost shouted out stop. Then reality came back. She didn't want Claudia to die. Emelia and Sarah seemed happy and healthy, very healthy. This was her last hope.

When Emelia was done, Sarah held Claudia close and kissed her check. "I love you" she said as she watched her fade away.

Emelia leaned over and held Claudia and Sarah. "It will be okay. I feel it."

Constance pushed the door open. As it creaked Emelia looked at her knowing she had seen everything.

"Now what?" asked Constance.

"We wait" said Emelia. "It will be tomorrow night."

It was a long rest of the night and even a longer day. They all sat in Claudia's room waiting, trying to sleep. The day ened and night began.

"I will hold her when she starts to come around. She will be hungry, hungry for my blood, but if she can't get mine, she won't care whose blood. The hunger will be strong and we will have to reason with her" said Emelia.

"Mother, you will have to stay back and let us talk to her" said Sarah.

Constance nodded in agreement.

They all sat still as Emelia listened close for Claudia's heartbeat. She heard nothing.

Time dragged on slowly. A couple of hours went by. Emelia listened again nothing. She looked at the wound on Claudia's neck. No healing yet either. It was getting late, almost morning. Nothing was happening.

Constance could tell Emelia was worried. "She was very sick" Constance said holding back her tears. "Maybe she was just too fragile."

Sarah was worried and tearing up. "It's sunrise. What should we do?"

Emelia saw the disappointment in Constance and Sarah's face as she said "I don't know."

They were all exhausted. Two days with little sleep. What would they do now?

Constance choked back her tears and said "Well, we will deal with this tonight. Right now I think we all need some sleep. She was just too sick." She joined Emelia and Sarah on the bed. She held Claudia in her arms. Tears were flowing from all three ladies. "It was worth a try. I know Claudia wanted to do this. She was just too weak, just too weak." She pushed the hair away from Claudia's face and kissed her check.

"I'm sorry" Emelia said as she lie down behind Constance holding her tight.

"If anyone is to blame, it is me" said Constance.

Sarah lay down on the other side of Claudia. "It's no one's fault. We tried to save her, but she was just too sick, I guess."

They all fell asleep as they held each other on the bed as the sun reached its height of the day.

Constance was dreaming when funeral plans popped in her head. She woke up and looked a Claudia. There was no change. The sun was going down.

"Mother, are you alright?" asked Emelia.

"Yes. I'm just going to miss her so much. Ever since you and Sarah moved out, we had become very close."

Constance looked at Sarah. She was holding Claudia, sleeping deeply. She looked at Emelia. "I probably should have told you this before. But I couldn't." She swallowed hard and added. "Emelia, your father was like you."

Emelia listened close to the words her mother was saying.

"I saw him change right before my eyes. My father had found out Emele killed people and drank their blood. He came to kill him. I saw him change when my father shot him in the back. Emele wanted to kill him and I saw him change. Emele was going to kill him, but I stopped him. I saw his heart break as he stood there in disbelief of what I had seen. Then my father killed him as I watched helpless in shock. I never knew how he came to be that way. I'm sure he was going to tell me, but Father interrupted."

"That's terrible, Mother."

"Yes, but it is such a relief to finally talk to someone about it."

All at once Emelia yelled "Mother get back! Sarah, hold her!"

Claudia was awaking. Emelia heard her heart pounding loadly.

Sarah quickly sat up and held Claudia by wrapping her legs around her waist and pinning her arms to her side.

Emelia pushed Constance off the bed as Claudia tried to lunge for her.

Constance was scared but at the same time she was happy to

see her daughter come back.

"Claudia!" Emelia said sternly. "It is us, your sisters, Emelia and Sarah."

Claudia looked at Emelia with hunger in her eyes as her fangs grew long.

Sarah was holding her tight, she was very strong. "Claudia, can you control the hunger?"

Claudia just licked her lips and ran her tongue over her new fangs, struggling to free herself.

"We don't want to hurt you, but you have to be strong and control the hunger, Claudia" Emelia said loudly. "Claudia, do you hear me?"

Claudia eased up a little and nodded.

"Can you control it?" asked Sarah.

Claudia was getting some control. "I'm so hungry, but I'll try. I can hear your hearts beating, and I can smell Mother's blood" as she looked at Constance.

"Mother, leave us now! Please!" Emelia said. She grabbed Claudia's face and asked once more. "Claudia can you control the hunger?"

"I think so. I'll try my best."

Sarah loosened her hold on Claudia. "Let's get you some blood."

Constance went to her bedroom and locked the door. It would be best to let the girls handle this.

Emelia and Sarah took Claudia's hands and led her to the car. Sarah quickly drove to the same spot she had had her first meal. Emelia was ready, just in case Claudia started to lose control. When they reached the spot, they saw a big man walking down the street. Emelia knew him, he was bad news. When Claudia saw him she lunged over Emelia to open the door. "Claudia, wait, this guy carries a gun" Emelia warned. She tried to hold

Claudia back. "Wait a minute. Let us help you with this one."

Sarah stopped the car and all the girls got out. Emelia and Sarah quickly got on both sides of the man. He could see they wanted trouble. He pulled his gun and shot at Emelia. She stepped out of the bullet's path. He could not believe he missed. Emelia's heart was beating wildly. She was actually a little scared. He fired a second shot and again Emelia stepped out of the way. Sarah was coming up behind him, when he caught a glimpse of her. He swung his fist around hard connecting and knocking Sarah off balance. Claudia went wild. She jumped on the big man before he knew she was even there and wrapped her legs tightly around his waist. She grabbed his shoulders and tilted her head and opened her mouth wide. She bit the whole front of his neck sinking her fangs deeply tearing a big piece of flesh loose. He cursed and tried to push her off him. Emelia and Sarah grabbed him from behind pulling him down to the ground. Claudia did not lose her grip. She was in a feeding frenzy. She loved the taste of the blood. As she drank, it made her feel so strong, so alive. She had never felt anything like this in her life. It was so intense. She drank every drop from his body.

"Okay, Claudia, take it easy. I think he's dry." Emelia said as she pulled Claudia from his body. "Now you need to remove the head from the body, or he will come back like us. Can you do that?"

Before Emelia finished her words, she saw Claudia tear the man's head loose. "Sorry big guy, but we don't want you hunting us down."

Sarah could not believe her eyes. "Wow, doesn't that bother you just a little?"

Claudia shrugged her shoulders, "Eeh."

"I think little sister will do just fine" said Emelia. "Now let's load this body and get you home. I know Mom is worried about us."

Claudia kept talking about how alive and energized she felt all the way home. She had been sick for so long. Emelia and Sarah were happy to see their little sister feeling happy again.

They drove out in the desert and buried the man as Emelia stressed the importance of disposing of bodies properly. Then they drove to Constance's house.

Constance was waiting up for them when they came in. She was a little scared from what Claudia had said, but deep down she knew she had nothing to worry about.

When Claudia came through the door, she saw Constance standing there. She yelled "Mommy!" and ran to her giving her a big hug, lifting her in the air and twirling her around. "I feel so alive. Words cannot describe how good I feel."

Constance was startled by Claudia's actions, but she let her have her fun. It had been such a long time since she acted like this. A smile came to her face as she told her "My goodness, you really are exuberant and I'm glad to see you like this, but I'm getting dizzy."

Claudia put Constance down and grabbed Sarah's arm. "I feel like dancing. Let's have a party, just us women" she said as she twirled her around.

Constance said, "That sounds like a wonderful idea. I think we do need to celebrate." She was so happy to have her girls all together. She was so excited to see her baby girl doing so well. She tried not to think about what she had become, or what she would have to do to maintain her life. She was just enjoying having her family together. Maybe this would bring Sarah and Emelia closer to their little sister. Claudia didn't really have any friends. Since she had been sick so long her friends had slowly drifted away from her.

"I'll put on some wild music" said Claudia as she turned to

put a record on the stereo.

"Don't have it too loud, we don't want the neighbors calling the cops and shutting down our party" said Sarah.

"I'll get some drinks going" said Emelia. "Just name your poison."

The women had a fun time dancing and drinking and just being silly. They all enjoyed letting themselves go. Constance could not believe the energy her daughters had. She could not keep up with them, but she did her best to try. Whenever she wanted to sit down one of the girls would just grab her by her arm and pull her back to the floor.

Constance was in awe of her daughters as she watched them dance. They were so sleek and svelte, so beautiful and graceful as they moved. Even Claudia had a new demeanor about her and her hair was so silky and shiny. She had always considered her girls beautiful but there was something more now. The girls had confidence she could see in them. She remembered how she loved to watch Emele walk or enter a room. She just realized it was the confidence he had that she liked. It was so sexy. While she knew Emelia and Sarah both worked as exotic dancers, she never imagined how it could be fulfilling for them until now. She was sure they were very good at their dancing after watching them move just goofing around. She was proud of them and she told them so.

After dancing for what seemed like hours, they all sat around the table to sip on their drinks and visit. This was Constance's time now. The girls knew it and they would have a heartfelt talk with her, talking about their lives as they had never talked before.

Emelia knew she needed to talk to Claudia more about her new condition. It was also a chance to let Constance know more about Sarah and her lives. She also knew her mother had many questions, and she was finally ready to answer them as best as she could. They talked for an hour about the jobs they had and the lifestyle they lived. They even talked a little about men.

Constance said she had been lonely at times since Edward's death, and though she dated a few men, none of them seemed right for her.

Emelia said she really wasn't in the market for a boyfriend right now. She would like to have her own club some day and she was saving her money for that dream.

Sarah said she wanted a rugged hunky man, one that could pick her up in his arms and carry her up the stairs to the bedroom, like that scene in Gone With The Wind. She couldn't help smiling as she thought of herself in a similar scene with a young strong man taking charge.

Claudia laughed and threw a wadded up napkin at Sarah. "I'm going to play the field and date lots of men. I think I like men a little older than me" she added. "They seem more mature, and have more money."

Everybody laughed as Sarah threw the napkin back at Claudia. "My sister, the gold digger" she teased.

Claudia stood up and shook her hips from side to side. "Well, they will have to have something to get all this" she said as she slowly slid her hands over the curves of her breasts down to her waist and over her hips.

"Oh my goodness!" exclaimed Constance.

"We've created a monster" said Emelia as they all laughed again.

They joked around a little longer.

The sun had been up for a while now and Emelia wanted to show Claudia the power of the sun. She took her hand and led her to the window. "The sun is very hot and can burn you if you're in it too long." She opened the drapes just a bit to let the sun shine in on Claudia's hand.

Claudia felt the sunlight go quickly from a warm pleasure to a burning pain, and she quickly pulled her hand away. "That's hot" she said.

"Don't ever try looking at the sun either. It can burn your eyes also."

Sarah and Emelia both talked to Claudia about the things they had learned. Constance was all ears listening intently as they told their stories to Claudia. She was glad to find out more about them. She also wandered what stories Emele might have told her if he had gotten the chance.

It was late in the morning and everyone was ready to call it a night. The girls stayed at their mother's house the rest of the day. When evening came they said goodbye and left to go to Emelia's house and get ready for work.

Constance knew she would be lonely, but she also knew Claudia would be better off living with her sisters. Claudia took some clothes and moved in with Emelia and Sarah. She would get more of her things later. She would leave some things there just so she could stop in and still feel like it was her house too.

At Emelia's, she had her own room to decorate the way she wanted. She liked living with her sisters. She settled in and the time came to get a job. She liked dancing and was not afraid to show off her body. She went to The Club and watched some of the ladies do their routine. Some of the girls were just there for the money and did not have fun, while they were beautiful and had nice figures, they almost cringed when guys would touch them and they were somewhere else in their mind. They were not tipped big. Claudia noticed the girls who were flirty and had fun made more money. These girls enjoyed their job. They liked showing off their bodies and were friendlier. These girls had guys line up for lap dances. She also noticed the crowd liked it when the dancers played fantasy dress up. She thought she would like working there.

The sixth day was here and Claudia would have to feed before the hunger took over. Emelia and Sarah would show her some good places to hunt. When Emelia and Sarah worked together, they were a deadly team. Now they would teach Claudia to be careful. They had to be sure of their victims and sure no one saw anything. They had to be unnoticed and get rid of the bodies, in the right way. They went to a place where drug dealers hung out. The girls did their homework and had watched things happen here. They knew who to take out. They waited for the right moment to strike. Tonight the three girls were like a pack of wolves, surrounding their prey. They moved silently and attacked from all sides. They did not need all the blood. They could share a victim when they had to. They took down the guy selling drugs. They let Claudia feed first. When she was finished she felt so alive again. She tore his head off and loaded the body in the trunk.

Now they moved to a different spot. Emelia and Sarah had to feed as well. Now they would show Claudia the art of seduction. They went to a bar Sarah knew about where one of the dancer's ex-boyfriend liked to hang out. He had beaten and raped her when she broke up with him. She didn't press charges or go to the police because she was too scared. She said she knew he would kill her if she did. Sarah knew who he was and she was ready to take him out. As Emelia and Claudia watched Sarah walked right up to him and whispered in his ear. The man stood up from his table and took Sarah's hand as she led him out of the bar. Emelia joined her as they took him down the dark alley. Emelia told Claudia to get the car and meet them in the alley. As Claudia drove in the alley with her lights off she could see her sisters sharing the man's blood. They each held one arm down and fed from opposite sides. She saw the man slump and the girls pull away from him. Sarah tore the head loose as Claudia popped the trunk then Emelia threw the body in.

They drove out in the desert and buried the bodies. Then went home, their hunger satisfied.

After a few days, Claudia went to work at The Club with Emelia and Sarah. She had come into her prowess and she knew it. She was very confident and seductive. The regulars still liked Emelia the best, but Claudia was becoming very popular. She showed off a bit more than the other girls and she definitely had the moves to draw a crowd.

Sarah was about to take stage. She had been working on a new routine. She came out jumping rope. Her long thick brown hair was in a ponytail that bounced as she jumped. She had a little rouge on her cheeks and a little purple eye shadow and clear lip gloss and pouted her lips. She wore a school girl uniform, a white button shirt that was tied in front to show off her tiny waist and had a small necktie left loose around her neck. Her pleated skirt was plaid and hung low on her hips and showed off her long legs. She wore white ruffle socks and black patent leather shoes that shined. She looked very innocent. She jumped the rope around the stage a couple of times. When she had them play one of her favorite songs, School's Out by Alice Cooper, she took out the scrunches' and shook her hair loose. The crowd went wild. She danced around the stage and swung on the pole a few times. She slowly unbuttoned her shirt and threw it to the crowd. Then she teasingly grabbed her skirt's zipper and shook her head as the crowd yelled "Yes!" Then she unzipped it and pushed it off her hips letting it fall to her shoes showing off her pink panties and she kicked it to the side. She unlatched her lacey bra and tossed it to the side, and then she danced around the stage one more time before stepping up to the pole. Then she put her finger to her mouth biting it slightly, as the crowd again yelled "Yes." Then she pushed her panties off as the lights dimmed and the crowd applauded as she stepped off stage.

Emelia was going on stage next. Her lustrous black hair was long and flowed over her shoulders. She wore heavy black eye liner that extenuated her big dark eyes and mascara that made her lashes long and thick. Her luscious lips were full and the red lipstick really drew them out. She was beautiful and truly a seductress. She wore a little white tank top without a bra and some tight pink shorts and her clear stilettos. She danced and moved around the stage and swinging on the pole a few times. Then she had one of her favorite songs play, Her Strut by Bob Seager. She strutted across the stage and slowly tore the tank top off, as the crowd started going wild. She crawled across the stage slowly swinging her hips from side to side and stretching one arm out in front at a time moving to the rhythm of the music. Dollars were being thrown on stage as she took off her pink shorts and strutted across the stage one more time in her black g-string. Pausing against the pole she unsnapped her g-string as the song ended and the lights dimmed, giving people a short glimpse of her beautiful naked body.

Normally Emelia was the last act, but tonight Claudia wanted to end the show. She had a tuff act to follow. The crowd was rowdy and feeling the alcohol. Claudia was ready. She came on stage in a cheerleader outfit, a short white sweater that barely covered her breasts from the bottom and showed plenty of cleavage from the top and a short white and red pleated skirt that hung low on her hips, fully exposing her midriff. Her shiny blond hair was pulled up in a high ponytail that swung side to side in perfect rhythm with her swaying hips as she walked. She wore blue eye shadow and dark eyeliner that brought out the sparkle in her blue eyes. She wore clear lip gloss on her pouty lips. She wore platform tennis shoes and carried pompoms. She went to center stage and stood at an erect stance, slapped her hands to her sides and did a cheer that ended with a cartwheel going into the splits. The crowd went wild as she held her hands high breathing deeply as her chest heaved. She smiled, exposing her perfect white teeth. She was every man's fantasy. She danced seductively, slowly undressing, removing her top exposing her breasts. She danced around the stage again, swinging on the pole until the song was almost over. She pushed her skirt down and kicked it aside. Then she stood center stage and ripped her red spankies off as the lights dimmed. The crowd went wild as she closed the show.

Steve Pierce

CLAUDIA'S DRUG

Things were going well for the sisters and they were getting along good. Claudia was working out well at the club, but one night while giving a young man a lap dance in the private room something happened. As Claudia was grinding on the young man she could tell he was becoming aroused. She could feel his erection growing and hear his pulse quickening. She smelled something different, something in his blood, something that excited her. She turned around and straddled his lap. She started to grind rougher and more vigorously on him. The smell of a chemical release in his blood was like catnip to a cat for her. She could tell the young man was about to climax as he reached his hands and held on to her hips. The smell of his blood was driving Claudia crazy. Her fangs grew long and her eyes turned red. She wrapped her arms around his shoulders and held him tight with her head next to his neck. The smell was so intense as he climaxed she lost control and bit his neck hard and sucked the blood. It tasted so good and gave her such a rush as she drank. Her eyes rolled back in her head as she felt the rush go through her entire body. The man was so caught off guard and Claudia held him tight in her grip, he could barely try to fight her off. He could not move. In another moment he was gone. Claudia was in a daze. She slowly loosened her grip and pulled her fangs from his neck. Her head cleared and she realized she had to clean up this mess quick. She took the body out the back and tore the head from the body and pushed it under some garbage in the dumpster. She went back inside and tried to stay out of sight. Her mind was thinking about what had happened. She had just fed the night before. Why did she lose control? She was trying to concentrate but her mind just kept going back to how great the blood tasted and how good it made her feel. All she knew was her body wanted more, and it would be hard to fight this craving.

One night after work, Claudia was not getting ready for bed and Emelia could tell something was bothering her. "What's up, Sis?" she asked.

Claudia looked at Emelia and asked "Do you ever, um, notice a change in the smell of a guy's blood when you're giving a lap dance?"

Emelia just looked at Claudia.

Before she could answer, Claudia added, "I mean when they get excited, a little too excited."

Sarah tried to hide her giggle, and turned her face, but Emelia knew Claudia was serious about her question and answered "Well, I've had a few that got a little too excited, and yeah I guess I did notice a different smell."

Sarah regained her composure and added "I guess I've noticed a little different smell, usually embarrassment, I think."

"No, not embarrassment, more of a lustful smell, I think" said Claudia.

Sarah thought a moment then agreed "Yeah I can remember a few times there was something different."

Emelia nodded in agreement.

Claudia just looked at them turning her hands and raising her shoulders."Well?"

Sarah was confused but Emelia knew what she was asking. "You mean does it make us want to bite them."

"Yes!"

"I have noticed it a few times. It is a pleasant smell, but it doesn't make me want to bite them." Emelia said. She could tell Claudia wanted to talk more.

Claudia did want to talk more but she wasn't sure she should. Maybe this should be her secret. She wasn't sure her sisters had

Steve Pierce

sensed what she had, or maybe she was just weaker than them.

"Claudia, did something happen?" asked Emelia.

Claudia started to squirm a bit wanting to avoid the question.

Sarah sat next to Claudia on the bed and put her arm around her. "Hey, Sis, you can talk to us."

Claudia felt a little more comfortable now. "Well, about a week ago, I was giving this young guy a lap dance. He was getting excited and I could smell something in his blood. I liked it. It sort of turned me on. As I ground harder on him the smell became stronger, and I started to grow fangs. I held my head against his neck so he wouldn't see my face, and held him tight so he couldn't move. Then he climaxed and I lost control, even though I had fed the night before, the smell was too strong. I couldn't help myself. I bit him and it was such a rush. The way it made me feel made me want more."

Emelia wanted to be supportive, but she had to ask. "Did you kill him in the back room?"

Claudia wanted understanding, but now she was getting defensive. "I handled it okay. I took care of the body."

Sarah didn't know what to say.

Emelia tried to salvage the conversation "Hey, I'm just a little concerned. We have to be careful. I know you know that. I didn't mean to snap at you."

Claudia felt a little better, but felt they didn't understand what she was saying. "I know. I just wanted to talk about what happened. I wanted to know if it ever happened to either of you."

"Well, I get urges but I fight them off I guess" Emelia said. She didn't want to lecture Claudia. She knew she needed to be supportive. "Maybe you need to tone down the lap dance a little." Trying to make it lighter she added, "Maybe you're just too sexy," and she joined her sisters on the bed and gave Claudia a hug.

Claudia knew her sister were concerned about her and didn't want her to be careless. She hugged her sisters and told them "Goodnight, I'm feeling kind of tired. She would have liked to talk more, but she decided to end it on the happy note. She went to the bathroom and brushed her teeth and hair and washed her face. Then she went to her room and closed the door.

Sarah and Emelia were still talking. When Claudia's door shut, Emelia whispered to Sarah, "Do you think Claudia can control her appetite?"

Sarah shrugged her shoulders and said, "I don't know. She was doing well, but I understand what she was talking about. Some guys have a very masculine scent when they get excited, but it really didn't make me want to bite them. Maybe he just had a strong smell. Hopefully it won't happen again."

"I hope not. We don't need her going wacko in The Club" Emelia said. "Well the sun is up. I'm going to bed. Goodnight, Sarah."

"Goodnight."

The two went to bed and were soon asleep, but Claudia couldn't sleep. Her mind was awhirl thinking about how much she craved that taste of blood again. She wondered if it was just a special thing that would not happen again. She secretly hoped not. She had to find out. She would control herself and give a lap dance to someone else tonight, and see if that smell came back. With her mind made up she was calming down now and soon she was asleep.

That night Claudia did give another young man a lap dance, and sure enough the same scent came from his blood. It was all she could do to fight her urge to bite and take of that forbidden fruit. She did not want to do this in The Club. She waited for the place to close and she quickly walked out the back and watched the young man leave. He was by himself. Claudia followed him to his car and asked "Hey there Mr., how about giving me a ride home?"

The young man was caught off guard, but very flattered. "Why sure! Hop in."

Claudia got in the car and he started driving. "Where to?" he asked.

Claudia just smiled and said, "I don't know. Just drive for awhile."

As the young man drove, all Claudia could think about was that lustful blood. She reached over and started kissing his neck and rubbing his thigh. He was becoming aroused and Claudia was picking up on the smell. She told him to pull in an alley. When he did she crossed over the console and straddled him. She kissed him hard and deep as she squirmed vigorously on his lap. When the smell was overwhelming to her she buried her fangs in his neck. She ravenously drank the blood from his quivering body. Her thirst quenched she released her bite and sat back in the passenger seat for a minute. She felt such a rush and her body was in a euphoric state, like a junkie getting his fix.

After a few moments she put the body in the trunk and drove the car to the dessert and dumped the body after tearing the head from it. Then she drove back to the city and parked the car in an alley not far from The Club. Then she ran home before the sun came up and sneaked in the house and into her room.

Claudia was restless. She had never felt so powerful. She craved lust blood. She liked the way it made her feel when she fed. She was becoming addicted. She was feeding more than she needed. She didn't tell her sisters. She didn't want to get lectured. She wasn't choosing the right kind of victims.

Sometimes the sisters hunted together, but Claudia was venturing out on her own now, walking the streets. She wore heavy makeup and skimpy clothes, low cut tops and short skirts with high heels. She had the look guys liked. She knew how to draw their attention with her walk, slowly swinging her hips from side to side. It didn't take long before some lost soul looking for a good time would pull his car alongside her and make their intentions known.

She would get in their car and have them drive to the part of town not so well lit. Sometimes she had sex with them and sometimes she pleasured them in other ways, but it always ended the same way. She could smell their blood as it sped through their body. She would start kissing their neck and teasingly bite it, until the precise moment. Then she held them tight with long claws and bit deep in their neck with her sharp fangs. They didn't stand a chance. They were helpless in their moment of ecstasy. They never saw what was coming. They didn't even have time to fight back.

After she feed, she always tore the head from the body, but she didn't always dispose of the body very well. She was getting careless.

THE SEARCH BEGINS

Emele and Gieves started the search for Constance. Gieves drove Emele to a library to try to find some information. Emele didn't really know what to look for. He was just wandering around, when the librarian asked him if he needed help finding something. Emele told her he was looking for information on someone who came to America about twenty years ago. The librarian told him he should go to the hall of records in the immigration office. She gave Emele an address and he thanked her for her help.

Emele gave Gieves the address and he drove to the Hall of Records. Emele and Gieves went in.

Emele walked up to a woman at the counter and said to her, "I'm looking for immigration records from twenty years ago. I'm looking for a woman I lost touch with. I'm afraid I don't know where she would have come into the country."

"Well it doesn't matter where she came in, if it was recorded, we have the information here. Just give me her name."

Emele told her "Constance Van Helsing is her name." Then he gave her a short time frame of when she would have arrived.

The woman led Emele and Gieves to a table and in another minute put two big books in front of them. "Here we go. This should cover all immigrations in the time frame you mentioned." She looked at Emele and added "If you need anything else, don't hesitate to ask for my help. I hope you find her." She gave Emele a little pat on the back and walked back to her counter.

"Thank you so much" Emele said. "You've been most helpful."

The two men sat down and started looking through the record books. They looked for hours. "Too bad these aren't in alphabetical order, huh?" said Gieves looking up from his book to Emele.

Emele didn't hear anything he was deep in concentration reading the names in the book.

Gieves just smiled and turned his attention back to the book.

After Emele turned several more pages, he felt a little discouraged. He started wondering. "What if she didn't report to the immigration, or what if she used a different name?" Emele asked.

Gieves could see the disappointment on Emele's face. "Hey, we're here. Let's just look through the books. You have to think positive. We will find her."

Emele looked at a few more pages. Suddenly a name stuck out, Constance Van Helsing. Emele felt such a relief. "Here it is!" he said excitedly. "Constance Van Helsing. She came here in Texas." He paused a moment, looked at Gieves and continued, "We need to go to Texas. Do you know how to get there?"

"I sure do!" exclaimed Gieves as he slammed the book shut and stood up. "Let's go!"

Emele told the woman he found out the woman he was looking for came through the Texas office and asked her how to get more information. She told him the office in Texas would have a complete record of details of her case. Emele thanked her once more.

They quickly left the office and went back to Emele's house, packed a few thing and were on the road. Emele took a heavy blanket to cover himself, but when the sun rose the rays did not penetrate through the darkly tinted windows. It was a long drive but their excitement made the time pass rather quickly.

They arrived in town late on Friday and rented a motel for a week. Then Gieves looked up the address of the office in the phone book. They drove to the address, but the office had regular business hours and was closed for the weekend.

Gieves started driving back to the hotel. On the way they drove past a steak house. "What say we have a steak? I hear Texas really knows how to grill a good cut of meat right."

Emele had a lot on his mind. "That sounds like a good idea." Hopefully this would help him take his mind off waiting until Monday.

They went to the restaurant and waited at the bar until a table was ready. They ordered a couple of Scotch on the rocks and soon a table was ready. They were seated and ordered. Gieves ordered a T-bone, cooked medium and Emele ordered a rare Porter-house. Soon they were served their meals. Gieves was right. They really could cook a steak and the meat was so tender. They had a couple more drinks then left. They went to the motel and had a few more drinks from a bottle Gieves had bought and talked for a while. The sun would be up soon and they were getting tired. They called it a night and went to bed.

They slept most of the day. Emele told Gieves "You may do what you wish tonight. I need to get some air. I think I'll go for a walk and see the town."

Gieves knew Emele needed to feed, but he also knew Emele didn't really care to talk about it, so he let it be and just nodded.

Emele walked around taking in the town. He didn't know it but he was in the very neighborhood Constance had lived. He walked a little farther to the restaurant they had eaten at the night before. It was a nice town. Constance would have liked it here, he thought. He also knew there would be bad people around; he just had to wait for the right place and time for them to present themselves.

He continued walking down the allies until he felt a knife prick his back. Emele was not surprised. He had noticed the man following him for a couple of blocks. "How about you hand me that wallet full of cash and that gold watch you've been showing off" came a voice from behind him.

"I don't think that will be necessary" said Emele.

Emele felt the knife push harder into his back. "It's up to you. You can hand them to me or I can take them off your corpse."

"Is that a threat?" Emele asked as he turned around and grabbed the mugger by his throat with his right hand lifting him in the air, before the robber had time to stick the knife in. With his left hand Emele squeezed the hand holding the knife crushing it, forcing him to drop the knife. He lowered the man a bit and released his grip on the crushed hand, as the man winced from the pain. Emele tilted his head and bit deep with his long fangs, taking the man's blood and his life. Then he shoved his clawed hand through the man's neck decapitating the body and disposed of them in a dumpster, covering them with garbage.

Emele walked back to the restaurant and sat at the bar. He ordered a scotch on the rocks and sat quietly with his thoughts. He thought about Constance, and tried to think of what he would say to her. Though it had been but a few months to him it had been over twenty years. Would he recognize her? Would she want to see him, or would she still be afraid of what he was?

He sat there looking at the people. He saw young couples on a date. He saw married couples with young children and older couples by themselves. He noticed they all looked at each other with love. It hurt as he knew he would never be like one of these young couples. He hoped Constance was happy and had children. She deserved to be a mother. He didn't like thinking of her alone all these years. If she were married and had a family he would just watch her from afar and leave her alone knowing she was happy in her life. Yet part of him secretly hoped she was not married, but waiting for that special someone. That special someone he had been all those years ago. Deep down he knew she would have moved on. After all as far as she knew he was dead, and that is why she came here. Emele had a couple more drinks then walked back to the motel.

After a while Gieves came in. They talked a while then went to bed. There was not much for them to do Sunday, but Monday Gieves went to the immigrations office and asked about Constance, telling them he was a relative that had lost touch when she came here. They gave him an address of where Constance lived and where she worked. Gieves went back to the motel and told Emele what he had learned.

When it got dark they drove to the address Constance had lived. There were no apartments, just a mini-mall. Emele told Gieves to take him to the next address where Constance worked. The office was still there. Emele went in and asked the receptionist "Is there a Constance Van Helsing working here?"

The receptionist said "There is no one with that name working here."

Emele added "She worked her about twenty years ago. She may be married with a different last name."

"There is no one named Constance working here now. I couldn't tell you about twenty years ago. I've only been working here for seven years."

"Is there anyone here now who would have been here twenty years ago?"

The receptionist thought a moment then said, "Mr. Price has worked here for twenty five years. He is one of the partners that started this business. He isn't in tonight, but he will be here tomorrow night. Would you like to come back then?"

"Yes. Yes, I would. Could you leave a message for Mr. Price, informing him I will be back to talk with him tomorrow night?"

The receptionist said she would leave the message.

The next night they went back to the accounting firm to visit with Mr. Price. Emele took a seat and waited for the receptionist to take him to Mr. Price's office. After a short wait, he was told Mr. Price would see him now, and he was led to an office.

Emele introduced himself and shook Mr. Price's hand, then sat in the chair in front of Mr. Price's desk.

"How can I help you, Mr. Dracula?"

"I'm looking for a Miss Constance Van Helsing. I was told she doesn't work here now, but I was also told she worked here twenty years ago. Could you tell me what happened to her?" He handed Mr. Price the picture of Constance.

Mr. Price took the picture and looked at it as he leaned back in his chair and thought a moment. "Now I remember her. She did work here for a little while." He handed the picture back to Emele. "She came here looking for a job. I hired her. She worked here for a year or two. She was a good worker. She really knew her stuff."

"Do you know what happened to her?"

"I believe she got married to some guy that owned a restaurant. She quit shortly after she got married to work with him at the restaurant."

"Is the restaurant still open?" Emele asked, hoping Constance would be close by.

"Yes, it is. I just ate there a couple of weeks ago. I think it changed hands a few years ago. I'm sorry, but I can't remember the name, but it's at the corner of Fifth and Hickory."

Emele was sad to hear it had changed hands. He would have to go and talk to the owner. He stood up and shook Mr. Price's hand. "Thank you for your time and the information."

"I hope you find her. She was a nice lady, a little shy but nice."

Emele went back to the limo and asked Gieves "Can you find Fifth and Hickory?"

Gieves nodded and said "I think I can find it." He drove east counting down the streets until they came to Fifth. Then he turned down the street and drove until it met with Hickory.

There it was, the Hickory Grill. Emele couldn't believe his eyes. It was the same restaurant Gieves and he had eaten at Friday night, and Emele had had drinks at Saturday.

Emele went inside and asked the hostess if he could speak to the owner. She told him to have a seat at the bar and she would check. Emele ordered a drink and soon the hostess returned and said "Mr. Alspeck, the owner, will see you when he gets a free minute. I can seat you at a table where you can talk." Then she led him to a small corner table.

Emele thanked her and sat down at the table and sipped his drink. Soon he saw a man come out of the office and walk toward him. When he got close, Emele stood up. "Mr. Alspeck?"

The man nodded and held out his hand "Yes, and who are you and how can I help you?"

"I am Emele Dracula. I'm hoping you can help me. I'm looking for Constance Van Helsing. I was told she married the man who owned this restaurant before you. I'm an old friend. We lost touch when she moved and I have been trying to reach her for some time."

"Constance Van Helsing. I never knew her maiden name, but if she's the one who married my old boss, Edward Johnson, then she would be Constance Johnson. She was a really nice person. She was a good worker. She could do any job in here and she also kept the books."

Emele felt good about getting some information. "Is she still around here?"

"Oh no, Edward sold me the Restaurant and took his family to Las Vegas, Nevada. He always wanted to open a steak house in Vegas."

"His family? They had a family?" asked Emele.

"Yes. They had three girls. Edward loved Constance and those girls so much. He would have done anything for them, and she loved Edward too. They were very well liked by the people they worked with and they were great to work for. Neither of them had any family, and they didn't have any close friends. That's probably why they were such a close family."

"Constance had three girls?" Emele asked.

"Yep, they had three beautiful little girls."

Emele tried to picture Constance with three little girls. He was happy to hear she was a mother. It also sounded like she had a nice husband that loved them all very much. Emele would go to Las Vegas. He would like to meet her husband and children, but most of all he longed to see Constance again.

Mr. Alspeck added "I'm sorry I can't give you more information. I bought the restaurant and they moved and we really never talked after that."

Emele thanked him for the information and went back to the limo. Gieves opened the door for Emele and asked "Well, how did it go in there?"

"We have more information. It looks like we're headed to Las Vegas, Nevada. Do you know the way?"

"I sure do" said Gieves enthusiastically. "This is going to be a great ride."

They drove back to the motel, settled their bill and packed up their things. Then they hit the road.

Emele was excited and hopeful.

Gieves was excited about Las Vegas. He hoped there would be time to stop at some casinos to have some fun, gambling, shows, great food and showgirls.

Emele slept most of the day while Gieves drove. That evening when Emele woke up he asked "Where are we?"

"Kansas City, not quite half way there" answered Gieves.

"If you would like to stop, we can get some food and a motel. You have been driving a long time. You must be hungry and tired."

"I'm excited to get to Vegas, but yeah, I could use some food. How about Italian? I could go for some spaghetti."

"Whatever you want. If you see a nice Italian restaurant, pull in."

After a short pause, Emele added, "I'd like to talk to you, over dinner."

What's going on?" asked Gieves.

"Just find a restaurant."

Gieves turned down a road that led to downtown. He wondered what Emele wanted to talk about. They had become a little closer over the past few weeks, but they still didn't talk a lot. He saw an Italian restaurant, but it looked expensive. "What do you say to this place?"

"It looks like a nice place."

Gieves pulled in and parked the car. They walked in and were seated.

Gieves noticed the door to the back room open and a waiter came out pushing a cart. He saw a glimpse of some guys in fancy suits sitting around a big table before the door closed. "Don't look now, but I think there may be some mobsters in the back" said Gieves in a low voice as he leaned close to Emele.

"Well, you wanted a good Italian place. If mob guys are here it must be good" joked Emele.

The waiter came and took their order. Gieves ordered a drink and spaghetti and meatballs. Emele ordered the same.

Soon the waiter brought their drinks and some bread sticks. Then he took some drinks to the back room.

Gieves looked back as the waiter opened the door. "Oh shit!

We need to get out of here! Now!"

"What's going on?" asked Emele.

"I recognized one of the guys in the back. He was one of the guys looking for me in New York. He found me about an hour before you did. I thought I lost him when I ran done that alley. Those were his goons working me over when you came along."

"That's the guy you tried to cheat?"

"Yes, we can talk about this later. Right now we need to get out of here."

Gieves was getting up from his chair and threw some money on the table to pay for the meals. When a man came up behind him and pushed him back down in his seat. "What's your rush?"

"We were just leaving" said Emele as he stood up looking at the man.

"Not so fast. You guys haven't had your dinner yet. Sit down. Enjoy your food. It is very good." The man said politely but insistently. "Besides, I'd like to talk to my old pal, Gieves, here" he added as he slapped Gieves on the back and shook his shoulder.

Emele looked at Gieves, who looked uneasy. He was sitting in his chair not knowing what to do. "I don't believe we've met" said Emele looking now at the mobster.

The man moved his glance from Gieves to Emele. "I don't think it's any of your business."

"Well this young man works for me now, so I believe that makes it my business" Emele said coldly staring the man down.

"Gieves works for you now. That's something" he laughed. "I still have some unfinished business with him, involving our last transaction" he added more seriously as his smile went to a stern look.

Gieves looked at Emele. "This is Mr. Granauldi, my former boss."

"Mr. Granauldi, why don't you join us and we can discuss this like gentlemen" said Emele.

Mr. Granauldi sat down in the chair next to Gieves. "I think the time of acting like gentlemen has passed." Then he reached across the table and grabbed Emele's drink and drank it.

"Now that's just rude. Might I suggest we move this party to a more secluded spot?" asked Emele. He was trying to hold his temper and himself from changing.

"Okay, Mr...." Mr. Granauldi looked at Emele. "What did you say your name was?"

"I didn't" said Emele coldly, not backing down.

"Fine. It really doesn't matter" said Mr. Granauldi as he stood up and pulled Gieves up by his shirt collar. "Let's go to the private party room" he said as he pointed to a door and pushed a gun in Gieves ribs. "You first" he added nodding to Emele.

Emele led the way and opened the door. He entered the room closely followed by Gieves and Mr. Granauldi, who closed the door behind them.

"What's the problem?" asked Emele.

"Your man here owes me a lot of money. And he needs to be taught a lesson."

"A lesson like your guys were trying to teach him in the alley in New York?" asked Emele.

"Don't tell me Gieves told you all about this."

"I happened across your men as they were, shall we say, educating your former employee."

"You were there? What happened to my men?"

"Let's just say they're retired from teaching."

"Sounds like this is the second time you've been in the wrong place at the wrong time." He pushed Gieves down to the floor and pointed his gun at Emele.

"Easy now" said Emele. "You don't want this kind of trouble."

Mr. Granauldi laughed. "It's no trouble." Then he pulled the hammer back on his thirty-eight revolver.

Emele grew fangs and claws instantly. His eyes turned red as he charged Mr. Granauldi as he fired his gun. The bullet hit Emele in the chest, but it did not slow him down. He grabbed Mr. Granauldi and bit him deep in his neck. Mr. Granauldi fired once more hitting Emele in the side. Emele quickly finished him and ripped his head from the body as Gieves watched, stunned in the horror he had just witnessed. "No time for clean up. Let's go now!" he ordered to Gieves as he lifted him to his feet with one hand.

They quickly exited the restaurant and got in the limo. Emele could see the other men moving to the room the shots had come from as they drove out the parking lot.

Gieves drove fast down the busy street. Emele kept an eye through the back window. "No one is following us, but I say we keep driving for a while anyway" said Emele.

Gieves was sort of in shock. "I've never seen anything like that. Are you okay?" he said as he looked at Emele in the rear-view mirror.

"I'm fine, although I could use a new shirt."

"How did you do that?"

"I don't understand it myself. It's all part of the change I went through."

Gieves nodded, remembering the story Emele had told him.

They drove in silence for a while. Then Gieves remembered Emele had wanted to talk about something over dinner. He looked at Emele in the rear-view mirror. He could see he had a lot on his mind. "Penny for your thoughts" said Gieves,

"I'm sorry. I have a lot on my mind. This just distracted me a little. Do you think there will be more trouble for you?"

"I hope not. I'm sure Mr. Granauldi told his associates about me, but they don't know where we're headed and they don't know you. Maybe we should avoid Italian restaurants for awhile."

"Perhaps" said Emele. He thought for a moment then he asked Gieves, "Do you think I was foolish to buy that house in New York?"

"It is a great house. If you're having second thoughts about it, I'm sure you could get your money back. But if you don't need the money, it might be nice to keep it until you know what you want to do."

"I've been thinking. If we do find Constance in Las Vegas, I will need a place to live. Even If we don't find her we will still need a place to stay."

"We can always rent some place that is secluded for a while. I hate to say this but so far we've been pretty lucky. You found information in New York that led us to Texas. Then we learned in Texas to go to Nevada. I hope this leads us to her, but it could just lead us somewhere else. They moved out here twelve years ago and we don't have much to go on."

"Yes, I have thought of this myself."

"Let's just rent a room at one of the casinos."

"I would like to have some privacy."

"Are you kidding? Privacy? No one cares what you do. People come and go all hours of the day and night. Vegas is the city that never sleeps. More people probably sleep all day and move around all night" said Gieves.

"I'm sure you know more about this than I do."

"Then it's settled. We'll stay at the casino. We should get there about two o'clock. It will be great to see those lights as we come over that last hill."

"Great, lights and the casino" said Emele, though he had no idea what a casino really was.

They drove through the day and stopped at a truck stop for a while. Gieves needed food and rest.

Emele stayed in the limo while Gieves got some supper. When he finished, he went back to the limo and got in the back. They both got some sleep. After a few hours they were back on the road.

It was just before midnight when they came over that last hill to see Las Vegas. They were in awe as they caught their first glimpse of the lighted city. The city was huge. Emele wandered just how many steak houses there could be in this city.

They drove down to the strip and found a casino and parked in the spot reserved for special guests, since they had a limo. Emele was a little uneasy about all the people that were about at these late hours, but Gieves was right. No one was paying any attention to them. They checked into a room and took their luggage up to the room. Emele couldn't believe how big the room was. It had been a long day and they were just going to relax and take it easy tonight. They settled in and Gieves looked through a phone book. He found two Edward Johnsons in different parts of the city. He would call them in the morning. He also looked for restaurants with the name Ed or Johnson in them. He found three. He would also check on them in the morning. There were so many restaurants in the city. It could take weeks to check them all out. It was three in the morning now, so they went to bed. They would start the search in the morning.

The next morning Gieves checked out the listings for the restaurants. No luck, neither place knew a Constance or Edward Johnson. The same with the home phone numbers, not the Edward they were looking for.

Gieves said "They could be unlisted." After a short pause he added. "If they were divorced, Constance could have the name Johnson or went back to Van Helsing. If she remarried, it could be anything." He didn't mean to sound so negative but he wanted Emele to be realistic. "If the restaurant didn't do so well they may have moved on again. Or if the place was going really good, they may have gotten an offer they couldn't refuse." Gieves also knew if the restaurant was wanted by the wrong people, they may have been forced to sell or worse yet if they wouldn't sell, they could be gotten rid of easy. The desert was an easy place to get rid of bodies, but he wasn't going to say this to Emele.

Emele was deep in thought. "I know you are right, but we have a little information. We know they were here and they had a restaurant. I believe someone at one of these places will know something about them. To find Constance, I will leave no stone unturned. We will check every restaurant in this city."

All the restaurants were open late so Gieves and Emele would go in the evenings and talk to the owners and workers. Some places were close together so they walked and when they were farther apart Gieves drove. They searched all night and slept all day. They were not having any luck the first few days.

A BIG BREAK

Emele needed to feed, so they drove to the seedier part of town. They parked on a busier street and walked down the streets. Emele was feeling down as they walked down some of the alleys. He was thinking he had come so far, but now it was looking like a dead end. He really wasn't paying attention to where he was going. He was just walking, deep in thought.

Gieves was following Emele a couple of steps behind. He had a lot on his mind too. He hoped Emele would find Constance, but so far they hadn't had any luck, and the list of restaurants they had left to check was getting short.

As they walked along, Gieves noticed a strip club. It was kind of a dump, but sometimes those kinds of places had some good looking girls that knew how to put on a show. They were usually friendlier and worked harder to get your money, which was always fun. Gieves noticed that Emele never seemed to really notice other women, but he did. He wasn't a womanizer, but he enjoyed seeing beautiful women, especially confident ones, and he loved to see their curvy bodies. Maybe seeing a few good looking girls would lift their spirits a little. It always made him feel better, or at least usually brought a smile to his face.

Emele was just a couple of steps ahead of Gieves when he said loudly "Hey, Mr. Dracula, what say we get a drink in here and take a little break and give our feet a rest?"

Emele wasn't weary, but he could use a drink. He looked back at Gieves, who was smiling pointing to a sign that read TOTALLY NUDE GIRLS. Emele had Gieves working hard without much of a break. Gieves was always talking about having some fun in Vegas. He was a young man. It would probably do him good to let him enjoy himself and blow off a little steam. He thought of

Gieves' enthusiasm and knew it would be hard to tell him no. Maybe things would go better after a break.

"Well, what do you think?" asked Gieves again still smiling and pointing at the sign.

"Okay, I could use a drink" answered Emele, "but I still need to feed."

"I'm sure there will be someone in here. There is always someone wanting to get mean and fight when they get drunk."

Emele looked at the sign. He had no idea what a strip club was. He had seen hookers in the alley around the bars, but they didn't flaunt themselves the way they did here. Here there were hookers on the street trying hard for business, wearing skimpy clothes that showed off their bodies. He did like seeing good looking women, who wore nice clothes and carried themselves well, but his interests lied in Constance. Gieves had put the idea in his head that she might be single, though he doubted it. Constance was the old fashioned type of woman who would take her vows very seriously. He was happy for her, but he was also sad for himself. She was his soul mate and it would be hard to move on from her. He would find her somehow.

"Hey, are we going in or not?" asked Gieves.

Emele came back to reality. "After you."

Gieves led the way and paid the cover charge. Emele followed him to a table close to the stage. As Gieves sat down Emele pointed to the bar and walked up to it. When the bar tender came over he said "Scotch on the rocks." When the bartender brought him his drink he gave her a ten dollar bill and said "Keep it." Emele took a sip and turned around to scope out the place. It was dark and noisy, but Emele's eyes saw perfectly and distinguish voices in the crowd. He saw a young woman wearing pink shorts that were so tight and short, the lower part of her butt cheeks were exposed when she bent over. She also wore a small white button shirt with three buttons and a big v-neck that barely contained her oversized breasts and showed off her midriff. She wore heavy makeup and smiled her white teeth at Gieves as she sat down the drink he had ordered. He saw Gieves hand her a twenty dollar bill and heard him say keep it.

Emele looked at the stage as a spotlight shined on a curtain and a loud song started playing. A young lady came out between the curtains swaying her hips as she made her way to the pole on center stage. She was wearing a tight skirt that went below her knees, and a white button shirt and a matching jacket. She wore a pair of horn rimmed glasses and had her hair in a bun. She looked like an old fashioned school teacher or librarian. When she reached the pole she bent over toward the crowd, put her finger up to her puckered lips and said "Shhhh." Then while moving to the music, she unbuttoned her jacket and took it off and threw it to the back of the stage. Then she unzipped her skirt and let it fall to her ankles kicking it to the back also. The shirt she wore was a man's shirt that was long on her body and hung down halfway to her knees. She took off her glasses and tossed them away. Then she took the pins out of the bun and shook her hair loose and let it fall over her shoulders.

Emele couldn't help but think of Constance. This young woman looked similar to her, the way she let her hair down and shook it free. He remembered how Constance had put on his shirt when she went to get more wine after they had made love. He looked away and turned around to face the bar. He finished his drink and sat the glass on the bar. When the bartender looked at him he pointed to the glass. She nodded and brought him another scotch on the rocks.

Gieves was captivated by the girl on the stage. She was beautiful.

She strutted across the stage, swinging on the pole from time to time, moving with the music. As she crawled across the stage she noticed Gieves stare at her face and gave him a quick wink. Gieves just gave her big smile and winked back.

The young woman was getting dollars from the men sitting around the stage. She held out her garter as they put the dollars in. After she made the round she went back to the center stage and slowly unbuttoned her shirt and took it off. She had on a matching lacey bra and panties. She reached behind her back and unfastened her bra and let it slide off her shoulders and down her arms exposing her breasts. Then she danced around the stage one more time, swung on the pole, then stood next to the pole and slid her panties down and kicked them to the side as the lights dimmed and she disappeared through the curtains.

When the lights came back up a few seconds later the young woman was semi dressed and walking toward Gieves. She could tell he was a bad boy. She came up in front of him, put her foot on his chair between his legs, bent over toward him and whispered in his ear "Would you like a lap dance?"

Gieves looked her over from her foot between his legs up to her eyes. When their eyes met he said "Sure."

She grabbed him by his arm and pulled him to a room in the back. She led him to a big arm chair and said "Hi, my name is Sarah" and she forcefully pushed him down in the chair.

Gieves was surprised how easily she pushed him down. "My name is Michael, but friends call me Gieves."

"Well, I guess I'm your friend now... Gieves" said Sarah and she gave him a wink. She could see he wasn't nervous, but he did look uneasy. "Don't worry, I won't bite," then she smiled showing her white teeth, and then added "unless you want me to."

Gieves' uneasiness left and he smiled his big smile and said "I'll let you know."

Sarah started dancing in front of him as she slowly removed her tank top and shorts. She sat on his lap and ground her body against his. Gieves put his hands on Sarah's sides and rubbed from her hips up to her waist, feeling the curves of her body. Then she turned around and put her knees deep in the side of the chair straddling him. "What bring you in here tonight?"

"My friend and I are looking for someone he lost touch with years ago. We just came in to give our feet a rest and have a drink."

Sarah was a little shocked. "You're here with someone?" Well, she wouldn't be dining on him tonight, she thought.

"Yeah he's up at the bar. This isn't really his scene."

Sarah started slowly rocking up and down and back and forth on top of him and pressing her breasts to his chest. She took his hands and put them on her behind and he softly squeezed her buttocks. She pulled his hair with a slight tug behind his ear, and then she leaned in and stuck her wet tongue in his ear.

Gieves was trying futilely to control his desire, which only made Sarah rock harder and faster as she felt him growing. She liked the way he smelled. He was a handsome man, and she was attracted to him. She wrapped her arms around him and hugged him tight as he gave up trying to control his desire and pumped his hips nervously.

He was a little embarrassed. That had never happened to him in a strip club before. Sarah gave him one tighter hug then said with a smirk "You can clean up in there" as she pointed to a restroom.

Gieves slowly stood up. He handed her a one hundred dollar bill and said "Thanks for the dance," but his mind was thinking Wow that was incredible.

"It was my pleasure."

When Gieves came out of the restroom, Sarah took his hand

and led him back to his table. She leaned over and whispered in his ear one more time "Just do me one little favor."

Gieves looked at her and said "You name it."

Sarah pointed to a beautiful young blonde woman and said "Keep away from her. That's my little sister Claudia. She'd eat you alive."

"Okay" laughed Gieves. "My friend is probably ready to leave anyway." He turned and walked toward Emele at the bar.

Claudia had seen Sarah point to here and she heard her whisper to the young man. She quickly plowed her way through the crowd to Sarah. "What's this all about?" as she grabbed her arm and pulled her around.

Sarah pushed Claudia's hand from her arm. "Look, Claudia, hands off this one. If he wasn't here with someone, I would have bitten him myself." But deep down she knew he was a good man and she wouldn't be able to take his life. She also knew Claudia wouldn't hesitate if she smelled his masculinity. Secretly she hoped she would run into him again.

Geives got to the bar and asked Emele "Are you ready to go?"

Emele finished his drink and sat the empty glass on the bar. Then he motioned for Gieves to lead the way. He did feel a bit better. "This was a good idea" he said to Gieves. "I feel a little more optimistic about our search for some reason."

They were walking through the crowd when something caught Emele's eye. It was the sparkle of light reflected off a necklace around the neck of a beautiful dark haired woman. He stopped dead in his tracks. "Take a seat" he commanded to Gieves, not turning form his gaze.

Gieves turned around. "Why? What's going on?"

"Just give me a minute."

"Okay" said Gieves. He worked his way back to the bar and ordered a drink.

Emele was still staring at the young woman. He knew that necklace. It was the one he had given Constance all those years ago. "Could it be?" he asked himself. His mind was going crazy with questions. How did this young woman come to possess this necklace? Had Constance sold it or given it to someone? Didn't it mean anything to her? Or maybe it had been stolen. This thought angered him. He had to talk to this young woman.

The young woman sees Emele staring at her and walks over to him. "Enjoying the show?"

"As a matter of fact it just became very interesting" answered Emele still staring at her.

Emelia was a little creped out by this guy. "Would you like a dance?" she asked as she touches him on his shoulder.

Emele grabs her arm and says "Maybe we could just talk somewhere."

Emelia pulls her arm away.

Emele is surprised at her strength.

"You must be new here" Emelia said thinking he was a nut job or pervert. He would be a nice meal. She will take him to the back room. "Okay, let's go in the back where we can talk."

Emele lets her take his hand and lead him to the back room, where he is seated in a big arm chair. Emelia sits on his lap. Curious about him she asks "What's your story?"

"I couldn't help but notice your necklace. It's very beautiful. Where did you get it?"

Emelia decides to humor him before she bites him. "It was a gift. It's very special to me" she said as her fangs started to grow.

Emele's heart was racing.

Emelia could hear his heart racing and the blood pumping through his veins. "Enough talk!" she says as she puts her hands on the sides of Emele's face and tilts his head. She bares her fangs. Her eyes red, she goes for his throat.

Emele can't believe what is happening. He throws her off his lap and stands up. "Who are you?" he demands to know.

Emelia stands up quickly "Your worst nightmare." With her mouth wide open showing her long fangs, she lunges at Emele.

He grabs her by her shoulders and holds her at arm's length, restraining her. She is struggling to free herself and becoming angry. He is so strong. She has never had anyone able to restrain her like this.

Emele's fangs are growing as he struggles to hold her. "Who are you?" he demands once more.

Emelia looks at him. She sees his fangs, his red eyes. She is stunned. She just stares in disbelief.

"Who are you?" he demands once more shaking her slightly. "I won't hurt you, but I need to know who you are."

Emelia knows she has met her match. "Emelia. My name is Emelia." She looks at him now knowing he will not hurt her. She calms down and Emele lets go of her. "Who are you?" she asks.

"I've been like this for a long time, but right now I need some answers from you. I've been looking for a woman I lost touch with several years ago, and she wore the necklace you're wearing."

Emelia is shocked. "Who are you and what do you want with her?"

"I am Emele Dracula, and I gave her that necklace years ago."

"Emele Dracula?" Emelia said with a puzzled look on her face. "That's the name Mother said. She said Emele Dracula, gave her this necklace, and that is the name of my father."

Emele dropped to his knees. He was speechless for a moment. "Constance is your mother?" he paused "and she said I was your father." He could hardly believe the words coming from his mouth.

"Yes, my mother's name is Constance." She paused a moment

then looked at Emele. "You're my father? But Mom said you died years ago, before I was born. She said you were like me, but her father killed you before she could tell you she was pregnant. She said she watched you die!"

Emele shook his head. "I almost did die. As far as Constance or anyone else knew, I was dead. I was buried and it took me a long time to heal. Then someone called to me, summoning me from my grave. When I awoke Constance was gone, and it had been twenty years." He swallowed hard and looked at Emelia. "I thought she had summoned me. I've been looking for her ever since."

Emelia held her arms out. Her eyes were tearing up.

Emele stood up and hugged his daughter. It felt so good. "You're so beautiful. I can't believe I'm a father."

"I can't believe you're here." She paused a moment holding tight to Emele.

Emele was so happy to learn he had a daughter with Constance. He told Emelia how he came to be this way.

When Emelia told Emele her story, he knew she was the one that summoned him. "I wish I could have been there for you." He paused a moment, then he asked, "Is Constance" he swallowed hard, almost afraid to press his luck, "here?"

"Yes she is."

Emele wanted to talk more. With all the exciting news he had so many questions. Emelia agreed. She said there was a coffee shop close by. They could talk more there.

Emele said "I have a car not far from here. My driver will take us there."

"Give me a minute. I have to tell someone I'm leaving for a while. I'll meet you outside."

"I'll have the car brought around to the front."

Emelia told Sarah and Claudia she would be gone for a while, but would be back before closing.

Emele left the room and grabbed Gieves by his shoulders. "I have great news! I have a daughter! I just met her! Constance was pregnant when she left, and she had a baby girl, my baby girl! And Constance is here in the city too!" he said excitedly. "We're going to a coffee shop to talk more. We need the car brought around to the front."

Gieves grabbed Emele and hugged him. "That's great! I can't believe it. You have a daughter, and Constance is here in Las Vegas. Unbelievable!" Gieves said. He got the car and parked by the front door. Soon Emele and Emelia came out. Gieves got out and opened the door for them.

"Gieves, I'd like you to meet my daughter, Emelia." They exchanged pleasantries and drove to the coffee shop.

Gieves waited in the car to let Emele and Emelia visit in the coffee shop. The place was not busy. They sat in a corner booth and ordered coffee.

"Tell me about Constance." Before he knew what he was saying he heard himself ask "Is she still married?" He was momentarily embarrassed and tried to recover the conversation, but it was too late.

"Mom was married to a wonderful man, Edward Johnson." Emelia said as she held back her tears. "I knew him as my father. He loved us all so much and he took such good care of Mom. We were so happy, then he got sick and he died. That was several years ago. We were on our own and we were so young. Mom was so strong and she did such a great job raising us. I know she had it rough, but she never complained, she just worked so hard." She couldn't hold her tears back any more and she started sobbing.

Emele reached over and held her. "I'm so sorry. I've been selfish. All I could think about was seeing Constance. Then I find out I have a daughter. I wish I could have been here for you and your mother. Edward sounds like he was a very nice man. I'm glad Constance had someone to care for her who loved her and raised you as his own."

Emelia wiped her tears and said "He was a nice man. He made sure Mom wouldn't have to work after he was gone. She only worked because she loved it. Edward even made a special room for us to be in while they worked." Then Emelia looked at Emele and said. "I use to feel different. I didn't look like Mom or Edward. I have such dark hair and my sisters have lighter hair and look like Mom. I never told Mom this, but one night Edward told me the truth. He knew I was feeling weird and thought I needed to know something. I wasn't that old but I understood. He told me he wasn't my real dad. He said my dad was killed in an accident before I was born, but he couldn't love me more if he were my dad. Then he hugged me and told me not to tell Mom. He said he knew she would tell me when she was ready. He also said my mother loved him very much and though she didn't talk much about him, he could tell he was very important to her and the few times she did talk about him, her face would light up. He said Mom always said I reminded her of Emele, with my dark hair and eyes. Then he got a little sad look on his face and said he was so glad he was the one who got to marry her and be my dad."

Emele was in deep thought. "I'm glad he was there for you and your mother. It sounds like you had a very special relationship with him." He paused a moment and asked, "You have two sisters that look like Constance?"

"Well, Sarah looks a lot like Mom, and Claudia has some of Mom's features too. You might have seen her at the club, before we left."

Emele remembered the beautiful young woman on stage that

reminded him of Constance.

"Don't cross them, they are like you and me." She continued telling her story about her sisters and how they came to be this way.

Emele was very intrigued by Emelia's story, and he was listening intently, but he wanted to hear more of Constance.

Emelia could see Emele was listening to her story, but she was sensing he wanted to learn more about Constance. She stopped talking and smiled. "You want to hear more about Mother, don't you?"

"I wondered if she ever talked to you about me."

"She only talked about you a couple of times to me, but when she did it was like she was reliving the moments." Emelia paused a minute then added, "Her face did light up when she talked about you. She told me the whole story as far as she knew it. How she was in love with you and waiting for you to ask her to marry you and move to America. She said the last night you were together she was going to tell you she was pregnant, but how her father butted in and told her what a monster you were, and she knew you were trying to tell her something about yourself that really bothered you, but her father killed you before you had the chance. She also said she was in shock seeing you change the way you did. She didn't know what to do. Then you were gone. She ran away to America to have me and be away from anyone that might hear about you. She never got in touch with anyone from there again, not her brothers, not even her father." She looked at Emele, who was hanging on every word she was saying. "I know she loved you very much, and she still feels guilty about not being able to reach out to you as you died. She was in shock. So much had happened so fast. She just wanted to get away. She came to America to get away from her past, and then she had me, and I looked so much like you, she named me

Emelia after you. She also told me while I was growing up, I reminded her of you so much it hurt sometimes."

Emele was saddened by this story. It was the first he had any light on Constance's state of mind over what had happened. His head was hanging low. "So how is Constance doing now? Is she lonely?"

Emelia tried to cheer him up. "Mom has an understanding of things better now, since her daughters are like you were. I know she doesn't like to think of us as monsters or killers, but she deals with it in her own way." She looked at Emele. "Yes, Mom is doing fine and she is single" she watched a smile come to his face, "but she is seeing someone." She watched as the smile left Emele's face. "I really don't know him that good. I haven't seen him much. Mom seems to like him though, but she says he's just a friend. Am I sensing there is going to be some competition?" Emelia asked with a sly grin on her face.

"Well I did come a long way to find her. I always told myself if she were married to good man and had a family, I would leave her alone. Just knowing she was happy would be enough. I just wanted to see her and know she was taken care of, but since she is not married, perhaps I will check out this friend of hers."

Emelia was excited and Emele could sense it. "This is so exciting"

Emele interrupted her. "Please don't say anything to Constance just yet. I would like to see her, from a distance, I mean, without her knowing. It has been a long time, and she thinks I am dead."

"Don't you want to talk to her? You've come such a long way and I'm sure you have a lot to tell her. I'm sure Mom would want to see."

"I don't know if you know this yet, but you will age slowly, very slowly. It could be a bit of a shock for her to see me not aged any. It has been over twenty years. I would like her address though, so I can see her."

"Mom is still a very beautiful woman. She told me you were older than her, but now it's like you're the same age." She gave Emele her mother's address and the address of the restaurant. "Mom usually works at the restaurant until about ten. That's when the dinner crowd is over. She usually heads home after that."

They talked a little more and it was time for Emelia to get back to the club. Gieves drove them back to the club.

As they drove back Emele said "I would like to talk to you more, if you don't mind."

Emelia gave Emele her home phone number and said, "You can call anytime, just leave a message if I don't answer."

Gieves pulled up to the front of the club and opened the car door.

"You could always stop by the club if you need to talk" said Emelia. Then she hugged her father and whispered, "You're not ashamed of what I do, are you?"

Emele hugged her tight and answered "Of course not. You are my daughter; I could never be ashamed of anything you do. The way you are, this could be the place for you. I'm glad you work with your sisters. You have each other's backs. I just want you to be careful."

Emelia said goodbye and went inside.

Gieves got back in the car and asked "Where to?"

"I think we have time to check out one more restaurant" Emele said and he passed the address up to Gieves. "I would like to see it."

Gieves drove to the address and pulled up front. The big sign read, The Hickory Grill. "Can you believe this? It's the same name as the one in Texas."

"That is something." Emele paused a moment then added

"I'm going in to look around. Care to join me for a drink."

"Sounds good." Gieves opened the door for Emele and then parked the car. He walked in and joined Emele. They went to the bar and Emele ordered two scotch on the rocks. Emele looked around. It was a nice place. He could imagine Constance working in a nice place like this. They finished their drinks and left.

Emele still needed to feed. He had Gieves drop him off at a rundown bar. Emele ordered a drink and flashed a lot of cash. He shortly left the bar and walked through the alley. Sure enough, he was soon followed by a rough looking character down the alley. When the man was close to Emele he pulled a knife and demanded "Hand over that wad of cash, Bub, and I'll let you be on your way."

Emele turned around and pulled the cash in his money clip from his pocket. "Do you mean this?" he asked as held it out toward the man.

"That's what I'm talking about" said the robber as he reached his hand for the money, still holding the knife pointed toward Emele.

With one swift move Emele knocked the knife from his hand, grabbed the man and turned him around. He pulled him close and bit his neck deep draining the blood and life from his body, then he propped the body against the wall. He walked out to the limo and told Gieves "I left something in the alley" as he got in the car.

Gieves pulled down the alley with his lights off. Then Emele quickly went from the car and picked up the body as Gieves popped the trunk, and through it in. They would stop out in the desert and get rid of the body after Emele tore the head free.

As they drove home, Emele told Gieves about the conversation he and Emelia had. Then he said they would go back to the restaurant tomorrow night and get a glimpse of Constance.

COMPETITION

That day Emele could not sleep. He was too excited, thinking about Constance and wondering if she had changed much over the years. Emelia said her mother was still a beautiful woman, but it would not matter if she did change. Emele was in love with her no matter what. The day dragged on and eventually it was evening. Gieves was up and ready to go.

Gieves drove Emele to the restaurant and let him out at the front door, then he parked the car and started reading a magazine with the dome light on, patiently waiting until Emele was ready to go.

Emele entered the restaurant and asked the hostess if he could have a corner table away from the kitchen. He was soon seated in a dimly lit corner, where he had a good view of most of the restaurant. He ordered a drink. As he sat there he wondered how he looked. He would go to the restroom to get a quick look. As he walked around the corner of the hallway to the restroom, he bumped into a man. "Excuse me" he said.

Emele was solid and the man almost lost his balance. Without looking up he said "Hey watch it, asshole!" As his eyes rose focusing on Emele's face, he was glaring with a mean look when their eyes locked.

He could not look in his eyes. Emele's stone cold stare was too much. He lowered his eyes and stepped aside. Emele could sense this man did not want a confrontation as he watched him walk away.

Emele continued his way to the restroom and checked his look in the mirror. His tailored black suit fit him well and the blue shirt really set it off. Satisfied he went back to his table and sat down. Taking a drink from his glass, he looked around the room and noticed the man he had bumped into sitting alone at a small table in the middle of the room. A waitress came over to Emele's table and he ordered a steak. When she turned to leave, Emele looked around the room. He noticed a woman walking through the crowd. Emele felt his heart beat a little faster. It was Constance, he knew it. She was a little older but Emelia was not lieing when she said her mother was still a beautiful woman. A smile came to his face, but quickly turned to a snarl as he watched Constance sit next to the man he had bumped into and give him a quick little kiss on the cheek and call him William. She looked happy, but seeing her again now, with this guy he was not sure he could walk away. He had gotten a bad vibe from this man. He would have to control his urge to feed on him for Constance's sake.

The waitress brought Emele's dinner and he ate while he watched Constance and the man have a drink. His food lost its taste as he watched them talking about their day. He wanted to leave, but he would have to wait until Constance left. He was not ready to reveal himself to her yet. He ordered another drink and soon the man put some money on the table and he and Constance got up and walked out the door. Emele gave them a couple of minutes to get to the parking lot and their cars. Then he got up and took his bill to the cashier.

Outside Constance had forgotten her purse and went back in the restaurant to get it from the back where she had left it. As she walked through the crowd she caught a glimpse of a man walking toward the door and she stopped dead in her tracks. He reminded her of Emele, his looks and the way he walked. She turned to try to get a better look, but he was through the door. Constance shook her head. That was silly. She watched him die over twenty years ago. Yet the thought of seeing him pulled at her heart strings. She wished she could have gotten a better look at this man. It was strange but she had a funny feeling in the pit of her stomach. She quickly grabbed her purse and headed back outside.

Emele got to the limo and got in. He told Gieves to wait for a minute, as he had seen William standing by a car, but not Constance. He watched as Constance walked over to the car next to William. "That's Constance." He paused a moment then added, "Unfortunately she is with that guy, William somebody...., for now."

Gieves looked at Constance and said "She is something." Hearing Emele's sarcasm he added, "But what's the story on the guy."

"I don't know. I ran into him in the restaurant and I got a bad vibe. I don't trust him." Emele and Gieves watched as William pulled Constance to him and gave her a hug and kiss and told her goodnight. Then they watched as he opened her car door and shut it after she got in.

"Oh ho, this guy is smooth" laughed Gieves.

"Not smooth enough" said Emele with disgust.

"Oh come on, Emele, this guy is a joke. I've seen his type before."Gieves paused as he watched William go to his car. "He's going to his car. Should we have him checked out?" Gieves asked as he wrote down the license plate number.

"That is a good idea."

"Once we find out who he is, I will ask around about him."

"Let's go to the casino. I've seen enough for tonight."

Gieves drove to the casino and they went to their room. He was hungry and asked "I'm ordering room service, would you like anything?"

"Have them send up a bottle of Scotch."

When the room service came, Gieves dug in to his food, and Emele had a few drinks. When Gieves finished his meal, he said.

"I know one of the security guys here at the casino. I'll go down and talk to him. He should be able to run the plates for us and give us a last name."

Emele didn't really know what Gieves was talking about, but he knew he would do his best to help him with this.

Gieves left the room and went to the security station of the casino. He talked with the guy he knew and gave him the license number.

The security guard called a friend of his that worked at the police department and had him run the number. After a short time he called back and had the name, William Beckett. The security guard said "I remember that name. William had a run of bad luck and had lost a lot of money in the casino. He became upset and started ranting about the casino cheating him. He had to be escorted out by security."

It would be sun up soon and Gieves went back to the room. "William Beckett" he said when Emele came over to him. "He may have a bit of a gambling problem. Seems he had a little run in with security when he caused a scene after losing a bunch of money. The security guard said he could call around to some of the other casinos and see if any other places had any similar experiences with him."

"What did you mean when you said you've seen his type before?"

Gieves didn't want to answer Emele, but he knew he had to. "Well, I've seen a few guys try to schmooze a lady that was pretty well off. They throw money around in front of them and act like it's no big deal if they lose some. He probably has a descent job, but he is spending more than he makes. Throw a gambling problem on top of that and you have a man in need of some cash, or assets. If his problem is bad enough, he might be in trouble with the wrong sort of guys."

"So you think he's after her money?"

"Yeah, probably, but he may know a good thing when he finds it. She's rich, good looking, and she is a nice hard working person. He may ride this pony for the long haul." He could see Emele's concern. "But hey, Constance is a smart woman. I don't see her caving in to help this guy unless" he stopped mid sentence, realizing he may have said too much.

"Unless what?" demanded Emele.

Gieves was slow to answer, but he did answer, knowing Emele would not like what he said. "Unless, she is falling for this guy."

Emele swallowed hard and said "Tomorrow we will check on Constance again, this time at her house."

They went to bed and would go to Constance's house that evening.

That night Gieves drove Emele to Constance's house. First they drove very slowly by her house and then they turned the car around and parked down the street, where they had a good view of the house.

Emele wanted to sit and watch the house hoping Constance would be home soon. Emelia had told Emele that Constance was usually home around ten, after the dinner crowd, unless there was something needing her attention. It was a little early and Emele was in deep thought, thinking how he could enter her life again and what he would say to her. His thoughts turned to seeing Constance with William, and he hoped she would not be coming home with him. The thought made him snarl and let out a "Humph."

Gieves was looking at Emele in the mirror. He could see the disgust on his face. "Something wrong?" he asked.

Emele looked at Gieves. "I just had an unpleasant thought."

WAS IT A DREAM?

Back at the restaurant, William was in a bad mood to begin with and when Constance told him she would be working a little longer than normal because one of her cooks quit without notice leaving her short handed, it only fueled his anger. He was hurting for money and was feeling the pressure from his lenders. He was drinking to try to calm himself. He had planned a special night with Constance and was going to ask her to marry him. He was hoping to whisk her away to a chapel for a quick marriage while she was feeling the thrills of the evening, even hoping the Champaign would help his plan. He was worried he would not be able to hide his financial state much longer. He thought of her restaurant and how much it was worth. "Once we are married it will be half mine, and I know she has money in the bank" he told himself as a little smirk came to his face. He had a few more drinks and left. He would drive to Constance's house and wait there for her to come home. On the way he stopped at a liquor store and bought a bottle of Champaign and a bottle of whiskey. As he waited outside her house he sipped on the whiskey.

William never noticed Emele's limo, but Emele noticed him. He could see him sitting in his car drinking from his bottle. This may not be good he thought to himself.

Soon Constance drove in the driveway and parked her car. She got out of her car and she waved at William and motioned for him to join her.

William grabbed the bottle of Champaign from the passenger seat and exited his car and followed Constance into her house.

Constance saw the Champaign in William's hand. "Are we celebrating?"

"Hopefully," William answered with a wink. He led Constance

to the sofa and sat her down.

Emele was sensing something wrong. He got out of the limo and moved quickly and silently through the shadows up next to Constance's house where he had a good view of her living room window. He could see William and Constance sitting on the sofa. He watched as William got on one knee and took Constance's hand. He listened closely as William professed his love to her. "Oh God, please, no. Have I waited too long?" whispered Emele to himself as he heard the dreaded words come from William's mouth, Will you marry me. He felt his heart sink at the thought of losing her again. Then he looked at her face. She did not show excitement or surprise. "Maybe not, she doesn't seem to be too sure."

Constance smelled the whiskey on his breath and could tell he had been drinking for a while. "Maybe we should not rush things" she said looking at him. "I'm just not ready. I think we need to get to know each other a little better first."

William was frustrated. He had not expected this. "Don't you love me, Constance?"

She could tell he was becoming upset. She tried to ease the situation. "I have feelings for you, but I'm not ready for marriage" and she pulled her hand from his.

William stood up and grabbed her hand and squeezed it tightly. "I love you Constance. I want to be with you and marry you."

Constance was a bit scared; she had never seen William like this. "I think you need to leave. We'll talk tomorrow."

Outside the window, Emele was becoming upset. He started to change, but he did not want Constance to see him like this their first time together again. What should he do? He listened intently as they spoke, trying to control his anger.

Constance stood up and tried to pull her hand from William's.

"You've been drinking. You need to leave before something is said we will both regret."

William squeezed her hand tighter. "I'm not ready to leave. We need to talk this through." He was panicking, but the whiskey was really kicking in now and he couldn't stop himself.

"You're hurting me. Let me go" Constance pleaded.

"What, now I'm not good enough for you?" he asked angrily.

Constance pulled her hand free. "Please leave!" she demanded.

At that William slapped Constance's face hard with the back of his hand, knocking her down.

Emele was around the house and through the front door in a second. He grabbed William, who was just standing there looking at Constance on the floor, by the back of his shirt collar and lifted him up.

"What the hell?" William hollered as he was lifted.

Emele used all his strength to control himself from killing William right there on the spot. He carried him to the door as William swung his fists wildly trying to hit however was holding him. When Emele got to the door he threw William out on the sidewalk. "I believe the lady asked you to leave."

William quickly stood up and charged Emele with clinched fists, until he recognized him as the man he had bumped into in the restaurant, and felt a cold chill go up his spine. He stood there glaring at Emele, but had to lower his eyes from Emele's stone cold stare. "This isn't over" he promised, and he got in his car and peeled out of the driveway and down the street.

Emele went back to the living room. Constance was still on the floor, leaning on her elbow and holding her other hand against her check, with her eyes closed. He could tell she was in pain. He kneeled down next to the woman he loved and gently touched her on the shoulder.

Constance twitched at the hand but felt the easy comfort of the touch. She slowly opened her eyes and looked upward. Seeing the face, not believing what she was seeing, she asked "Emle?"

He nodded and Constance fainted. He carefully picked her up in his arms and carried her to the bedroom and softly laid her on the bed and sat next to her. He couldn't believe he was finally by her side. It felt so good to be close to her again. He carefully brushed the hair from her face with his fingertips as Constance let out a soft moan. As he stared at her he wondered if she could love him again. Then he remembered Emelia telling him how her mother had lit up when she talked about her time with him and how sad she got when she talked about him being killed in an accident. Emele went to the refrigerator looking for an ice pack. Not finding one he took a frozen bag of peas and held it on Constance's cheek, to help the swelling. He was hoping this would wake her up, but it did not. He held it there for twenty minutes. When he moved it the swelling had gone down. There was a bruise, but she looked better. He just sat there staring at her.

Gieves had been waiting patiently in the car, but it was getting late now. He drove the car to Constance's driveway. Seeing the front door open he entered the house and slowly walked through the bedroom door. "Mr. Dracula, the sun will be up soon." Then seeing Constance lying on the bed he asked "Is everything okay? Is she alright?"

Emele didn't turn around. He just sat there staring at her. "She had a rough night, but she will be fine after a little sleep. Look at her Gieves. Isn't she beautiful?"

"Yes she is" he answered. "What happened?"

"I let him hurt her." He paused a moment then continued. "I waited too long. I knew it was not going good, but I waited. I wanted her to see the real him. Then it was all I could do not to kill him, only I was afraid she might see me like that and be scared again. I couldn't let her see me for the first time like that."

"You did the right thing, but unless you're going to stay here we need to get going, the sun is rising."

Emele didn't want to leave her side, but he knew he had to. He leaned over and kissed her gently on the lips. "Sleep well my love." Then he stood up and he and Gieves went to the car and drove home.

The next morning Constance woke up with a headache. What had happened? She remembered William hitting her, but then what? How did she get to her bed? Was it Emele, or had she walked in her sleep and dreamed about him? Was her mind playing tricks on her?

Emele did not sleep well that day. Thoughts of Constance raced through his head. He was excited about finally being near her. He was trying to think how he could tell her what had happened. He hoped she would be a little more open about this, since her daughters were like him. He wanted to talk to her about Emelia and her other daughters. He longed to be with her the way it was before. He would have to tell her everything he had wanted to tell her all those years ago had they not been interrupted by her father. For now it would be wise not to mention her father, after all she had not been in touch with him since that dreadful night.

When night came Emele asked Gieves to drive to a flower shop. He wanted to get a bouquet of flowers. He couldn't wait to see her again and talk to her, even though he wasn't sure what to say. Emele didn't want to wait for Constance to get off work so he had Gieves drive to the restaurant. "You might as well come in and have a drink" he said to Gieves, "I may be a while."

They both went in, the hostess greeted them. She asked if they were there for drinks or dinner. Gieves went straight to the bar and Emele asked if Constance Johnson was working tonight.

The hostess said she was cooking. Emele said he would like

to have dinner when a table was available. The hostess said he could have a seat at the bar and she would get him when a table was ready. Emele went to the bar and ordered a scotch on the rocks. He sat there staring at his drink, taking a sip now and then until the hostess came and told him his table was ready. He carried his drink following the hostess to a small table that was close to the kitchen. Emele sat down facing the kitchen. The kitchen had two swinging door that each had a small window toward the top. Soon Emele's waitress came over and took his order.

Constance was cooking and thinking about Emele, when she heard the cook next to her say "Wow, a thick cut porterhouse steak, rare. I love the easy ones."

Constance remembered that was Emele's favorite cut of meat, and he liked it rare. She almost burned the dish she was preparing, and pulled herself back to reality. It couldn't have been Emele she told herself and she got back to work.

Soon Emele's dinner was brought to him. As he ate he started thinking this was probably not the best place to talk to Constance. He did not want to cause a scene. He would finish his meal and wait for her at her house and if she didn't want to talk to him she could just shut the door.

He had just finished when he saw the kitchen door swing open. As he looked in he caught a glimpse of Constance. She turned around and locked eyes with Emele for a split second just as the door swung back shut.

The waitress brought Emele the check and he handed her a hundred dollar bill and told her to keep the change. Then he quickly got up and walked out, calling to Gieves on his way out. Gieves downed the rest of his drink and followed him out to the car.

Constance had convinced herself she had had a dream, but

now she was not so sure. She asked the cook next to her to cover for her as she was not feeling well. She quickly opened the door and looked at the empty chair. She looked around the restaurant, but didn't see anyone looking like the man she had just seen. She walked over to the table and picked up the glass. It smelled of scotch, Emele's favorite drink. "Could it be Emele?" she asked herself, "I saw him die. There's no way that was him." A tear came to her eye and she wiped it away quickly. She asked the waitress to describe the man who had been seated at this table. When the waitress described him, Constance pictured Emele as she described him perfectly. That was silly. Emele would be much older now. Her head hurt, she couldn't think. She was rattled. She needed to go home and get some rest. She called Beth, the night shift manager and told her she needed to leave, could she come in a little early to cover things. Beth said she could be right there.

AN EXPLANATION AND A QUESTION

Emele told Gieves to drive to Constance's house. They parked a little way down the street and waited for Constance to come home.

Within minutes Constance drove in her driveway. She got out of her car walked up to her house unlocked the door and went inside to the living room and flopped on the sofa. Her mind was going wild with thoughts of Emele and questions she now had.

Emele watched as Constance had come home and entered her house. He was nervous.

Gieves had watched also. "Looks like that's your cue" he said looking in the mirror at Emele, and he turned the car around and pulled in the driveway.

Emele got out of the car and carried the flowers up to the door. He rang the doorbell. He felt like a school boy about to ask a girl for his first date. His knees were trembling.

The door knob twisted and the door opened slightly. Constance peeked through the gap. "Who is it?" she asked.

Emele forgot his mane for a second. "I would like to talk to you...its Emele, Emele Dracula."

Constance's heart raced wildly. Could it really be him? She opened the door wider. "Is it really you? How can this be?"

Emele wanted to take her in his arms, but he knew he had to go slow. He could see the puzzlement on her face as her eyebrows lowered. "Please hear me out. May I come in?"

Constance remembered the last time she was with him, how he changed in front of her and Emele watched as her puzzled look started to turn to fear.

"I won't hurt you. I need to tell you what happened." His heart started to break as the thought of losing her entered his mind. "If you want me to leave, I will go right now and never bother you again."

Constance also remembered how gentle he was with her and how he had stopped when she told him the man he was about to kill was her father, and how she had cried on the ship for not being able to reach out to him. She opened the door wide and said "No, please come in." She stepped aside to let Emele enter her home.

When he did she closed the door. He handed her the flowers. Things were very awkward, but she took the flowers. "Thank you, they are lovely. Let me put them in a vase."

Emele stood still while she took care of the flowers and placed them on the kitchen table.

As she turned from the flowers to Emele, she looked closely at his face. "My God, you haven't aged a bit." He was a handsome man, and her heart beat a little faster as her old feelings were rekindled. She wanted to kiss him and hold him in her arms, but her mind would not let her.

Emele got a good feeling as he saw a little smile come to her face. "Could we sit and talk?"

Constance led him to the living room. When she got to the sofa, she turned around. Emele was right behind her. She couldn't fight the old feelings anymore. She leaned toward him, wrapping her arms around his neck and pulled him toward her and she closed her eyes.

Emele put his arms around her waist and pulled her close as their lips met. He held her tight and lifted her up as their kissing became ravenous.

Constance had forgotten what a good kisser Emele was and how strong he was. She could feel the muscles in his arms as he held her and the muscles of his back as she ran her hands over them as they kissed.

Emele thought he could remember her lips and her touch, but her lips tasted sweeter than he remembered and her touch was driving him wild with passion. She had hardly aged herself. He slowly lowered her back to the floor, and their kissing became softer. She was in great shape and still had her small waist and Emele loved feeling it as he moved his hands over her curves.

It would have been easy to be caught in the moment and let the passion sweep them away, but Constance needed to hear what he had come to say. They stopped kissing and she looked in Emele's eyes. He was smiling staring back in her eyes. He was her first love and her soul mate, and it felt so good to be back in his arms. She wanted to kiss him more. She wanted him now, but she had to stop. She took her arms from Emele's back and took his hand and sat down on the sofa. "I need you to tell me what happened."

Emele sat down next to Constance. He took a deep breath. He knew he had to tell her everything as hard as it would be to explain it. He wasn't really sure about part of it himself. "Do you remember that night so long ago?"

Constance nodded. She could see this was hard for him.

"I knew I was losing you when I saw the horror and disbelief in your eyes. I didn't care if I died at that moment. I had such plans for us. I was going to tell you about myself and ask you to come to America as my wife."

Constance was starting to tear up, but she held them back and let Emele continue.

When your father stabbed that poker through my heart, I thought I was dying, and I could feel I was losing you. I don't remember anything after that. It was like I was sleeping. Then I awoke to someone calling me for help. It was like a dream. I had been buried. I used every ounce of my strength to push myself through the soil. To me it was like the next day, but my clothes were rotted and when I called for Rhensfield, an old man came to my side. It had been twenty years. I was weak but someone had summoned me. The only thing I could think was you were in trouble. Now I have finally found you."

"But I watched you die. I was sure." Constance said. "I felt there was nothing there for me anymore, so I left. I couldn't bear to be there without you."

"To the world I was dead, but somehow my body slowly healed itself over time."

Constance interrupted; she needed to say this right now. "I need to tell you something." She took a deep breath and continued "You have a daughter. I was pregnant with your child when I left. I was going to tell you that night, but"

Emele interrupted Constance "I know. I have already met her. She is a very beautiful young woman." He watched as her eyes grew wide with surprise.

"How do you know this and how did you meet her?" Constance demanded.

"In my search to find you, my driver wanted to take a break for a drink in a club we were passing by. When we were leaving a sparkle caught my eye. When I looked to see what it was, I was surprised to see the diamond I had given to you, as a necklace on a young woman. I had to talk to her to find out where she had gotten it. She told me her mother had given it to her. When I asked her who her mother was, she told me her mother's name was Constance. It hit me hard. I had almost given up the idea of ever finding you. Then she told me how it had been a special gift to her mother from the man who was her true father. We talked for a while and she told me about you and about herself. I know she is like me. I don't know if she has told you the story about when she changed, but it was the exact time I was awakened. It was her who was in trouble and summoned me."

Constance was glad to know Emele had met their daughter, but she was amazed to hear this. "About a year after it happened she told me a little, but not much detail about that night." Constance looked deeply into Emele's eyes. "I think I have a better understanding of you because of her and her sisters. Did she tell you I have two more daughters?"

"Yes, and she told me they were like her. She told me she changed Sarah because of her loneliness and Sarah's fear."

Constance butted in "And she changed Claudia for me." Her eyes were welling up with tears as she continued "Claudia is my baby and she was dying. She had been sick for so long and she didn't have much time left. I asked Emeleia and Sarah to change her for me. She was such a good girl, but she hadn't lived yet. I couldn't stand the thought of losing her. I had lost so much in my life already. Now she is so full of life. She danced with me the night she changed. Isn't that silly?" Her tears stopped and she smiled. She even let out a little giggle.

Emele wiped her tears away. "I wish I could have been here for you." He paused a moment. "Emelia told me about your husband."

"Edward was a wonderful husband and father. He took such good care of us, and he loved Emelia like she was his own."

"I was glad to hear you were married and had a family with a man who took good care of you,"

Constance knew Emele really was happy for her. "Why did you wait to come see me? I thought I was losing my mind. I was seeing you, but I knew it couldn't be. I was so confused."

"When I awoke, I wanted to find you, but when I found out how long it had been, I told myself if you were married or had a family I would not bother you. I didn't want to cause you any pain. I wasn't sure if you would ever want to see me again. I just wanted to know you were happy. Then Emelia told me you hadn't dated much until William. I didn't want to bother you if you were happy in love. Then I had to be sure he would treat you good and well.."

Constance was deeply touched by his confession.

"Before we go any further, I have to tell you a little more about myself. I don't know how much your daughters have told you about our condition." This was extremely hard for Emele to say, maybe even harder than it was twenty years ago, but he knew he had to continue. "I tried to tell you about myself that night." He was looking at Constance, watching all her expressions as he spoke. "Your father was right, I am a monster. I would change if I could, but I can't. I do kill people and drink their blood. I have to or in seven days I will lose control and be overtaken by the hunger and kill anyone around me, but I learned this early and now I choose my victims. I'm a vigilante. I have seen a lot of evil things done by men over the years and now I try to help the innocent by getting rid of those who choose a life of debauchery and preying on them."

Constance looked at Emele very intently and nodded. "Emelia has told me a similar story. I know what my daughters do. I have seen them change. While I may not like it, I do accept it.

With that said Emele took Constance's hand and kneeled down on his knees. "I also want to ask you something else. Something I wanted to ask you long ago." He reached in his pocket and pulled out a small box and opened it.

Constance's jaw dropped. It was a very beautiful diamond ring. It was crafted with great detail and sparkled flawlessly. It was a big diamond. It had to be at least three carets, maybe four.

"Constance, I love you. I have always loved you, from the first moment I saw you. Will you marry me?"

Constance was speechless. Her heart was beating wildly. Was this too soon she wondered? He had just come back into her life. Her mind told her to wait, but her heart longed for true love again. "Yes!" she said and she held out her left hand spreading her fingers apart so he could put the ring on.

Emele pulled the ring from the box and softly slid it on her finger. It fit perfectly. "My mother gave this ring to me before she died. She told me to give it to the one woman I would always love, and now I have." He leaned close to Constance and hugged her tight. She hugged him back and they kissed once more. He felt like the luckiest man on earth. He was truly happy.

They sat on the sofa holding each other and filling each other in on their lives. Emele told her about his journey to the United States and how he had met Gieves and became trusted friends.

Constance was sad to hear of Rhesfield and Jenny's deaths, but she was anxious to meet Gieves. She told Emele the story of her life for the past twenty years as he hung on every word she said. It was so exciting for him to hear about her life and how she came to be where she was now. They talked for hours. It would soon be sunup, so Emele said goodnight and Gieves drove him back to the hotel.

When they got to their room Emele poured them both a drink and they sat as Emele filled Gieves in on his engagement.

Constance wanted to have a small dinner party with her daughters to let them know about her engagement to Emele as soon as possible. She would use the small dining room Edward had made next to the living quarters. She knew Emelia would be home now so she called her.

When Emelia answered the phone they exchange greetings and made a little small talk. She could sense excitement in her mother's voice. "What's going on, Mother?" she asked.

"I have some news I would like to share with you girls as soon as we can all get together!" she said excitedly. "I was hoping we could all have dinner soon."

Emelia could hear the happines in her mother's voice. "What is it Mother? You sound so excited."

"I don't want to spoil the surprise; anyway it's not something you tell over the phone, okay? Talk to Sarah and Claudia and find out when we can all get together and let me know."

"Okay, Mother, I will talk to them right away and call you back."

"The sooner the better" said Constance. "I love you. Bye-bye"

"I love you too, Mother. Bye-bye."

As Emelia hung up the phone, she wondered what the news could be. Her sisters were asleep, so she would talk to them when they woke up tonight. Right now she would go to bed and get some sleep herself.

When night came Emelia woke up. She yelled to her sisters. "Wake up sleepy heads. It's time to get moving."

Sarah got up right away, but Claudia rolled around in bed grumbling "I'm tired." After a couple of minutes she came out of her room to join her sisters.

"Hey! What the deal? Where were you last night?" asked Sarah.

Claudia got a guilty grin on her face. "I just needed some air, so I went for a walk."

"We have to be careful" said Emelia.

"I can take care of myself!' snapped Claudia giving Emelia a cold stare.

"I know. That's what worries me about you. If you go looking for trouble, you will find it. I'm worried what someone else might see."

"You worry too much" said Claudia as she rolled her eyes.

Emelia looked at Sarah, who was looking at Claudia and said in a baby voice "You worry too much." Then she rolled her eyes.

Claudia wasn't paying attention. She was thinking about last night, remembering that sweet taste of the man's blood she had seduced. She turned her head away and licked her lips.

"Mom wants us to get together for a dinner and tell us something important as soon as we can all make it. She sounded pretty excited on the phone" said Emelia.

Sarah looked confused. "I wonder what it could be" she said. "I just hope it doesn't have anything to do with William. He gives me the creeps."

"All I know is Mom just said it wasn't the type of thing you tell someone over the phone. I'm supposed to phone her back and let her know when we can all get together."

Sarah thought a minute then said "How about Thursday. I don't think any of work Thursday."

Emelia nodded. "Sounds good." She looked at Claudia. "Hey girlie, how about you?"

Claudia wasn't paying attention.

"Claudia!" shouted Emelia.

Claudia turned around startled. "Huh?"

"She hasn't heard a word you've said" said Sarah.

Claudia looked at Sarah. "What's so important?"

"I swear, sometimes I don't know where your head is" said Sarah shaking her head.

"I was saying Mom wants to have a dinner with all of us to tell us something important" said Emelia.

"And I said how about Thursday?" added Sarah.

Claudia thought a moment, put her finger to her chin then said "Yep, I guess Thursday would work."

"Great. I'll call Mom and see if Thursday works for her as well" said Emelia.

The call was made and Emelia could tell Constance was really excited about the dinner.

THE DILEMA

When Thursday came Constance wanted everything to be perfect, and it would be. She was so excited she couldn't stay still. She was buzzing around the restaurant all day. When the sun went down, she knew the girls would soon be there. She had asked Emele to give her a little time by themselves; then she would have him come in and tell them of their engagement.

The girls all came in together. They saw their mother and exchanged hugs.

"It is so good to see you all together" said Constance. She led them to the dining room where they got a drink and sat at the table. They visited for a few minutes.

Constance was beaming and the girls were anxious to hear her news.

Sarah couldn't take it any longer. "Okay, Mother, I know you have exciting news and you are beaming so I know it is something major, but good. Can you please tell us what it is before the suspense kills us?"

"Okay, I will tell you. Someone from my past has come back in to my life."

Emelia knew her father was going to talk to her mother, but she had not heard from him to see what happened. "That's great mom."

Constance continued "I don't know if Emelia has told you much about her father, but he is like you. I was in love with him many years ago, but things happened and we lost touch. Now he has come back to me."

Constance got up from her chair and walked to the door of the adjoining room and opened it. "I would like you to meet Emele Dracula." Constance couldn't hold back anymore. "Emele has asked me to marry me and I have accepted." She held out her hand and showed off her engagement ring.

Emele walked through the doorway and stood next to Constance. He was dressed in a black suit, tailored in the old European tradition that fit him well.

Emelia had told her sisters about her dad, but they had never seen him until now.

Claudia leaned in close to Sarah "Wow, Emelia never told us how handsome her dad is" she wispered.

Sarah nodded in agreement and shushed Claudia.

The girls were a little stunned, but they all got up to congratulate the happy couple. They gave hugs and kisses, but they were a little weary of their mother marrying a vampire. Did she know what she was getting into?

They all sat down at the table and ordered dinner. Emele knew the girls would have a lot of questions for him.

Soon the question came up from Claudia "Mother do you want to become a vampire now?"

Constance answered "Emele and I talked about this, even though he thought it might be best if I were, I said no. I love you all and I understand, but it's just not me. I don't think I could hurt anyone. I know you will stay younger and I will become older, and that is okay" she said with a smile. "Let's just enjoy our evening."

The meals were brought in. Emele took off his suit coat and draped it over his chair.

Everyone was enjoying the conversation and food. No one noticed when the door opened and William walked in. He was next to the table before Constance saw him. She could smell the whiskey on his breath as she got up to ask him to leave. Emele stood up quickly next to her, but Constance said "I'll handle this."

He was not expecting a big confrontation, but he was ready, against his better judgment he stepped aside and let her take lead.

Constance reached her hand out to turn him around. "William, you've been drinking. You need to leave. I'm having dinner with my family" Constance said as she grabbed his arm to lead him out.

William had seen Emele stand up. After a couple of steps he looked at Constance with disgust. "You bitch" he said as he jerked his arm from Constance's grip.

Emele was next to Constance in a second, but Constance held her hand out telling Emele she would handle this. "Just let him leave" she said.

"Okay, sir, please leave" Emele said with a cold stare. He was doing his best to control himself.

William looked at Emele then quickly turned to Constance. He shook his head and turned around.

Just as Constance sighed in relief, William turned around as his hand was pulling a nine millimeter hand gun with a silencer from the pocket of his suit coat. He had lost it. He didn't care anymore. He was desperate and mad. In his mind his problems were her fault. She had let him down. Now she wanted someone else. No! That was not an option. He aimed the gun at Constance. "If I can't have you, no one will" and he shot.

Emele stepped between Constance and the gun as it fired. Two more shots fired, piercing Emele's body as Emelia bit into William's hand that held the gun. Claudia jumped over the table as Sarah shoved it to the side, tipping it over, and both girls bit their fangs deep in William's neck, one on each side of him. Emele raised his right hand between the two girls as his claws grew long piercing William's neck tearing the muscles and tendons loose, ripping the head from the body with one upward motion. The blood squirted from William's body spraying on the girls as they pulled their fangs from the stump of his neck allowing the body to collapse to the floor.

Emele's shirt had thick blood around the bullet holes, but the bleeding had stopped as his wounds were healing. Everything had happened so fast. Emele turned around to face Constance. She was just standing there in shock with a blank look on her face from what she had just seen. Her hands were pressed hard against her chest. Emele was reaching for her as he stared in to her fear filled eyes.

Emelia gasped as she watched her mother's white blouse turn red from the blood as it flowed quickly from her body.

As Constance pulled her hand away from her chest in dismay, she saw the blood on her hands. Then she looked up at Emele. She saw the fear in his eyes as he saw the blood run from the bullet hole in her chest. One of the bullets had gone through Emele's body mushrooming slightly, causing a bigger hole in Constance's chest.

Emele caught her as she fell and he laid her softly on the floor. He ripped the shirt from his body and held it tight to Constance's wound to try to slow the blood loss.

"What do we do?" asked Emelia.

Sarah and Claudia turned to see what the commotion was about.

Sarah asked "Should I call for an ambulance?"

Claudia just stared in disbelief, not knowing what to do.

Emele looked at Sarah, then Emelia. "There's no time. She's fading too fast.

One of the waitresses who had heard the loud noises was knocking on the door. "Is everything alright in there?"

Claudia was at the door holding it shut. "Everything is fine" she said. She knew they couldn't let anyone see what was actually happening. "We tipped over the serving tray."

"Do you need some help?" the waitress asked.

"No thank you. We can handle it" answered Claudia.

"Are you sure?"

"Yeah. We've got it" insisted Claudia and she listened for her to walk away. Then she slowly locked the door.

"What do we do?" asked Emelia again.

Sarah and Claudia were at her side leaning down close to her.

Emele looked at the girls, all teary eyed. Then he looked at Constance. "Forgive me." Then he lifted her shoulders off the floor.

The girls all knew what Emele was about to do. It was their mother's only hope.

Constance's eyes opened as Emele's fangs entered her neck. "NO!" she said in a weak voice. Then she closed her eyes.

Emele's eyes filled with tears as he drank the blood of the woman he loved and watched her fade away.

Emelia remembered that night when Sarah had been in a similar situation. She was still worried, but not as much as the rest of them. She had faith Constance would come back. "It will work" she said looking at Sarah and Claudia. "It may take an extra day, but it will work. Just like it worked with you two. You were both weak, but it worked."

Emele picked Constance up and was about to lay her on the couch.

"No. Bring her in here" said Emelia as she opened the door to the next room. "Put her on the bed."

Emele carried her in the next room and laid her on the bed. It was so sad to see her like this, lifeless. It hurt. He leaned over her and kissed her softly on the lips. "Now we wait. It's going to be a long day."

"I will clean her up and change her blouse" said Emelia.

"We had better clean ourselves up too" said Emele. He went to the bathroom and cleaned himself. Then Emelia handed him one of Edward's black tee-shirts and he put it on. It was a little snug, but it looked good on him.

Emelia took Constance's blouse off and washed the blood from her mother's body. When she finished, she put on a clean blouse and put the wash cloth over the wound on her neck. She looked like she was sleeping. Then she cleaned herself up.

Back in the dining room Sarah said to Claudia "Let's get this mess cleaned up, before someone else knocks on the door."

"Good idea" said Claudia. "It will help us to stay busy."

The girls were busy setting the table back up and picking up the mess from the floor when Emele came back in the room. He picked up William's body and head and opened the outside door. Gieves had fallen asleep in the car and was awakened when Emele knocked on the door.

"What's going on?"

"It's a long story. I'll fill you in inside. Pop the trunk please." Emele threw the body and head in the trunk and the two men went back in the room to help clean up.

A knock came to the door. "Is everything alright in there?" a voice asked as the doorknob twisted.

The body was gone, the table was set back up, most of the mess was cleaned up, and Constance was lying on the bed in the next room, but there was still a big red stain on the carpet where William's body had been.

"It's Beth" said Emelia who was coming out of the next room. "She is Mom's friend and the night manager."

Emele grabbed a bottle of red wine from the liquor cabinet and wrapped a towel around it. Then he took it by the blood stain and squeezed the bottle, breaking it over the stain and let the pieces of glass slide from the towel around the stain. He motioned for Sarah and Claudia to get to the bathroom to clean themselves up. Then he opened the door.

Beth looked in. "Is everything alright?" she asked walking in.

"We dropped a serving tray. I was just cleaning it up" answered Emele.

"Who are you and where is Constance?"

"I'm sorry. I am Emele Dracula" Emele said as he offered his hand to Beth. "And you are?"

"I'm Beth Richardson. The night manager" she said taking Emele's hand. "You're Constance's fiancée right?"

"That's right. Pleased to meet you."

"Pleasure to meet you. Constance told me about you. She said you were going to celebrate tonight."

Emelia said "Hi Beth."

"Hello Emelia" said Beth still looking around the room seeing the broken bottle on the floor. "Where is your mother?"

"Well don't say I told you this, but Mother celebrated a little too hard. She got a little tipsy and knocked over a tray and dropped a bottle of wine. She is resting in the next room." Emelia opened the door and let Beth peek in just long enough to get a peek at Constance lying on the bed. Seeing Beth's fears subside she shut the door.

"Well, I won't bother you any further. Are you sure you don't want me to send someone to help clean this mess?"

"We can take care of it" answered Emelia.

With her fears satisfied, Beth left to go back to her other duties.

Emelia locked the door behind Beth. "Whew, that was too close" said Emelia. "Beth is a good manager, but she can be a bit nosey."

Sarah and Claudia were cleaned up and changed, and came back in the room. "It's a good thing we left some clothes here huh?" said Sarah.

"It sure is" answered Emelia. "Now let's finish cleaning this place up."

The girls scrubbed the floor and got the stain out of the carpet. The place looked as good as new.

"Well, I don't know about the rest of you, but I could definitely use a stiff drink" said Emele.

"Sounds good" agreed Emelia.

"I'll second that" said Sarah.

"Me too" added Claudia.

"Name your poison" said Gieves as he stepped over to the mini bar.

He mixed their drinks and they all sat around the table, filling Gieves in on the events of the night.

The sun would be up soon. Emele told Gieves "Can you get rid of the body. I will stay here today. You can spend the day with us or do whatever you wish, but I would like you back here at dusk."

Gieves answered back "Sure thing Mr. Dracula. Consider it done."

Constance had told Beth to come in a little early the next couple of day because she was taking a little time off.

The girls made a call and they were off for the night also.

Emele laid on the sofa and the girls all laid on the bed next to their mother.

"We will have to be ready when she wakes up" reminded Emelia.

Sarah and Claudia nodded in agreement. And Emele nodded his head as well when Emelia looked at him.

After a couple of hours, Emelia thought about the events of the day. She looked over at her father. He was just staring at the ceiling. She got up and walked over to him. He looked tired, but she knew he would not sleep. "You know, if you hadn't bit Mother, I know I would have." She said trying to relieve him a little.

Emele looked at Emelia. He knew she was trying to ease his mind. "It all happened so fast. I saw her fading away. I had to do something fast, it was the only choice I had." Saying the words did not make him feel better. He knew Constance would not be happy. "I knew it should have been her choice, but I couldn't let her die."

Emelia touched him on the shoulder and nodded. "Try to get some sleep, okay?"

"I will. Good night, Emelia."

"Good night Father." Emelia turned around and went back to lie on the bed by her mother and sisters, putting her arm over Constance's stomach. It was going to be a long day.

Emele did manage to doze off. When he did, he had a dream. Constance was very upset that he had changed her. She said she would never forgive him for what he had done. Then she said she would kill herself before she would feed on and kill another person, and she held a knife to her throat and started to cut herself. Emele woke with a start. He crept across the room to the bed. He looked at Constance's lifeless body. Had he done the right thing, knowing how she felt about this, or was his act of love simply a selfish act of his own? He closed his eyes and pictured Constance's eyes opening as he bit her neck while the word NO rang out so loudly. Would she forgive him? His heart was in turmoil. He opened his eyes and looked at the beautiful daughters she had raised, all lying close to her side. Surely Constance was not ready to leave them. She was so happy and excited to share their news with them. Why did this have to happen? He turned around to go back to the sofa.

"Dad?" said Emelia seeing him out of the corner of her eye.

"What is it?" he asked as he turned to face her.

"You look so sad."

"I was just wondering if I did the right thing. We had just talked about this." Emele looked at Constance. "But I couldn't let her go. She had just come back into my life." He looked back at Emelia.

"I've known Mom longer than anyone. She may be angry at first, but she will come around." She looked at her mother then back to Emele. "Just be careful when she wakes up. It seems the weaker ones are always the strongest with the hunger."

The rest of the day dragged on. The girls were trying to sleep with only a little dozing off here and there. Their minds were busy with anticipation of their mother's awakening. They all knew she accepted their lifestyles, but could she be like them and take someone's life? They would find out soon enough.

Slowly the day turned to night. The girls were all around their mother ready to restrain her, to fight off the mad cravings to bite the one who changed her.

Emele was slowly walking around, pretending to check out the pictures on the walls and the furnishings of the room, but his mind was thinking of just one thing. Would Constance forgive him and be okay with her new life?

Emelia was the first to change when she heard Constance heart start to pound in her chest as the vampire blood coursed through it. She held tight to her mother's side pinning her arm tight to her side as she started to twitch. Sarah and Claudia turned as well and Sarah pinned Constance's other arm to her side as Claudia wrapped her arms around her legs.

Constance was waking up fast now. The girls could hear her heart pounding wildly as she squirmed violently trying to free herself from their grips. Constance opened her eyes slightly showing their red. She moaned as her fangs started growing.

She stretched her mouth wide as she felt them growing longer. She straightened her fingers stretching them tightly as her nails turned to sharp black claws.

The girls all tightened their grip.

"Mom!" Emelia said "Can you think clearly?"

Constance screamed and fought to free herself as the hunger grew within her.

"Mom, you have to stop fighting us and listen to me. You must concentrate and fight the hunger" said Sarah. "We don't want to hurt you, but you have to be able to control it, then we can help you."

Gieves had the car next to the family room door and was awaiting the signal to open the door fast and drive them to the appropriate location.

Emele had turned, but he was giving the girls their space to let them try to talk to Constance. It was hard to stand back, but he knew it was better to give them room right now.

"Mom, can you control the hunger?" asked Emelia.

Constance did not answer she just struggled to free herself.

"Mom, I know it's hard but you have to fight this and be in control" said Claudia.

Constance opened her red eyes wide and raised her head focusing on Claudia. "You don't know anything" she said as she fought with all her strength to raise her head higher. She could see Emele now and she stared at him coldly with hatred in her eyes. She opened her mouth wide, showing her fangs and said "You, you did this to me. I will have your blood."

Emele stood motionless. He could see the rage in her eyes as she stared without blinking, burning a hole through his very soul.

"No, Mother" said Emelia as she tightened her grip around her mother. "I know you crave blood. We will help you if you will let us."

Constance used the hunger to fight with all her being and pulled her arm loose from Sarah's grip and swung her elbow hard into her face knocking her back. Then she grabbed Claudia's hair and yanked it hard causing her to loosen her grip. Then she turned her attention to Emelia. She rolled her body a little and tried to pull her other arm free. Emelia was holding tight and her claws dug into Constance's side, but Constance freed her arm and she stood up as Emelia hung on.

It happened so fast. The girls were shocked at their mother's strength, and tried to regain their hold on her as she lunged toward Emele.

Claudia grabbed her mother's foot as she jumped, and Emele caught her at arm's length. Sarah reached out and took hold of Constance's arm again, and the girls tried to pull her down.

Constance's eyes were still fixed on Emele and she used all her new found strength to reach her hands around his neck.

Emele did not want to hurt her, so he restrained himself and Constance took advantage and pulled herself forward taking the girls with her.

"NO!" screamed Emelia as the girls watched as their mother opened her mouth wide and buried her fangs deep in Emele's neck. The blood tasted so good, she couldn't stop. It made her feel so alive, so powerful. She wasn't thinking this is the man I love. She could only think how wonderful the blood was.

The girls all pulled hard together as Emele pushed against Constance's shoulders, forcing her back. Sarah and Emelia unwrapped her hands from around Emele's neck.

As her hands came loose her fangs ripped a piece of flesh from Emele's neck and the blood sprayed out as Emele reached his hand to cover it with pressure until it could heal.

The girls pulled Constance to the floor. Her face now covered with Emele's blood. Constance licked her lips then laughed out loud.

"She should be somewhat satisfied for the moment" said Emele as he pulled his hand slowly away from his neck, feeling it had healed. "She has fed."

"Was it enough?" asked Emelia.

"It should be enough to control her hunger if she wants it to" answered Emele.

"Can you control it now, Mother?" asked Emelia still holding tight to her.

"I don't know" answered Constance, as she was starting to realize what she had done.

"Try hard and we will help you" said Sarah.

Emele's neck had healed but he needed to feed for the blood he had lost. "She still needs more and I need to feed also" he said. "Let's get her to the car." Emele knocked on the door and Gieves opened it and then the car door, then he stood back.

Constance was still a vampire and she let her tongue feel the fangs. Then she regained control. "I'm okay now."

The girls lifted her and led Constance to the car and helped her in.

"You better ride up front" said Emelia to Emele.

Emele didn't argue. He just walked around the car and got in the front seat. He knew Emelia was right.

"You better put up the divider" said Sarah as she looked at Gieves "just to be safe.

Gieves drove fast to the corrupt spot Emelia had told him of, where the girls could always find an easy meal. He stopped a block away from the alley where the dope dealers and prostitutes hung out.

All the blood had made Claudia hungry and her stomach growled loudly as she opened the car door. They all exited the car staying in the shadows. Emelia was in front holding Constance's hand followed shortly by Sarah and Claudia. "I see four people" said Emelia. "Looks like a couple of pushers and a couple of drugged out hookers. I don't see anyone else."

Claudia sprang into action hitting one of the dealers and taking him down hard as she bit his neck.

The other drug dealer tried to pull Claudia from his buddy and one of the hookers grabbed the other's hand and pulled her along running down the alley.

Emele ran around the building to cut the hookers off before they got through the alley.

Emelia pulled Constance ahead and said "Go get him."

Constance hesitated.

This was going to be harder now that her hunger was somewhat satisfied. "Look Mother, he's trying to hurt your Claudia."

"Mom, get him now" said Sarah as she gave Constance a little shove. "He's going to hurt her," but she knew he was no match for little sister, hoping this would motivate her mother into attacking.

It worked. Constance's motherly instincts kicked in and she charged the man quickly and jumped on his back, bringing him down quickly while her vampire ways kicked in also making her bite him. He was quickly drained of his blood and his life. The blood was warm and sweet and it empowered her as she drank.

Claudia finished and looked at her mother. "I think that's good enough" she said as she tapped Constance on the back.

Constance opened her mouth and took her fangs from her victim's neck.

"I'll check on Emele" said Sarah as she ran through the alley. She saw Emele tear the head from the hooker. She opened her eyes wide and saw the second hooker standing in the shadow against the wall motionless, trying to hide. Sarah ran over to her and grabbed her and was about to bite when she looked at this young woman's eyes. She wasn't hiding. She was so stoned she was leaning against the wall so she wouldn't fall over. She hadn't seen anything. Sarah punched her face, knocking her out. Then she sat her down next to the dumpster. She would have a black eye but she would sleep it off and be okay in the morning.

Emelia and Claudia were teaching their mother how to decapitate a body, and why it was so important.

Claudia showed her how easy it was to rip the head loose with one quick thrust of her clawed hand.

Emelia could tell this was not going to be easy for Constance.

Constance took a deep breath and plunged her clawed hand into the dead man's neck. It didn't tear loose. Her hand got stuck. Constance got a disgusted look on her face. "Gross" she said as she pulled her hand out.

"It will get easier" promised Emelia.

"Let me show you Mommy" said Claudia as she shoved her hand palm up into his neck. "With one swift move you shove your hand in and thrust upward and Wala, there it goes" as they watched the head fly free from the body and land a few feet away.

"Now for the cleanup. We can't leave any evidence" Emelia said as she picked up the two heads. "We can put them in the trunk for now and bury them in the desert later."

Claudia picked up one body by the back of his pants with her hand and pointed to the other body. "That one's yours."

Constance picked him up like Claudia showed her. She couldn't believe how easy she lifted him. She carried it to the car as Gieves opened the trunk and she threw it in as did Claudia and Emelia.

Gieves drove to the other end of the alley. Emele was standing holding the body and head of his victim. Gieves popped the trunk and Emele tossed them in. Then he and Sarah got in the car and Gieves drove out of town to the desert. He drove off the road a bit and parked. He opened the trunk and took out two shovels. He and Emele quickly had a hole dug and the bodies were thrown in and covered up. Then Gieves drove to Constance's house.

As they drove Constance was getting nervous. It was really sinking in that she had just killed someone. She started to cry.

Emelia gave her a hug and softly said "It will be alright, Mother."

Constance looked Emelia in the eyes. "No it isn't. I killed a man. I feel terrible." Then she looked at Emele, who was watching from across the seat. "This is all your fault" she said as her sorrow turned to rage. Her eyes turned red as she glared at him. "I didn't want this and you knew it. I told you this."

Emele looked down from Constance's cold stare. "I'm sorry" he said looking back up at Constance. "I didn't know what else to do. It may have been selfish, but I couldn't lose you." He paused a moment then continued. "I just got you back in my life."

Emelia tried to ease the tension. She put her arm on Constance's shoulder, leaning toward her. "Mother, I know you don't want to hear this right, but if Father hadn't bit you, I would have. I'm not ready to lose you either." Emelia hugged her tight. She could feel some of the tension leave her. Then Constance hugged her back.

Sarah was sitting on the other side of Constance. She leaned over and hugged her mother. "I'm with Emelia, I'm sorry Mother, but I would have bitten you too."

Claudia was across the seat and she crawled across the car on her knees. "Don't forget me Mommy. I'd bite you anytime."

This made Constance and the girls all laugh. They opened their arms to include Claudia in their hug.

"Don't be mad at Emele" said Sarah. "We all just love you so much."

Emele felt fortunate to have Constance's daughters sticking up for him. In his heart he knew Constance wasn't ready to leave them yet either. He just hoped he was included.

Emelia looked over to Emele. She could see him in deep thought, looking at them. When he looked up at Emelia, she was looking at him. She smiled and winked at him. "It will be okay" she said as she squeezed her mother, but she was talking to Emele.

Emele smiled a little smile. He hoped so.

Gieves rounded the corner to Constance's house and pulled in the driveway. Constance and the girls got out. They would all stay together today. As Sarah and Claudia led their mother to the house, Emelia poked her head back in the car. "She will come around, you know" she said to Emele. "It may take a while, maybe a week or two, but she will come around. Give her some time to get used to her new life." She smiled and reached her arms toward Emele.

Emele reached his arms toward Emelia. They hugged and he said "I hope so."

"Good night, Father."

"Good night, Emelia."

Emelia closed the door and walked to the house. She opened the door and went inside.

Emele knew they were a close family, and he knew the daughters would take good care of her. He looked in the front seat to Gieves, who was looking at him in the mirror.

"Home?" asked Gieves.

"Yes" said Emele. "It's been a long day."

Gieves drove them home and they went inside.

"How about a drink?" asked Gieves.

Steve Pierce

"Sounds good" answered Emele.

Emele opened a bottle as Gieves got two glasses. Then Emele poured the scotch.

"Well, what do you think?" asked Emele as Gieves handed him a glass.

"I think your daughter is right. Love can endure anything."

Emele touched his glass to Gieves' and said "To the power of love" and they both drank.

A DIFFERENT LIFE

Back at Constance's house, the women were having a drink also and talking about the events of the night.

"Well, Mother, looks like you'll be a night shifter too" said Sarah.

Constance was feeling a little better now and this made her smile. "If my girls can do it, so can I."

They continued talking for a couple of hours. They started to get tired.

"It won't be so bad" said Sarah.

"It gets better with time. At least you know what's coming" said Emelia.

"And the energy you get" chimed in Claudia. "The strength, the agility, the speed, the power and the seduction."

"Yes" said Emelia "the power of seduction."

They all laughed.

"You know, Mother, you have more of a prowess now" said Sarah.

"The men will come a running!" exclaimed Claudia.

"Oh, you girls are so silly, you make me laugh. Seduction, prowess, I'm too old" said Constance, "and I'm tired. I think it's time for bed."

The girls agreed with their mother and went to their rooms. Constance went to her bedroom. She looked in the full length mirror. She had not seen herself since she changed. "My goodness" she whispered to herself as she saw her reflection in the mirror. She did look a little different. She liked it. She did feel a little sexier. She remembered back to the day after Emelia's attack. Though she didn't know what had happened at the time she remembered how Emelia looked different, in a good way. She remembered Sarah and Claudia looked different too. The more she thought about it, the more she realized it was prowess, a new found confidence that made them seductive. Could this be happening to her now? She took her clothes off. Was it her imagination? Her breast seemed a bit perkier. She turned around and rubbed her hands over her butt. Could it be? She did some exercises, but she thought she felt a bit firmer back there. A smile came to her face. "It's just your imagination" she told herself. "All this talk of seduction and prowess is silly." She shook her head. "You need sleep woman."

She put on her pajamas and got in to bed. A little smile came across her face as she closed her eyes. "Maybe, who knows?" she thought, then she drifted off to sleep.

As Constance fell asleep, she started to dream. She dreamed she was in Venice, leaning back in a seat of a gondola under a big umbrella, as she was gently pushed through the streets. She was wearing a big straw hat, sunglasses and a white wrap over a white one piece bathing suit. She was hot and put her hand in the water to help cool off. The water was cool and felt so good on her hand. She swirled her hand in it making little waves. She wet her lips with her tongue and tasted blood and felt her fangs as she ran her tongue over them. The gondola slowly stopped moving. She turned to look at the young man who was pushing her through the water streets. He was laying there lifeless. She reached her arm from the shade of the umbrella and gave the young man a gentle shake. His head rolled away from the body it had been ripped from. She could see fang marks in the stump of the neck. Suddenly she felt a burning sensation on her arm. She pulled her arm back to the shade of the umbrella and looked at it. It was charred and burned. She rubbed her arm lightly and watched in horror as her arm turned to ash and fell apart. She screamed loudly, waking herself up with a start. Her heart was beating wildly as she felt her arm.

Emelia ran in to her mother's room. "Are you alright?!" She asked seeing her sitting up in bed holding her arm.

Constance took a deep breath, feeling relief seeing her arm was okay. "I just had a freaky dream, but I'm alright, just a little shook up."

Emelia sat on the bed next to her mother. "I guess I should have warned you, you might have some weird dreams." She put her arm around Constance. "Do you want to talk about it?"

Constance was still holding her arm. "No, I just need a minute to calm down. It really got me going there for a minute. It seemed so real." She took another deep breath. "I'm alright now."

Emelia lay down next to her mother and pulled the sheet over both of them.

Constance snuggled up next to Emelia and put her arm over her. She smiled as she closed her eyes. She was so calm now and she soon fell sound asleep. When she woke up several hours later it was getting dark.

The girls all had to get ready for work. They said their goodbyes to their mother and said they would visit her throughout the week. They got in the car and drove home.

Emele stayed away from Constance to give her time to deal with her reality. He knew the girls would help her get through it. Emelia had told him she and Sarah would help explain things and take her to feed the next time befor the hunger took control. He also knew she would help heal his and Constance's relationship. He wanted to believe that everything would be alright, but part of him had doubts. Either way it was very hard for him to stay away and give her time.

He had talked to Gieves about this one night and Gieves reassured him she would come around. Gieves told him, "She fell right back in love with you after twenty years. Give her some credit. She just got dealt a new hand. She had a lot of things happen in the past week. You came back in her life, her ex-boyfriend tried to kill her and now she has been turned into a vampire and had to kill to survive. Just give her some time and flowers. Send her a big bouquet of flowers. Send an I'm sorry note with them." Then he leaned back in his chair and laughed a little then he added. "It doesn't matter if you are right or wrong. Flowers and an I'm sorry go a long way."

Emele smiled at this young man's wisdom. He wasn't sorry. He wasn't ready to lose Constance yet. If the same situation arose again he would do it again in a heartbeat. He looked at Gieves. "You are quite the philosopher." He paused a moment thinking, then continued. "I am sorry for changing her life so much. Constance is probably the warmest, kindest person I've ever known." Now he was starting to understand her frustration.

"Yet another reason she'll come around and forgive you."

"What would you have done if you were in a situation like that? The woman you love with all your being is about to die right in front of you. You will lose her forever. Knowing you would never love like this again. Knowing how she felt about being bit or killing" asked Emele.

Gieves felt Emele's pain. "Wow." He thought about Emel's question. He had been in love and he had been heartbroken, but he knew he had not been in love on this level. "If I were in love, like you..." He thought a little deeper, then continued. "People say they would cross the world for someone, but very few really would, but you did. You crossed thousands of miles, searching for months, just to see her face and know she was happy with a nice life. You even came back from the grave when you thought she was in trouble. You told me you could walk away if she was happy. But she wasn't happy, until she met you again. If I were in that situation, I couldn't let her go. If I had the ability to save her at any cost, I would do it."

"You don't think I was being selfish?"

"Not if something is done out of love."

"I may not look it, but I was over eighty years old when I met Constance. It was love at first sight. I tried to put her out of my mind, but I could not. She was all I could think about. I know she is the only woman I will ever love."

Gieves didn't know why but Sarah's face came to his mind. She was a beautiful woman. He remembered a few days ago when he had driven Emele over to Emelia's house so they could talk, and how Sarah had come out to the car and asked if she could come sit and talk to him while Emelia and her dad were talking. They just sat there talking for a couple of hours. They didn't talk about anything deep, just light conversation and he really enjoyed that time with her.

"Have you ever really been so attracted to someone you couldn't get her out of your mind?" Emele could tell Gieves was having pleasant thoughts as he watched a smile come to his face. He had not heard Emele's question. Perhaps Gieves understood better that he thought.

A CLOSE CALL

Over the next couple of days, Sarah and Emelia visited their mother to make sure she was doing okay. Claudia stopped in once, but she was busy sneaking around on her own. Sarah and Emelia talked about some things to help their mother cope with her new life. Constance had learned about the need to feed once a week or lose control to the hunger and take a chance, from Emelia's stories she had told her before.

On Tuesday night they stopped in again. When they got in the house, Emelia noticed a big bouquet of flowers on the counter. "Wow, these are beautiful. Who are they from?" asked Emelia.

"Emele sent them" answered Constance with a look of indifference.

"How is that going?" asked Sarah.

"I don't know. I'm still upset. I had talked to him about this before, and he knew I did not want this" said Constance with distain.

Emelia read the note. "Well at least he's trying. He didn't know what else to do that night. He just didn't want to lose you."

Constance just rolled her eyes.

"Maybe you should talk to him" said Sarah. She could see her mother wasn't ready to talk about Emele yet.

Seeing no reaction, Emelia changed the subject. "You know Thursday you will have to feed. Sarah and I will help you."

Constance just stared forward. "I wish he had not bitten me. I don't think I can kill again. It has bothered me a lot."

Sarah said "I know it is hard, but if we can make the world a little safer, isn't it worth it. Think of the lives we're saving."

Constance did not look enthused as she gave Sarah a doubtful look.

"Sarah is right. The night she was attacked, those guys didn't care if she was killed. It was like a game to them." Emelia paused a moment then continued. "Wheather you want to believe it or not we are helping some people."

Constance pondered the thought and remembered Sarah's story. "I know you are right, but it is still hard to convince myself it is all right to kill."

Emelia answered back, "I know you think there is good in everybody, but try telling that to the parents of a young girl on the morgue slab who was repeatedly raped then killed by gang members having fun, or a bunch of rowdy guys who had too much to drink and got carried away then paniced. I have seen this Mother." Emelia was becoming a little upset now. "How about a wife or girlfriend who is beaten so close to death they are afraid to leave or contact the police. I"m sorry but a restraining order does not put a protective shield around a person." Emelia thought she might be pushing it but her mother needed to understand. "Look what William did. He was going to kill you, and for what, not marrying him. How many of us would he have killed in his panic?"

These were very harsh words and they did sink in to Constance. "Okay, just help me to know the one we choose is a bad person."

Sarah told her mother "I do some research in the library and read the papers. It bothered me a little at first so I try to check on people. Most times there are people who hang out in bad places, repeat offenders who don't want to change but just go out looking to cause trouble."

The girls could see their mother agreed, but was not enjoying talking about this, so they talked about more pleasant things that would take her mind away from this for a while. They were sure she would worry enough about this on her own.

Constance talked about switching to the night shift and how

happy Beth was when she called her and asked if she would work during the day. That worked out well, so she would start this weekend.

The girls agreed that was great. Now they could stop in late after work sometimes and catch a little visit with her. Constance liked the sound of that. They talked a little longer then the girls had to leave for work.

"Remember we will be here Thursday night" reminded Emelia.

"Yes, Thursday" sighed Constance. "Good night."

Thursday night came along with a thunder storm. It was one o'clock. The wind was howling through the streets. The rain was torrid but short lived as the storm moved its way; sending fresh smells in the air. The sky was alive with dark heavy clouds you could see moving fast as lightning illuminated the sky. The lightning was steady and intence with deafening thunder. Although the rain was moving fast, the storm was growing in strength.

Emelia pulled her car in to Constance's driveway. She and Sarah ran to the house as a few sprinkles fell on them.

Constance was startled as the door flew open and the girls ran in.

"Wow, this is some store, huh?" said Sarah.

"Yes it is. It's been a long time since I've seen lightning like this" answered Constance.

"Well, I think the rain is over. We should get going" said Emelia.

Constance was uneasy, but she knew she had to go with them. She knew they were here to help. She said nothing as they walked to the car and started driving down the street, but soon she was figidity. "Where are we going?"

"There is a community center that has become a local hangout for teens. There are a couple of guys who deal drugs. Lately they have been hanging around the community center late at night trying to get kids hooked on their stuff. Most of the teens are gone by one o'clock, but these guys stick around for a while to sell to older customers" said Sarah. "I have told Emelia how to get there."

The farther they drove the more lightning there was.

Emelia pulled the car over parking a couple blocks away from the center. She looked over at Constance. "Are you ready for this?"

Constance felt something stirring within her. Maybe the hunger was coming, or maybe it was her will not to kill stirring her emotions, or it might be the conflict of what her mind wanted and what her body was craving. "Yeah, I guess so" she said nervously.

They all exited the car and sneaked around the building moving in the shadows between lightning strikes.

Emelia moved with her mother as Sarah moved in front letting them know when to move. Sarah motioned for them to stand still as she came into view of the drug dealers. She watched as a young man exchanged a hand ful of wrinkled bills for a small plastic bag, then run off quickly. No one else was around now. It was time to make their move.

"Remember these are not nice people. They probably have weapons. We need to hit them fast. Okay?" said Emelia as she tugged her mother's hand.

Sarah gave the signal and she ran toward one of the dealers.

Emelia had Constance's hand and pulled her out of the shadows toward the other man. Constnace was feeling the excitement and the hunger. Her fangs were growing and her claws were sharp. When Emelia was close, she let go of her mother's hand giving her room to move on her own. Constance grabbed him, digging her claws into his shoulder and turning him around to face her, pulling him close to her. He was caught off guard with no time to react. Constance was focused on his neck and opened her mouth wide and was ready to bite when a bright lighning flash distracted her and she focused on the man's face. He was terrified and in pain. Constance froze for a split second and let her claws loose from the man's shoulder. He started to run as he saw his partner being taken down by Sarah.

"Mother, are you okay?" yelled Emelia.

Constance just stood there.

Emelia ran past her and took the man down and fed on him. She turned around to see her mother, but she was not there anymore. She quickly tore the head free. She looked over to Sarah who was tearing the head free from her victim. "Where's Mom?"

Sarah looked around. "Isn't she with you?"

"She froze and I had to step in. Now she's gone."

Sarah ran over to Emelia. "Maybe she went to the car."

The girls ran around the center from different directions meeting at the car. Constance was not there.

"We need to get those bodies, then we can find her. She couldn't be far, right?" said Emelia.

Sarah got in the car and drove over close to the bodies. Emelia had one and threw it in the open trunk. Sarh grabbed the other and did the same. With the bodies hid in the trunk, the girls felt a little safer about yelling and hollered for their mother.

"Mom, where are you?!" yelled Emelia. "You can't run from this. The hunger will find you!"

"Mom!" yelled Sarah. "This is serious!"

With no answer they had to move on quickly.

"Where could she be?" asked Sarah nervously.

Emelia knew they had to keep calm if they were going to handle this. She thought a moment. "I bet she's heading for home. You drive slowly toward Mom's house and watch the roads. I'll check some of the off roads" Emelia told her sister.

The storm was at its peek and the wind was whipping up trash form the streets and whirling it upward.

Sarah drove down the road looking down the streets for her mother, and Emelia ran through some of the alleys, both heading toward Constance's house.

Emelia was worried. "She's going to lose control soon. She needs to feed" she said to herself. She was over half way to Constnce's when she had a premonition. "Sarah." She ran as fast as she could straight to her mother's house. When she got close she could see Sarah pulling in to the driveway. She could see Constance sitting in the passenger seat. She watched as Sarah got out and walked around the front of the car as Constance opened the door to get out. Emelia ran as she saw Constance's eyes turn red and saw her open her mouth. Before she could get to them, Constance grabbed Sarah, catching her off guard. The lightning flashed brightly as it struck a light pole. The light bulb flashed brightly before it exploded, but Constance did not lose her focus this time, and she stayed focused on Sarah's neck. She had surrendered to the hunger, and did not know what she was doing. The memory of the old woman in the restaurant that night came to Emelia's mind. "No Mother!" yelled Emelia. Emelia tackled her mother taking her to the ground as she bit into Sarah's neck, taking her down with them. They all crashed to the ground. Emelia pulled her mother's hands from Sarah, and Sarah pushed Constance away from her, ripping her fangs from her neck. Sarah rolled away from them and held pressure on her wound. Constance rolled Emelia over and got on top of her. Emelia kicked her leg upward and threw Constance over her landing her on her back, then she kicked once more flipping herself on top of her mother. She pinned her arms down to the ground and squeezed her body with her thighs. "Is this what you want, Mother?" she asked her intensly looking her in the eyes.

Constance was not listening. She was just fighting with all her strength.

Emelia looked over to Sarah. "Are you okay?"

Sarah pulled her hand from her neck. The wound was healed. Sarah nodded her head.

"I don't mean to be rude, but if you're okay, don't just stand there go get her some food while I hold her here. She needs blood now."

Sarah got in the car and quickly drove to a man on her list that was close by. Luckily she saw him walking alone outside. She pulled over next to him. When he bent down by the window Sarah pulled him through the window and held him to the seat as she quickly drove back. She pulled the car in the driveway, opened the door and pulled the man out. Emelia let Constance up as Sarah shoved the man toward her. Constance grabbed him and bit his neck deep, draining his blood and life quickly, then let his body fall to the ground. Her hunger satisfied, she slowly regained her composure. She suddenly saw what had happened and it all came together. She relived it in her mind just as it had happened. She looked at Sarah and started to cry. "I'm so sorry." Then she looked at Emelia. "Thank you." She continued sobbing as she fell to her knees. "This will never happen again" she swore.

Sarah took her mother's hand and pulled her up. "I know" and she hugged her tight.

"Take her inside" Emelia said, "I'll take care of this body." She quickly ripped the head from the body and put it in the trunk. Then she quietly looked up and down the neighborhood at all the houses. All the windows were shut and drapes drawn. Feeling safe that no one had seen anything that just happened, she went inside to join Sarah and her mother.

The girls knew Constance had learned her lesson the hard way. There was no need to lecture her. She would not lose her focus again. She knew she had to kill and she understood the consequenses if she tried to put it off. This was her life now and she would deal with it, whatever it took. She would never lose control again.

The girls stayed for a while until the storm passed. They tried to take their mother's mind off the events of the evening. They both knew she would go over and over it in her mind as soon as she lay down in her bed.

When it was about four- thirty the girls said goodniight to their mom and left. They drove out to the desert and burried the bodies, then they drove home.

They had just sat down at the kitchen table when Claudia came through the door.

"Where have you been Girlie?" asked Emelia, knowing Claidia wasn't working.

Claudia shrugged her shoulders "Nowhere, just walking."

"You do a lot of walking, don't you?" asked Sarah.

"I need to move around okay."

Sarah and Emelia both knew she had been out feeding again.

"Well, you be careful on your little walks" demanded Emelia.

"Don't worry about me. I'm always careful" said Claudia with a little smirk on her face. But she wasn't being careful at all. She was not choosey with her victims and she was hastely deposing of the bodies. Then she tried to change the subject away from herself. "How did it go with Mom tonight?"

"Well, we got through it, but it was a little rough for a while" said Sarah as she touched herself on the neck.

Claudia wasn't listening. She had turned her back to Sarah and was rumaging through her purse.

This frustrated Emelia and she grabbed Claudia's arm and turned her around. "Hey, Sarah is talking to you! Do you even care about Mom?"

Claudia grew fangs and opened her mouth slightly to bare them a bit to Emelia.

Emelia slapped her face. "Don't even think about it. We could have really used your help tonight."

Claudia was mad now, but she wasn't ready to cause a scene. She swallowed her pride and said "I'm sorry, I should have been there."

Sarah was too shocked to say anything for a moment. She couldn't believe what had just happened or what could have happened. She stepped over to Claudia and gave her a hug. "Hey, it's okay. We just want you to be more involved with us and Mother. Mom is going through a lot right now. She could use some support from you. It wouldn't hurt for you to try to get Mom and Emele back together. You saw how excited she was to share her news. He really loves her and he would treat her right." She looked at Claudia and smiled.

Claudia smiled back at Sarah and said "I know, it's just that I'm going through some stuff myself right now."

Emelia glared at Claudia, "Humph."

Claudia added "But I will visit Mother more. I promise."

Sarah knew Claudia meant well, she was just easily distracted.

"I'm going to bed" said Emelia.

When Emelia's door shut, Sarah touched Claudia's shoulder. "Hey, Emelia went through a lot tonight. We lost Mom for a little while and she was really scared."

Claudia nodded like she understood what Sarah was talking about. But she was still holding on to her anger against Emelia.

She finaaly calmed down when Sarah told her the rest of the story. She showed real concern and asked "Are you alright? That must have ben scary" when Sarah told her about Constance biting her.

The two sisters talked for about an hour as Sarah tried to smooth things over. The sun had been up for a while now and the girls decided to call it a night. They said good night and went to their rooms.

Things went pretty well over the next week. Constance went out to feed with all three of the girls. This time she caught her victim as they watched. She fed and decapitated the body and put it in the trunk. She thought about how taking this guy out of action would be good for this neighborhood.

Constance was coming in to her new life, and seemed to finally have a handle on it. Now they just had to get their mother and Emele back together, which they were working on. The girls thought their troubles were over. They were wrong.

THE TRAP

Claudia's careless behavoir was catching up to her. The police had found a few bodies in dumpsters in a small part of the city. They were sure there was a serial killer at work. The shape the bodies were found in led the police to believe these were hate crimes, as the victims heads had been ripped from the bodies. The police were pretty sure the killer was a woman, a strong woman, or maybe two women working together. They also knew the killer was preying on men looking for prostitutes off the main roads. They had gotten information from some of the working girls on some of the victims. These men had been cruising the streets looking for fresh young faces late at night on the darker streets, so the police were looking for one or two pretty young women who were prostitutes or posing as prostitutes. The victims had also had some kind of sexual activity either as they were killed or shortly before. The only baffeling part of this case was the lack of blood. When someone's head gets ripped from their body there should be blood.

The police came up with an area most likely worked by the killer, and a trap was set. An undercover police officer wearing a wire would drive around the dark streets late at night and try to pick up any prostitutes in the area. If he felt they were not the killer, he would say he changed his mind and drop them off and continue his search. There would be backup officers listening to the transmission not far away to swoop in and take the killer down.

The first two nights were a waste of time. The officer did pick up a couple of hookers, but soon found they did not fit the profile. The third night the officer was driving along the dark street when he noticed a scantily clad woman moving seductively along the road, slowly swinging her hips from side to side as she walked.

The cop pulled along side her and asked "Looking for a ride?"

The young woman turned toward the car, showing her beauty to the driver. She leaned down by the window and said coyfully "Maybe." She smiled, showing off her white teeth and asked "You looking for some company?"

The cop felt an uneasiness in his gut, telling him this was the one. "Sure" he said. "Come on in." And he reached over and opened the passenger door.

The young woman walked around the front of the car letting the headlights help show him her body. She got in the car, shut the door and said "Drive."

The cop started to drive. "Where to?" he asked.

"Let's go some place a little less social" she said as she put her hand on his thigh. "Take a left up here."

The cop turned left down a road that led out of town.

"In a couple of blocks there will be an old rundown warehouse. Pull around to the back" she said as she rubbed her hand higher on his thigh.

"You seem to know your way around. Do you live around here?"

Claudia touched her figertip to his nose and slid it off the end. "Naughty boy. I'm not telling you where I live" she said, but she was thinking it wouldn't matter if she did tell him.

As the cop pulled in Claudia could hear his heart pounding in his chest, but the smell was not right. He smelled more of adrenalin than lust. She thought maybe he didn't want sex, maybe he was a killer preying on prostitutes. She would be ready for anything, even more of a challenge.

The cop pulled along the side of the old warehouse and asked "Does this work for you?"

"It works for me, but is it working for you?" Claudia asked

as she ran her hand up higher cupping his genitals and giving a light squeeze.

He flinched slightly. "Yeah, that works for me."

Claudia started massaging and felt him growing. "I guess it does." Claudia was hungry for the lust blood she could smell now. Her fangs and claws were growing.

The cop started running his hands over Claudia's body seductively, but he was really feeling for a weapon. He didn't feel any weapon. Maybe his gut was wrong this time.

Claudia was getting a bad vibe about this guy. She would finish him before his lust ended. She started kissing his neck and her fangs grew longer.

The cop was thinking she was no killer. "Maybe we shouldn't do this."

"Too late" said Claudia and she bit deep into the man's neck.

The cop was shocked, but he pulled his gun from along the side of his seat and put the barrel against her side and pulled the trigger, shooting her in the stomach.

Claudia felt the rush of pain as she heard the gun fire. She couldn't believe she wasn't ready for this. She grabbed his hand and squeezed hard as he pulled the trigger again sending another bullet into her stomach. She heard the bones of his hand breaking as she squeezed harder.

She quickly drained his blood, but lights and sirens were surrounding the car as the back ups were closing in fast pulling up close.

Claudia kicked the door hard and it broke free from the latch and hinges and fell to the ground as she stepped out.

The policemen could see their co-worker slumped in the seat. They identified themselves and told her to stand still and put her hands up.

Claudia started to run and the police opened fire sending

several bullets into her body. One man shot her in the chest as she came toward him. Claudia shoved him out of her way sending him flying back twenty feet until he hit another police car just pulling in. She grabbed the next policeman as he shot her in the chest and broke his neck.

The police were everywhere now. Claudia was caught off guard. She paniced. She tried to run through the cars, but the police were shooting at her. She jumped over one of the cars.

One of the newer officers was on the radio calling for more back up. He was ranting from the shock of what he was seeing. "Officer down! Officer down! We neeed backup now."

Claudia ran fast but she was running straight away from them. She felt the bullets hitting her in the back, knocking her forward and she fell. She was quick to get back on her feet, but now the cops had a better aim on her and fired rapidly emptying their guns.

Claudia's bullet riddled body could not heal itself fast enough. She couldn't breathe as her lungs were filling up with blood. Her clothes were drenched as the blood ran down her legs. She couldn't think. Everything was going dark. She was going down. Her body crumpled as she collasped to the ground.

The police swarmed around her body making sure she was done. One officer felt for a pulse. "She's dead."

Anoother cop checked the officer in the car. He was dead. His throat was ripped out but there wasn't any blood in the car.

The cops were stunned at the amount of force it took to take this small woman down. She had to be on drugs to be so deranged and so powerful.

Am ambulance came in fast from the call of officer down, and the EMTs rushed to check on the downed policemen.

Meanwhile Gieves had driven Emele out to feed. He was

261

sitting in the car with the police scanner on. The scanner was going wild. Back up was being summoned to a location Gieves had heard of.

Emele had fed and was just bringing the body to the car and threw it in the open trunk.

"Mr. Dracula, you may want to hear this."

Emele and Gieves listened as the officer ranted over the radio. "Officer down! Officer down. We need backup. This young lady is going through our men like nothing I've ever seen. She's taken several shots but they don't slow her down."

"The location he gave is Claudia's hunting ground" said Gieves.

Emele got in the car and said "Drive!"

Gieves hit the gas and the tires squeeled as he pulled out.

A minute later the scanner came back on "She's down! She's finally down."

Emele and Gieves could see the flashes of the cop cars and ambulances as they got close. "Slow down" said Emele. "We don't want to get too close yet. There are too many of them."

Gieves slowed way down and pulled over shutting the lights off. They could see police walking around.

After evidence was gathered and pictures taken, the police cars started to pull out and go back to their normal routine. What ever happened was over. The two ambulances pulled out one behind the other and headed down the road without their lights or sirens going.

"This doesn't look good" said Gieves.

Emele was so upset it was hard to control his anger. The thought of Constance's daughter possibly killed was more than he could take. He started to change.

"Now what?" asked Gieves. He could see Emele was losing control.

"Follow those ambulances. We need to know." Emele said through his fangs.

Gieves turned the car around and followed the ambulances. Sure enough they both slowed down and turned in the driveway to the morgue. Gieves turned and parked a couple of blocks away. They watched as the EMTs unloaded the stretchers and wheeled the zipped up body bags inside. They waited for what seemed like forever, but was actually only about ten minutes, while inside the paperwork was being filled out and bodies tagged. The ambulances slowly pulled out and dissapeared over the crest of the road.

"I may need some backup" said Emele.

Gieves knew the seriousness of the situation. "Let's go" he said as he put a pistol in the back of his jeans.

"We need to see if it is Claudia, and if it is we need to get her out of there before they do anything to her body."

"We need to sneek a peek and see what we're up against."

Emele pushed on the door, breaking the lock and carefully looked both ways. It was clear so they walked in. They walked softly down the hallway. Emele saw one security guard sitting at a desk doing some paperwork. He was the one who signed for the bodies. They had to act fast the sun would be up before long.

The guard got up and went to another room. Emele and Gieves went to the cold storage room.

"We need to check those bodies" whispered Emele.

Gieves nodded in agreement.

There were six body bags on slabs. Gieves unzipped the first one. "It's a cop."

"Has he been bitten?"

Gieves looked him over good. "No. His neck is broken."

Emele unziped a bag. It was Claudia.

Gieves could tell by the look on Emele's face it was her. "Is she" he swallowed hard "dead?"

"I don't know. She doesn't look good" Emele said as he looked at all the bullet holes in her pale blood covered body. "I don't see any healing going on here." He put his ear next to her chest. He heard nothing. "We need to get her out of here."

"We need to check those other bodies in case she bit one of them." Gieves stepped over to another bag and unzipped it. He looked closely but didn't see any bite marks. He zipped it back up.

Emele checked the next one. "Another cop, but looks like his body is crushed. No bite marks." Then he unzipped another bag. It was okay so he zipped it back up.

Gieves opened the last bag. "Here we go" he said as he saw the fang bites in the man's neck. He watched as Emele reached his hand across to the bag and saw his hand grow claws and rip through the neck setting the head free and zip the bag back up.

"Are we taking him too?" asked Gieves.

"No. I have an idea" said Emele and he opened one of the cooler doors and pulled out the body. It was an old man. He pushed it back in and shut the door. Then he opened another drawer. It was a young woman. He picked the body up and said "Take Claudia out of that bag."

Gieves lifted her body from the bag and watched as Emele put the other young woman's body in the bag and zipped it up. "Ah the old switcheroo" Gieves said as he nodded in agreement. "But won't they notice the difference?"

"Not if this place is burned to the ground."

"What about the guard?"

"We need to get rid of him." Emele looked at Gieves. "Can you handle that?"

"I got it." He sat Claudia's body down and went for the guard. He sneeked up behind the guard and hit him on the head knocking him out. Then he carried him ouside and sat him under a tree away from the building. He went to the car and got the gas can from the trunk and went back inside.

Emele was setting up for the fire. He found some old rags and dirty smocks and piled them next to the inner wall.

"The guard is out cold clear from the building. I brought some gas too" said Gieves as he held up the can.

"That will do fine."

Gieves poured the gas around the rags and splattered some on the walls. "Ready?"

Emele picked up Claudia and nodded as he walked out.

Gieves pulled out his zippo lighter, flicked the lid open and sparked the flame and threw the lighter on the gas soaked rags. The flames shot up as the fire spread wildly to the walls.

Emele kicked the door open and he and Gieves walked to the car. Gieves opened the car door and Emele laid her on the back seat and shut the door and got in the front seat by Gieves.

Gieves started the car. "Now what?"

"Pull away a little, but not too far, I want to watch it burn."

Within minutes the flames were coming through the roof. Emele could hear sirens of the firetrucks and soon the flashing lights were visible in the distance. The fire would not be easy to put out now.

"Let's go to Constance's house" Emele said to Gieves.

The sun was rising, taking away the light of the fire, replacing it with its own as Gieves sped away.

The fire fighters fought the blaze keeping it from taking other building with it, but the morgue was totally destroyed.

FORGIVENESS

When they reached Constance's house Emele quickly picked up Claudia and carried her inside the house and laid her on the sofa. He hollered "Constance!"

Constance was asleep, but woke to Emele's loud voice. She ran down the stairs to see what was going on. She saw Emele leaning over the sofa. Then she saw the bloodied body. As she looked closer she screamed "Claudia! My baby." She cried loudly as she saw her body full of bullet holes and covered with dried blood. She fell to her knees. "NO!" She reached her hands to Claudia and shook her. "Claudia! Claudia! Come on you can do it." She let her face fall on her daughter's chest and cried uncontrollably.

Emele would have traded his life for Claudia's if he could, just to save Constance from feeling this pain. He just stood there helpless knowing nothing he could say would make her feel better.

Constance was still crying uncontrolablly. "What happened?"

"I'm not sure, but I think the police caught her feeding and gunned her down."

Gieves was next to Emele now. "We heard it on the scanner. We went as fast as we could, but we were too late. We followed the ambulances to the morgue and stole her."

"She'll be okay, right?" asked Constance looking to Emele for hope.

Emele hated the answer he had to give her. He wished he could tell her everything was going to be fine. But he couldn't lie. "I don't know." He put his hands on Constance's shoulders. "She was shot up really bad." Staring at the unhealed bullet holes he suddenly got an idea. He rolled his sleve up and bit his wrist and as the blood started to run he held his hand over the bullet holes and let his blood drip into them. His wound healed and he bit it again and repeted this process until he had filled most of the holes and was starting to feel the blood loss himself.

Constance watched as Emele tried to save her daughter's life. She stared at the holes hoping to see any sign of healing. The blood started to clot on the outside of the holes and a couple of the bullet holes started to close. A smile came through Constance's tears as she saw the healing start. "She's healing!" She stood up and wrapped her arms around Emele. "Thank you so much."

Emele listened closely. It was true. He could hear a very faint heartbeat. He hugged Constance back. "Yes she is."

Constance realized she was wrong to be angry with Emele for biting her and changing her. She would have done anything to save her daughter and not think of the consequences. She looked deeply in Emele's eyes. "I'm sorry for being angry with you. I was wrong. Can you ever forgive me?"

Emele could see the sincerety in her eyes. "How could I not forgive you? Constance, you are my life. I love you." His heart was beating with happiness again. He lifted Constance up and twirled her around.

Constance tilted her head back as he twirled her around. She felt like her eyes were opened seeing things more clearly now. She held Emele close and tight. "Please, stay with me today. I want to hold you while I sleep." She got a dishpan and a washcloth and a big towel. She sat down next to Claudia and washed her carefully.

"It's been a long night. I'm going back to the casino. I'll be back tonight" said Gieves knowing he would just be in the way.

Constance and Emele sat on the other sofa facing Claudia. She felt relieved as she leaned her head on Emele's chest. He had his arms around her shoulders and she had her arms around his waist.She loved the smell of Emele, it soothed her now, but other times it excited her. They just sat there holding each other for hours until they fell asleep.

Gieves was driving to the casino and wandering if Sarah and Emelia were worried about Claudia's abence. Maybe he should stop by and let them know what was happening. He also thought it would be a good excuse to see Sarah again. A smile came to his face as he pictured her in his mind. He drove over to Emelia's house. He walked up to the door and knocked loudly. "Sarah, are you awake? Sarah, are you awake?" he shouted.

The door opened slightly as Sarah peeked out from the shadow. "I thought it was you" she said seeing Gieves standing there.

"Can I come in? I need to talk to you."

Sarah pushed the door open and Gieves walked in. He saw Emelia sitting on the couch.

"Hi Gieves. What's going on?" asked Emelia.

"I thought you both might be up" Gieves said. "Claudia is going to be alright. I just wanted you to know this. I thought you might be worried about her."

Emelia stood up and Sarah walked in front of him. "What do you mean, she is going to be alright?" asked Sarah.

"Well, she is healing now. She was shot up pretty bad by the police. Emele and I stole her body from the morgue."

Emelia pushed Sarah to the side and stared at Gieves. "You stole her body from the morgue?"

"Yes, we thought she was dead and we had to steal her body before they cut into her. So we switched her body then burned the morgue down. Then we took her body to your mother's house."

Sarah pushed Emelia out of the way. "It doesn't sound like Claudia is alright, her body."

Gieves was smiling, feeling they did a great thing. "We put

her on the sofa and Emele let his blood drip into her bullet holes. After a little bit some holes started to close up. We think she will be okay. She just needs time to heal.

The girls were up becasue they were worried about their sister, but they didn't know what to do.

"How did you know about this?" asked Sarah.

"I heard some stuff on the police scanner about a young woman, and it taking a lot to bring her down. The cops were calling for backup in the area you told me Claudia like to go for walks in. I told Emele about it and we checked it out. We found Claudia in the morgue and stole her body and took it to your mom's house."

"We have to go to Mom's house, now!" demanded Emelia.

"I have the limo right outside" Gieves said pointing his thumb over his shoulder. "You girls can get in the back and I'll drive you over there. The dark windows will keep you girls cool."

Gieves went out and opened the car door and the girls ran quickly from the house to the car and got in. Gieves shut the door right behind them and got in the driver seat and started driving.

As Gieves drove they talked through the moniter. "I thought you also might want to know Constance made up with Emele. She asked him to stay with her because she didn't want to be alone. She told him she finally understood why he did it when she saw Claudia just lying there like that. She said she would have done anything to get her back."

"That's great. I knew she would come around" said Emelia.

Sarah was interested in what happened to Claudia. She asked Gieves, "So what happened at the morgue?"

"Well, we went in and there were six body bags on the slabs. We checked them out. It looked like your sister may have been caught feeding. One of the guys had his neck ripped out. When

Emele saw it he ripped his head off, so he wouldn't come back. I think she must have put up a fight, because one cop had a broken neck and another one's body looked like it had been mangeled, a lot of broken bones and very bloody. I'll ask around a little tomorrow and find out what happened."

"I told her she needed to be more careful" whispered Emelia to Sarah.

"I told her too, but we both knew she was feeding a lot more than she needed to. I wonder if they know who she is" whispered Sarah back to Emelia with a worried look on her face.

Gieves couldn't hear what they were saying, but he could tell they were concerned. "I don't think she was carrying any I.D. so hopefully they don't know who she is. With the place burned down and the bodies switched, they'll have a hard time identifying her."

They reached Constance's house. Gieves pulled the limo up close and opened the door and the girls ran inside and stood by the sofa where Claudia was laid. They didn't really know what to expect. They were a little shocked to see all the bullet-hole marks and how pale her body was.

Emele and Constance were still sitting on the other sofa and they could both tell the girls were shocked.

"She will be alright, won't she?" asked Emelia looking at Emele.

Emele answered "She is healing. She was shot up really bad. She even took a few bullets through her heart. It will take a while for her body to heal. She just needs time."

Sarah was looking at Emele now too and asked him "How long?"

Emele thought of his own situation healing in his grave for nearly twenty years. He could not hide the concern in his eyes as he did not answer her.

Constance looked at Emele and his story came rushing back to her as her eyes started to tear up.

When Emelia saw her mother tear up, she rememberred her father's story also. "Don't tell me it could take twenty years."

Emele didn't know what to say. "She is young and strong. That will help a lot, I'm sure."

Sarah didn't know the whole story, but she didn't like what she was hearing. "Twenty years! Are you serious?"

Everyone was looking at Emele. "I don't know. With all the damage she got it could take a long time" he said somberly.

Gieves looked at Claudia. "But you said your blood in the bullet holes may have help start the healing process. Maybe she just needs more blood."

Once again all eyes were on Emele. He thought about it a minute then said. "Maybe Gieves is right. I was trapped in my grave with no one to help me. When I did heal I was so weak I could hardly move."

BRINGING CLAUDIA BACK

Emelia leaned over and whisperred something to Sarah.

"Don't forget we have remarkable hearing" said Constance hearing the plan. "I say give the plan a try."

Gieves asked "What plan?"

Sarah walked over to Gieves and took his hand. "I'll explain it to you in here" and she led him to the kitchen. She closed the door behind them and put her arms around Gieves and started kissing him.

"There are people in the next room" said Gieves uneasily.

"They won't bother us" Sarah promised. Then she gave him a real kiss and held him tighter. She stopped kissing and softly blew in his ear, then she sniffed and said "That's it."

Gieves was confused. "That's what?"

"The smell."

"What smell?"

"The smell of arousal or passion."

"You can smell that?"

Sarah laughed. "Sure we can, and we can taste it in your blood."

"In my blood? I don't like the sound of this" said Gieves in a concerned voice.

"It gets worse. At the moment of ecstacy, it can be overpowering" Sarah said as she slid her hand over his genitals. "That's what little sister craves."

Gieves was a little worried and Sarah could smell that too. "Don't worry big guy. She's not getting you, but we might try this with someone else. And I know who that someone else could be."

Gieves was relieved to hear this.

"We will need a driver though" said Sarah.

"I'm your man, as long as I'm not on Claudia's menu."

"Don't worry" said Sarah as she smiled at Gieves. "You're only on my menu."

Gieves looked at Sarah. She winked at him. He smiled, but he didn't know if he should be relieved or not.

Emelia and Sarah talked about the plan. There was a guy who came to the club a lot, Robby. He was a good looking guy, but he was arrogent and rude and they heard he liked to hit woman. They figured one night with him was all any girl could stand because he never brought the same girl twice, but somehow he brought a new girl to the club every week, and they were beautiful girls. He would always ask Sarah or Emelia for a lap dance, and then he would always ask if they would like to have a three-some with him and his new girlfriend. For some reason he stayed away from Claudia. Sarah thought he might have been scared of her. If he was at the club tonight, they would set their plan in motion.

Sure enough that night, there he was with a very attractive date. This time he asked Emelia for a lap dance. She took him to the back room and started dancing for him. When she sat on his lap he asked her if she would like to join his new girlfriend and him for a threesome. This time instead of saying no, she said "How about this? Instead of a threesome with your girlfriend, why don't you come here alone tomorrow and my sister Sarah and I will rock your world. After we are done here we can go to my place.

Robby could not believe what he was hearing. He considered Emelia and Sarah to be two of the hottest girls he had ever seen. A three some with these two would be a dream come true. "Hell yeah!" he exclaimed.

"Just one thing. Make sure you don't mention this to anyone or the deal is off. We wouldn't want people to think we do this all the time. You got that?" Emelia put her hand on the back of his head and grabbed his hair and gave it a good yank and asked again "Do you get me?"

"Sure!' Robby said with a big smile on his face. "I get you. I won't say nothing to nobody."

Emelia gave his hair one more good tug. "Swear it."

"I swear!"

After they closed that night, Emelia told Gieves "Tomorrow you need to move Claudia to my house and put her on the couch. Sarah and I will have it turned away from the door. Then have the limo waiting outside the club in the alley right before closing time."

Gieves agreed "Consider it done."

The next night at the club, Robby was there alone. Emelia walked by him and pinched his butt. "Did you keep our little secret?"

"You bet I did. You ladies are in for quite a treat tonight."

Emelia walked away rolling her eyes and shaking her head as Sarah watched.

Just befor closing Sarah went over to Robby. "There's a limo outside in the alley. Just tell the driver your name and he will let you in. Emelia and I will be out shortly."

Robby went out and Gieves let him in the limo. After a few minutes Sarah and Emelia joined him in the limo. Gieves drove them to Emelia's house. He parked the car and opened their door. "Will you ladies need anything else tonight?"

Before they could answer, Robby slapped Gieves on the back. "I've got it from here, Pal." Then he put one arm around each of the girls' waists as they walked to the house.

Gieves would pick up Emele and Constance and bring them

274

to Emelia's house.

Emelia led Robby through the door and next to the couch. She took her shirt off, showing her sexy black bra. Sarah came up to Robby on his right side and reached over and unbuttoned Robby's shirt and took it off and started rubbing his chest feeling his chest hair between her fingers.

Emelia stood on Robby's left side opposite of Sarah and started kissing him. She held his left arm still with one hand and started rubbing his genitals. He was becoming aroused and the smell was strong.

Sarah bit him teasingly on his chest then his arm and took his hand and bit his wrist just enough to get the blood to run. Robby twitched a little but didn't seem to notice it, or it just didn't bother him. Sarah moved his arm over the couch and held it over Claudia's mouth as Emelia kissed him more passionately as she rubbed his crotch a little faster and a bit harder to distract him. Sarah watched as the blood dripped on Claudia's lips and her mouth instictively opened. Claudia's fangs started to grow as the blood landed in her mouth.

Robby was getting into it and moving with Emelia's motion. When the time was right she gave Sarah a little kick to the leg. Sarah was ready. Emelia stopped massaging his manhood and stopped kissing him. Sarah spun him around and Emelia pushed his head toward Claudia. "You remeber my little sister Claudia, don't you?" asked Emelia.

Robby screamed as he saw Claudia's red eyes open wide and the long fangs growing as he was shoved her way. He tried to get free but the girls were too strong.

"He's for you Claudia" said Sarah.

Claudia tried to grab for his arms, but she was too weak. Emelia shoved his body lower and Sarah positioned his neck right over Claudia's open mouth close enough she could dig her fangs in deep and she fed ravenously. Her eyes rolled back as she drank his lust blood.

Robby's screams subsided as the life ran from his body norishing Claudia's back to health.

"Looks like little Sis has her appatite back" said Emelia. "I think she's going to be just fine now."

Claudia's strength was growing and she reached her arms up and grabbed Robby as she finished him. She pushed his body back and licked her lips. She hadn't spilled a drop. She closed her eyes as a smile came to her face. Her body was healing fast now and she would be her old self once again very soon.

After a few minutes Claudia had enough strength to sit up. Emelia sat next to her on the couch and asked "What happened?"

Claudia didn't want to talk about it but knew they would never stop asking until she told them.

"Yeah, what the hell happened?" asked Sarah as she stood next to Emelia. "We were really worried about you. Emele and Gieves thought you were dead. Mom was so worried about you. Then we didn't know if you would heal yourself and if so how long it would take, maybe years."

Claudia shrugged her shoulders.

"Don't give us that!" snapped Emelia. "You need to tell us. Now!"

Claudia rolled her eyes. "Okay." She took a deep breath and started telling them her story.

"I knew it" said Emelia interupting Claudia's story. "You need to be more careful out there. And I knew you were feeding way more than you should be."

Just then Constance ran in followed by Emele and Gieves.

"We're not finished here. I want to hear all of it" said Emelia.

Constance ran to Claudia and hugged her. She was surprised to see how much she had healed. "You're up, and you look so good."

"Yes, Mother, I'm feeling pretty good."

"We were so worried about you. We weren't sure if this would work" said Constance as she teared up, but this time she was crying tears of joy. She paid no attention to the body on the floor. Her baby was going to be fine and that was all that mattered.

Emele and Gieves walked over to Claudia. "Let's get rid of this body" said Emele. "We will be back tonight so you ladies can talk."

"I'll grab the door" said Gieves. He opened the door and looked around outside. He didn't see anyone. "All clear." Then he opened the trunk and Emele threw the body and head in. Emele closed the trunk and they got in the car and drove out to the desert and buried the body, then they drove to the hotel. Emele went to the room, but Gieves wanted to do a little investigating of his own.

Gieves went down to talk to his buddy that worked as security guard in the hotel. Gieves asked him if he had heard anything about the incident a couple of nights ago. His buddy told him what he had heard from his police connections and what he had heard from other people. The papers hadn't had much at all about it. Gieves went to his room and told Emele what he had found out.

That night Emele and Gieves went back to Emelia's house. It was early and Emelia and Sarah had a little time before they would have to get ready to go to work. Constance and the girls were sitting around the table talking when Emele and Gieves came in.

Emele walked over to Constance and squeezed her shoulder lightly. Constance reached her hand up to Emele's and gave his hand a squeeze. Emele looked at Claudia and said "It's good to see you doing so well so fast."

Claudia looked up at Emele from her seat "Yes I heard you had a lot to do with my recovery. Mother filled me in. I want to thank you. You saved my life." Claudia got up and walked over to Emele and gave him a hug. "Thank you so much for what you did for me. I'll never forget it." Claudia gave Gieves a hug too and thanked him as well then she sat back in her chair.

Gieves said "You really had us worried there for a while."

Claudia sensed he had more to say. "What is it? You have something else to say don't you?"

Gieves looked from Claudia over to Constance, then to Emele and Emele nodded to him. Everyone was looking at Gieves now. He said "Well, I found out some infromation. The police were investigating a string of murders in the area they had found some bodies in dumpsters around and set a trap with an undercover cop. He was wearing a wire when he picked you up and you attacked him. That's how the cops got you surrounded so fast. Then they shot, when you went wild and attacked them, until they took you down."

Everyone was looking at him listening so intently. "There is a big investigation over the fire at the morgue." He took a deep breath and continued. "It gets worse. One of the cops on the scene that night is saying you were a stripper at The Club. Seems the cops were there late last night after you girls left, talking to some of the workers. My friend said it turned out this girl they were asking about was one of three sisters that work there. Right now they don't have any proof this girl is you; since the fire destroyed the bodies and no one at the club knew the girl's last name. The owner is in trouble for not haveing the proper information on his workers. He paid them in cash to save money on taxes and benifits. One of the girls said as long as the girls were good looking and showed up on time and drew a crowd; the owner didn't ask a lot of questions."

Sarah was the first to ask a question. "Now what can we do?"

Gieves answered "Like I said, the police are just going on a hunch from one of the cops. They don't know who the young woman they gunned down really is. They didn't find any identification on her. There is no evidence to tie anyone to The Club, is there?" Gieves looked at Emelia then Sarah.

Emelia said "When I started, the owner didn't ask a lot of questions he just said I needed a name so he could introduce me and asked if I had a problem being paid in cash." Emelia thought a minute then added "I never told anyone there my last name or where I lived or anything else about me. I only told people that Sarah and Claudia were my sisters."

Sarah and Claudia told them the same thing as Emelia.

Gieves said "If you don't mind answering a few questions from the police, you could go to work like nothing happened. Once they see Claudia there they will just think she looks a lot like the woman they gunned down. You may be in a little trouble for not paying taxes though."

Constance didn't like the sound of what Gieves was saying. "I think it's too risky. We don't need the police asking a lot of questions of you girls. If I'm right about what I think I know. The club will probably be shut down and the owner arrested for tax evasion. The cops or IRS will be checking on everybody that works there to see if they are legal to work in the U.S. and are reporting their income." Constance looked at her girls. "What if any of you were arrested for something? We cannot chance that."

"What are supposed to do?" asked Emelia.

"We can't stay here" said Constance. "We need to get away from here."

"Where would we go?" asked Claudia.

"How about New York City?" asked Emele. "I think we could

fit in there easily with the nightlife I've seen there."

"Okay, I say we go to New York City. All in favor" said Constance as she held up her hand.

"Can we talk about this?" asked Sarah.

"We have to move fast on this. This is hitting too close to home" said Constance.

"Speaking of home" said Emele. "What about your home and the restaurant?"

"I've had some very good offers on the restaurant. It would be easy to sell and the house will move fast too." Constance added again "All in favor."

"Are you sure about this Mother? I know how much the restaurant means to you" said Emelia.

"My family is more important to me than a restaurant."

The girls knew she was right and they each raised their hand.

"It's settled. We will move to New York" said Constance. Her mind was made up.

"I have a place in New York we can stay" Emele said. "It's big enough for all of us." He thought a moment then added. "There is also the castle."

"New York will be fine" said Constance.

Gieves chimed in "Emele's place in New York is a mansion. It's great! Constance, if you're serious about selling I know a thing or two about setting up a transfer that can't be traced."

Everyone laid low except Constance and Gieves. They sold the restaurant and house just as easily as Constance had said.

A NEW LIFE

Constance and her girls left their lives behind in Las Vegas to begin new ones in New York City. Although it was sad for all of them, they were also excited to see New York. They packed up a few belongings in their cars as Gieves drove the limo with Emele, leading the way. They drove at night and stayed in a motel during the day.

After four nights of driving they arrived at Emele's mansion and were quickly settled in. Everyone had their own room. Constance and the girls couldn't believe how big it was and how nice.

Emelia had saved a lot of money and was looking forward to buying her own club. Gieves drove her around the area and she found a place that was off the main road. It was a little run down, but Emelia saw the potential and the price was right. She bought it and she and her family started fixing it up. She found out Emele and Gieves were skilled carpenters. Some of the work had to be hired done so Gieves lined that up and was around to make sure it was being done right.

Emelia was interviewing a lot of beautiful young women for her club. She would talk to them and have them do a dance routine. There were some girls who just didn't have the moves, but were very sexy. She could hire them to be bartenders and waitresses. She found the amount of women she wanted. She still had a little work to do, but felt things would soon be finished and would have the grand opening the first Friday of June. Emelia had hired some kids to put flyers up around the area and she had put ads of the grand opening in the papers, giving the address and boasting of having the hottest girls on the planet. The club would be open Wednesday through Saturday at dusk, with Friday being theme night.

Now that everyone was settled in and things were going well. Emele and Constance decided it was time to finish their wedding plans. They would have a small wedding, just the girls and Gieves. Emele wanted Constance to have a fancy wedding even though it was going to be small. He told Emelia to take Constance shopping for a beautiful dress and bridesmaid dresses and not to worry about the cost. He said if she liked it, buy it.

Constance asked Emelia to be her maid of honor and Sarah and Claudia would be bridesmaids. Emele asked Gieves to be his best man.

Emelia found an elegant shop that was open late. Constance and the girls were impressed with the selection the store had and they all found dresses to wear. Constance was so excited. The dress she found was so beautiful.

It would be an evening wedding in the garden behind the mansion. It had a lot of beautiful flowers and shrubs with a cobble stone walk running through them that led to a gazeebo. Gieves rented several candelabrums to line the path and light the gazeebo.

Emele lined up a preacher and someone to play a few songs he and Constance had picked out. He had Gieves order a small cake and some flowers and line up a photographer. Gieves and Emele bought tuxedoes and everything was ready.

That eneving everything was in place. The cake had been set up in the dinning room on the table that was enhanced with blue and black decorations. Outside it was a calm night with an almost full moon shining. The candles were lit illuminating the garden. Music was softly playing in the background. The preacher was standing next to Emele in the gazeebo. Emele was waiting to see the love of his life make her entrance. He was wearing a long tailed tux with a bright blue comberbun, a white ruffeled shirt and a black bow tie.

The music was a little loader now and Gieves started walking Sarah and Claudia down the ailse. He was dressed in a black tux with a bright blue ruffled shirt and a black bow tie. Claudia was dressed in a sleeveless full length gown, bright blue with a black lapel around the deep v-neck. Her hair was teased full with little baby breath flowers mixed throughout. Sarah was dressed in a bright blue strapless full length gown that had a black sash tied tightly around her waist and hung on her left side half way down her dress. Her hair was in an up do with curled ringlets held in place by a black bow with a strand of hair spiraling down both sides of her face. Both girls carried bouquets of blue and black roses. They walked slowly down the path and took their places in the gazeebo.

The music switched to the wedding march as everyone watched Emelia escort her mother down the ailse. Emelia wore a sleeveless full length gown that had a black lapel around the v-neck and a black sash tied tightly around her waist that went the lenght of her gown on her right side. Her hair was done up in riglets held with a bright blue ribbon with spiraling locks of hair on each side of her face.

Emele felt his heart beat fast from excitement of seeing Constance in her beautiful gown. A big smile came to his face as he stared at the most beautiful woman he had ever seen.

Constance's gown was white satin with old fashioned lace on the bodice. The sleeves and upper part of the dress were tulle with a satin collar and cuffs. She wore a bright blue sash tight around her waist that tied in the back and flowed the length of her dress's train. She wore a veil that was held in place by a comb in her hair that was curled in waves. She was all smiles as she was led down the ailse to the man she loved.

When they enterred the gazeebo Emelia put Constance's hand

in Emele's hand, hugged them both and kissed her mother, then took her place next to the other girls.

The preacher started the ceremony. Constance's and Emele's hearts were pounding in their chests as Constance raised her veil and they exchanged their vows. It was such a happy rush for both of them. Then the preacher pronounced them man and wife and introduced them as Mr. and Mrs Emele Dracula, and said kiss your bride.

Emele held Constance close and softly kissed her as she closed her eyes and leaned to him.

Gieves knew what a huge thing this was for his friend and he couldn't contain himself anymore. "Wooo Yeah!" he yelled.

Constance started to laugh and had to stop kissing. Everyone laughed. They all took turns hugging and congradulating Emele and Constance. Then they posed for the pictures in the gazeebo and the garden, then they went in the house to the dinning room and the photographer took more pictures of the couple cutting the cake and giving each other a small taste of it. Then Constance stood next to the table turned her back to her daughters and tossed the bouquet over her shoulder. She quickly turned around to see Sarah jump and reach above her sisters to catch the bouquet.

A few more pictures were taken and the photographer and the preacher left.

The man with the music played a special song for the new couple that Constance had told him to play, I Honestly Love You by Olivia Newton John. Emele took Constance's hand and pulled her close to him putting his hand around her waist as she put her arms around his his back. They danced slowly to the song just holding each other as they swayed with the music. When the song ended Emele dipped her elegantly and kissed her once more.

The music man packed up his equipment and left as the

wedding party sat and ate their cake and sipped champaign.

Gieves stood up and raised his glass. He looked at the couple and said. "Constance, I have only known you for a short time, but as much as I have heard about you from this guy," as he patted Emele on the back. "I feel I know you very well. You were all he talked about as I traveled with him across this country in seach of his one true love. I saw his face light up when he thought of you. He is quite a guy and I am proud to call him my friend. I can truely say I have never met a family quite like this one." Everyone laughed a moment then Gieves continued, "I'm so happy that you two have found each other again. To the bride and groom" and they all clanked their glasses and drank.

They sat around visiting for a while then Emelia said "Well, I'm sure the bride and groom would like to have a little time to themselves." The girls and Gieves gave hugs and left the room. Emele had a special honeymoon planned. He and Constance packed their bags and were on their way.

"Hey I have a great idea" said Gieves. "Let's go clubbing."

"Sounds great" said Claudia "and we can all wear our fancy outfits and have everybody staring at us all night."

The girls ran to the limo and piled in. Gieves put down the window and said "Where to ladies?"

Sarah looked at Gieves and said "Isn't this your town?"

Gieves smiled "Yes it is." And he drove to a fancy dance clud he had been to before. "I must warn you I have been kicked out of this place for being too rowdy."

Sarah smiled showing her fangs and said "Don't worry big guy, we've got your back." Then she winked at him.

Emelia rolled her eyes. "You're starting to sound like Claudia now."

"Hey!" said Claudia. "What's wrong with that?"

They all chuckled as Emelia said "Not a thing."

They went from club to club dancing and drinking until they closed the last place down. They drove back to the mansion said good night and collasped in their beds.

The next night Emelia and her sisters had to be at the club to make sure everything was ready for the grand opening. All the ladies Emelia hired would be there too, to have their music and outfits ready. The club would open in only two more days.

Friday night came and Gieves drove the girls to Emelia's new club. He was going to help out as a bouncer when Emele didn't need him. It would open shortly after dusk. The club was fancy inside. There was a long bar with stools running half the length of the building on both sides, with tables and chairs in between them. Waitresses and female bartenders dressed in tight, short white button shirts that had big collars with low cut v-necks, that showed off there midriff and cleavage. They also wore black short shorts and black bow ties.

There were rooms for private dances and dressing rooms on both sides of the rear of the building that led up a few stairs to two stages connected by thin runways to a larger stage in the middle forming a v-shape with several chairs along them. The larger stage had an entrance of it's own from behind. Emelia had her own dressing room for her and her sisters that connected to her office in the back next to an exit.

The club was packed. The lights dimmed and a spotlight came on from the back of the building showing an outline of a woman on the center stage. The crowd was silent as three more spotlights came on shining brightly on the dancer. "Hello" she said. "I'm Emelia" as two of the spotlights moved to the other stages showing two more dancers, "and these two lovely ladies are my sisters" she pointed to her right, "Sarah" then pointing to her left "and Claudia. My sisters and I along with the most beautiful women in the world would like to welcome you to" a neon light lit up behind the center stage "Queen of the Night." The song Queen of the Night by Whitney Houston played loudly as the lights came up showing all the dancers, as they all started dancing on the runways and the three stages. The crowd went wild.

Emele hired a private jet to fly Constance and himself to Transylvainia. The windows on the plane were shut to keep the sunlight out, until the plane landed at dusk. Emele had the caretaker of the castle pick them up from the airport. He drove them to the castle were the horses were hitched to the carriage and they took a midnight ride through the countryside under a full moon. Emele sat tilted slightly toward Constance who was leaning her back against his chest. Emele had his arm around her shoulder as Constance held his hand.

Constance was looking out the window at the moonlit woods and hills along the way. "Isn't this a beautiful sight?" she asked.

Emele was looking at Constance and he answered, "Indeed it is."

Constance turned her head to see Emele's face still staring at her. "Are you listening to me?"

Emele smiled and said. "Yes, I was just enjoying the most beautiful sight as well."

Constance smiled and turned around. "That isn't what I was talking about."

Emele pulled her close in his arms and kissed her and held her there until they were back at the castle.

When the driver opened the carriage door, Emele stepped out and took Constance's hand and helped her out. Then he led her to the castle door and opened it. He picked Constance up in his arms and she wraped her arms around his neck. He carried her through the doorway, up the stairs and to his bedroom. He pushed the door open with his foot and carried her in and gently sat her on the bed. "I have dreamed of this moment for a long time, having you as my wife and carrying you to our bedroom." He took Constance's hand and kissed it.

"I have dreamed of something like this myself, you carrying me into a bedroom on our honeymoon" and she winked at him.

Emele had the caretaker put a bottle of champainge in an ice bucket. He took the bottle from the bucket and opened it. The champainge sprayed out for a second then Emele poured two glasses and handed one to Constance. "For making my dream come true" he said as he held his glass closer to Constance.

Constance stood up and added "And mine." Then she clanked her glass to Emele's and they drank.

Emele took the glass from her hand and set them down. He took Constance in his arms and pulled her to him holding her tight against his body. He kissed her passionately. He slowly ran his hands over Constance's body as he undressed her.

Constance tore his shirt off and rubbed her hands over him feeling the muscles of his chest and back, then she romoved the rest of his clothes. She put her arms around him and pulled him to the bed ontop of her.

They made love. Constance started to turn and her fangs started to grow. She became embarassed.

Emele whispered "It's alright" and he bit Constance's ear teasingly.

She grabbed Emele and flipped him over roughly with her strength and got on top of him. They made love unrestrained.

As they lay there exhausted, Emele looked Constance deeply in her eyes. "Mrs. Dracula, you are now and will forever be my Night Goddess."

Would you like to see your manuscript become a book?

If you are interested in becoming a PublishAmerica author, please submit your manuscript for possible publication to us at:

acquisitions@publishamerica.com

You may also mail in your manuscript to:

**PublishAmerica
PO Box 151
Frederick, MD 21705**

www.publishamerica.com

CPSIA information can be obtained at www.ICGtesting.com
Printed in the USA
LVOW120125280812

296245LV00001B/2/P